DEFIANCE PRESS
& PUBLISHING

Public Land
Warrior In The Woods

D1228119

Matthew Rudolph

PUBLIC LAND

Copyright © 2023 Matthew Rudolph

First Edition: 2023

All rights reserved. No part of this publication may be reproduced, distributed, or transmitted in any form or by any means, including photocopying, recording, or other electronic or mechanical methods, without the prior written permission of the publisher, except in the case of brief quotations embodied in critical reviews and certain other noncommercial uses permitted by copyright law.

This book is a work of fiction. Names, characters, places, and incidents are either products of the author's imagination or are used fictitiously. Any resemblance to actual persons, living or dead, or locales is entirely coincidental.

ISBN-13: 978-1-959677-17-8 (Paperback)
ISBN-13: 978-1-959677-16-1 (eBook)

Published by Defiance Press & Publishing, LLC

Bulk orders of this book may be obtained by contacting Defiance Press & Publishing, LLC. www.defiancepress.com.

Public Relations Dept. – Defiance Press & Publishing, LLC
281-581-9300
pr@defiancepress.com

Defiance Press & Publishing, LLC
281-581-9300
info@defiancepress.com

Dedication

This book is dedicated to all the hunters that came before me. To all those who actively hunt every year to feed their family and friends. The men and women who shared their wealth of knowledge, passing down the strategy and tactics used to the next generations so that we may keep our way of life and traditions alive.

Chapter 1

The light from the sun was fading. It was late in the evening in late September and David was hunting out of a two man pop up blind with his brother Zander. This was Zander's first time bow hunting with his older brother, and David was eager to help him get his first buck. They had left early in the morning before the sun rose and after spending the entire day in the woods, both were hungry and tired. David was thinking to himself: *Probably about twenty more minutes before we have to pack up and head back to the truck.* David, now seventeen years old, had started hunting when he was thirteen with his father.

David's grandparents used to own a farm where they had plenty of land to hunt on, but after his grandfather passed away when he was fifteen, his grandmother sold the farm since all her children had moved away and it was too much work to take care of on her own. David was really the only grandchild that had an interest in hunting and fishing, so when his grandparents sold their land, he was crushed. David started to hunt primarily on public land after his grandmother sold their farm, rarely getting permission to hunt on private land owned by someone his father knew. Since their father had to work on the opening day of bow season, David decided to take his brother deer hunting for the first time. David had some success hunting the past four seasons and had harvested a few deer of his own. He felt confident that if they came across a deer this season, between the two of them, they would be able to harvest it on their own. The enthusiasm that Zander had early in the morning was starting to fade. The ambition of getting his own wall hanger like his older brother and father was all Zander could think about. Zander was twelve years old and started rabbit hunting with his older brother and father two years ago. Zander really took an interest in hunting other animals after he went rabbit hunting a couple times. While he enjoyed hunting with dogs and moving around in the woods and fields, the thought of getting a trophy buck was the only thing Zander was focused on.

As it was getting darker, David could barely see the large oak tree directly in front of him that he estimated was about thirty yards away. David knew the range of the crossbow he was letting his brother use was about thirty yards, and considering he was hunting off the ground, he didn't really feel comfortable taking a shot with his own compound bow much further than thirty yards either. "We should probably pack up and head back. I don't know about you, but I'm starving," David told his brother. The boys packed snacks to eat throughout the day but hadn't had a full meal since breakfast.

"Ok, me too," replied Zander. The two unzipped the pop up blind and placed their bows against a large log that was nearby. They gathered their chairs, and Zander grabbed the backpack with their hunting equipment as David folded up the blind. Once they had secured all their gear, they headed toward the trail they followed in to get to their hunting spot, and they started walking back toward the parking lot where David's truck was parked. It was about a fifteen- minute walk without any gear, although both of them were healthy and very active, so even with all the gear they were carrying it would likely not slow them down much. David led the way because he had a head lamp and had hunted the area several times, so he was somewhat familiar with where he was going.

Zander was hunting there for the first time, so everything was new to him. Even with David's knowledge of the terrain, it amazed him how different everything looked at night compared to how things looked during the day. All the trees, bushes and other landmarks he noticed on the way in earlier that day he could no longer see, so there were times during their walk back when he was not exactly sure where they were or how much farther they needed to go to reach the large field that eventually led to the parking lot where David's truck was. Zander was using his own flashlight although the light was much dimmer than the head lamp David was using. Zander just followed his brother and trusted David knew where he was going.

About five minutes into the walk back, David noticed another light farther back along the trail as they looped around a turn near a creek. David remembered they had not noticed anyone else cross their path in the area where they were hunting all day, so he was wondering where exactly this individual came from that he was noticing late that evening. While David thought it was a little suspicious and odd that someone else was in the woods with them that he hadn't noticed before, he also didn't want to alarm or scare his younger brother.

Probably just another hunter, David thought to himself as he picked up his pace a little bit hoping Zander would follow suit.

"Hey, I think someone's following us," Zander said quietly, sounding a little concerned.

"Yeah, probably another hunter. It happens," David replied. He had come across other hunters while hunting on public land, although he tried to avoid it as he did not want to ruin anyone's hunt; nor did he want another hunter potentially ruining his. As David and Zander picked up their pace hoping to separate the distance between themselves and this random person, David noticed that the light from the stranger was steadily getting closer. David didn't want to run and give away that he was a little scared of the stranger following them in case the stranger wished to harm them. He also didn't want to scare his younger brother even more than he probably already was. David had hunted many times when he came across coyotes and bobcats, and it never seemed to bother him. They always seemed to run away after they saw him anyway. The thought of being followed by a stranger who most likely had at least a bow or knife on them worried him. *Damn, this guy just keeps gaining on us,* David thought to himself. He knew even if they tried to run, it would be difficult with all the gear they were carrying. He wondered what all the stranger was carrying and started trying to figure out if they could reach the field that led to his truck before this stranger caught up with them. The moon was pretty bright that night as it was a full moon, and David felt confident he could see better if they got out of the thick wooded area and into the field. He started to wonder if the flashlights would give away their position and if they should turn them off to at least give themselves somewhat of an advantage, making it harder to be seen.

"Turn your flashlight off," David told his brother.

"What? Why?" replied Zander.

"I don't know what this guy's up to; if our lights are off it will make it harder for him to find us," David whispered to Zander as they walked up a steep hill along the trail they were following.

"But then I can't see," Zander told David.

"Don't worry. I can see enough," replied David. The more David had hunted, the better his eyes adjusted to the dark. Most mornings when he hunted, David would get into the woods at least thirty to forty-five minutes before sunrise. If he hunted in the evening, he wouldn't leave until it was dark. Usually that meant at least a ten to fifteen-minute walk in the dark. As the boys turned their lights off, David glanced over his shoulder as he walked and noticed the stranger's light was getting closer. *We should be getting close to the edge of the tree line along the field,* David thought to himself. As they were approaching the field, David was trying to figure out a plan in case this person was in fact following them for whatever reason.

David had hunted on private property before and never had an issue coming across other hunters. It seemed that only when he hunted on public land, he would come across strangers. Sometimes it would be a couple walking their dog; sometimes it would be a group horseback riding through the trails, or sometimes it was just a random group of teenagers going into the woods to smoke. Regardless of who he came across, David usually just minded his business and politely said, "Hello" as he walked by. Some of the people he encountered were rude toward him, most likely because they were anti-hunting. Every now and then when he crossed paths with a stranger, they would ask him what he was hunting and then ask him generic questions about it.

David started to remember some horror stories he heard about hunting on this state park. Residents that lived nearby West Spoon Lake would talk about random people going deep into the woods to practice shooting, and they would see people carrying rifles that were illegal to hunt with. West Spoon Lake was built by the Army Corps of Engineers, and when the lake was dammed, it became the largest state park in Ohio. They called it West Spoon because the lake was in the shape of a spoon with the river (handle of the spoon) flowing into the lake coming from the west. David noticed they were almost to the edge of the woods when he looked up through the trees and could see the full moon. When the two reached the edge of the forest and David could now see his truck was the only vehicle in the parking lot, he became even more suspicious of the random person following them.

"Zander, listen to me. We don't have a lot of time," David said as he took a knee. "Take my keys, go straight to the truck, and lock the doors. Give me your crossbow; take my compound bow with you. Don't look back while you're walking in the field, and when you are in the truck, look straight ahead. If you look around trying to locate this guy, he may notice and be onto us. I'm going to hide in the woods and wait to make sure he doesn't follow you. If he follows you and approaches the truck, let me handle it. If he attacks me, call the police," David told his brother.

"But . . ." Zander started to say.

"Just listen to me," David sternly told his brother while trying not to make too much noise.

"I'm scared," Zander softly admitted.

"I know. It's ok. Just do as I say, and everything will be fine," David replied.

David moved up to the side of the hill facing the field, concealing himself between two large trees and a couple of thick bushes that as long as he sat on the ground would keep him hidden. He knew if he sat up, his head would be slightly exposed; yet if he laid down, he was completely hidden. He wanted to be able to see where this stranger went as he approached, and the spot he chose was perfect. David decided to give his compound bow to Zander, because David wanted to use the crossbow. He didn't want to have to draw an arrow if the stranger attacked him.

Zander had to cross a stream that led into the lake in order to get back to the trail that led through the field and directly to the lot where David's truck was parked. David watched as his brother headed to the truck. From the edge of the forest to the parking lot was a little longer than a football field, David estimated, and he knew if this stranger headed that way, he could reach his brother in about twenty seconds based on the time he ran one-tens with the football team plus the added weight he was carrying. As David watched Zander walk to the truck, he was also looking for the light behind them coming from the stranger. David quickly realized the person following them had also turned his light off which made him even more suspicious of the stranger's intentions. Zander reached the truck, and as David heard the door close, he saw a dark shadowy figure approach. David could tell it was a man most likely in his mid to late twenties with dark hair and wearing camouflage. David saw the outline of a crossbow next to the man's body and could see the man looking around in the direction of the field.

The trail leading out of the woods split into two directions once the edge of the forest met the field. Going straight, the trail led through the field and to the parking lot. Turning left along the trail led across the main road and along another trail and David was unsure about where it led. The stranger turned left and walked along the trail that headed toward the main road; then he stopped within about eight yards of David and had his back turned to him as he was looking at Zander in David's truck.

"Where the fuck did the other one go?" the stranger said in a raspy voice to himself.

David remained still for a few seconds although it felt like an eternity to him. Aware of how easily he could give up his position, David held his breath. He could feel his heart pounding worse than ever before, even worse than the time he shot his first deer. The adrenaline pumping through his body was more than he ever felt in his life. The pressure he felt from wrestling or playing football was nothing compared to the thought of possibly having to fight for his life. Still unsure of this stranger's intentions, David was extremely concerned this guy was going to go after his brother. The stranger looked right, then left, then did a complete 180 and was looking up the hillside David was lying in.

David, once confident he was completely hidden and concealed, was now wondering if maybe his boots or some part of his body was exposed as the stranger was looking around scanning the area for him. David was fairly confident he could defend himself considering his wrestling and football background, not to mention the stranger was about his size. David also thought of the worst outcome and what could possibly happen if this stranger attacked and killed him, then went after his brother. David's truck was a manual and Zander didn't know how to drive a manual yet. David realized his brother could not drive away to safety even if he wanted to. *Did I make the right decision sending my brother to the truck?* David wondered as his heart was beating faster and faster. *Please just leave us alone,* David thought as the stranger kept looking around trying to find him.

Just when David was afraid the stranger was going to head toward his brother, the man kept walking down the trail toward the main road that was parallel to the parking lot where his truck was. David waited until he could no longer see the man, which meant he either crossed the road or was far enough away that David would be able to see the stranger come toward him as he walked through the field toward his truck in the parking lot. David got up very quietly and headed back to the main trail walking quickly to his truck. As he walked through the field, he kept looking in the direction the man went just in case the stranger tried to ambush him.

David was aware that the man could hide in the woods and try to shoot him with the crossbow he saw the man carrying. David walked quickly without running, so that he would not make too much noise and expose his location. When he reached his truck, he quickly put his gear in the bed of the truck, had Zander unlock it and put his crossbow in the back seat.

When he got in the truck, Zander handed David the keys and immediately started the truck. David looked over at his brother and said, "Hey, you did good. Let's get out of here." As David drove off and they headed toward the park exit, he looked over and could see how scared his little brother was. Zander was visibly shaking, and his face looked like he just saw a ghost. David wanted to say something before they got back on the highway, so he pulled off the side of the road in the gravel and said, "Zander, look at me." Zander looked over at David with watery eyes and David noticed a couple tears streaking down his face.

"It's ok. We are safe. He's gone," David told his frightened brother. Zander didn't say a word. As Zander was looking at his brother, he nodded and then slowly looked back down at his feet. David placed his hand on his brother's shoulder for a moment and then patted him on the back and said again, "We are safe now" as they drove off.

Chapter 2

When the plane touched down, David looked out the window to see if he could recognize the landscape near where he once called home and spent the majority of his life. He was returning home permanently after serving in the Army Special Forces. After graduating high school, he enlisted and was sent off to basic training, spending the past five years in the Special Forces. He had a hard time sleeping on the plane ride which was unusual for him. Throughout his career in the military, David had no problem sleeping on flights regardless of whether he was traveling to base for training or overseas for deployment. *I jump out of these damn things; why can't I sleep?* David wondered. The guy's David served with in the Army would always joke around about how easily he could sleep just about anywhere. Instead of resting or dreaming, David was thinking about the conversation he had with his parents when he decided to join the Army against their wishes. The decision was triggered by seeing a Chick-fil-a sign at the airport. David remembered that was the last meal he had with his parents before he left for basic. "Why do you want to go into the military?" David's mother asked. "You got accepted to every college you applied to."

"I think everyone should serve their country in some way; besides I have no interest in college," David replied.

"Do you know what branch you want to join and what exactly you want to do?" David's father asked.

"Yeah, I want to join the Army and work my way into Special Forces" David had said. His father dropped his head, and his mother turned away, clearly upset.

"Do you have to pick something so dangerous?" his mother asked.

"Look, a lot of people have certain skill sets and depending on what the military needs, they can find a position for them. Combat is the only thing I'm interested in and honestly the only thing I feel I'm good at. I've been fighting my whole life, been hunting my whole life. How many eighteen year olds do you know that have two state championships in wrestling, have been hunting since they were twelve, and are certified scuba divers? This just feels like it's something I'm supposed to do," David told his parents.

"If you are worried about finances, don't be; you got a lot of financial aid because of your grades and test scores. Plus your father and I have been saving money for you and your brother to go to college ever since you were born, so money isn't an issue. Most kids that join the military after high school only do so because they are poor and cannot afford college; we don't have that problem," his mom replied. That last comment set David off.

"I'm not joining because I can't afford college!" David replied sternly. "That's disrespectful as hell to say that only poor kids

join the military." His mother was silent. After a brief moment of silence, his father spoke up.

"Look. As much as I hate to admit it because you're my kid, I do think you would be perfect for the military," David's father said. "The skills you have picked up and learned over the years would help you a lot in any branch of the military, and I think you would make a great soldier because you have an incredible work ethic and you're a quick learner. What concerns me is the real possibility of something happening to you overseas. Our country has been at war for a long time, and I don't see that changing anytime soon. Depending on how long you'll be in the Army, the same war may still be ongoing after you retire or leave the military. So honestly, what's the point? You are smart enough to get into college, and you have many talents that would just be wasted if you went over there and got killed. Also a lot of troops return home with severe PTSD because of what they see over there. Even if you see combat and nothing happens to you physically, I would hate to see you mentally affected by what you could potentially see during your time in the military," David's father told him.

David sat in silence for a moment, as did his mother and father. After a brief pause in the conversation, David finally spoke up, "I don't expect either of you to understand my decision and that's fine. The important thing is that it's *my* decision. I would never tell either of you where to work or what career to pursue, so I would appreciate it if you could respect my decision and support me the same way you have done throughout my life. You came to every game and practice I ever had since I first started playing sports when I was five years old. Anytime I needed something for school or athletics, you were always there to help me, and you provided me with any equipment or supplies I needed. All I'm asking now is that you continue to support me and don't tell me what to do with my life," David told his parents.

He began to drift back to the present and looked across the plane at some of the other passengers who were gathering their carry-on items before he could get up and start walking. Once all the people in front of him got off the plane, he grabbed his carry-on bag and walked off the plane to head outside of the airport so he could wait to get picked up. David's parents told him they would pick him up and there were fewer people outside, so David decided to find a bench as far away from the crowd as possible to sit and wait. He checked his watch and realized the flight was quicker than expected, so he had about half an hour to wait for his family to pick him up. He began to drift off again.

David thought about the first time he flew out of CVG airport in Hebron, Kentucky when he was leaving to go through basic training at Fort Benning, Georgia. Instead of going off to college like the rest of his friends, David was leaving home to go serve his country. He remembered his parents dropping him off at the airport and how emotional it was. He expected his mother to cry a lot which she did; however he did not expect to see his father with tears in his eyes. Throughout his entire life, David could count on one hand how many times he saw his father cry. It didn't happen often, and David understood how difficult it was seeing their oldest son leave for military service. Zander didn't cry, but David could tell he was bummed to see his brother leave.

After spending about four and a half months in Fort Benning for basic training, advanced individual training and basic airborne training, David was sent to Fort Bragg, North Carolina to start his training for Special Forces. He talked with several military recruiters while he was in high school, and while every branch of the military seemed interested in him, he decided the Army was probably the best fit for him. After more research he decided he wanted to challenge himself and become a Green Beret. David was slightly more nervous when he was sent to Fort Bragg than when he left for Fort Benning, and even though his training at Fort Bragg was significantly more physically and mentally challenging, he found that one of the biggest challenges was simply how long Special Forces training lasted. It was easy for David to get lost in his training and not get distracted too often, but every now and then he did miss his family and friends.

One of the most helpful conversations he had while in the Army was about six months into his training at Fort Bragg. During dinner one night, he and his friend Danny started talking about their family and friends when David said, "You know I was aware of how challenging our training was going to be. I just never thought I'd get homesick at times and miss my family and friends as much as I do."

"Yeah, that's probably part of why our training lasts as long as it does though man. Think about it; our deployments are pretty long, so if you can't handle how long it takes to complete the training, going overseas for many months at a time is going to be a problem," Danny replied.

"True. How do you and your girl handle it?" David asked.

"Well we do everything we can to communicate as much as possible, or at least as much as they will allow me to and I remind myself every day that I'm here learning how to fight and defend my country because I'm also defending and providing for my fiancé and son," Danny told him. David nodded and those words stuck with him. David knew he always wanted to be a soldier and serve his country; fighting for his family and friends helped give him that extra motivation when things got really tough. Whenever David thought he was too exhausted to keep going or when he would feel any fear, he thought about what Danny said and kept pushing himself through whatever adversity he faced.

After David became a Green Beret, he went back home to spend time with his family and friends before going back to Fort Bragg to get ready for his first deployment to Afghanistan. While he was home visiting family and friends, his mom asked him, "Would you like us to have a going away party for you? We can invite some of your friends and our family to come over for dinner or something."

"No, I don't think me being sent to war is really anything to celebrate. I shouldn't have to do this," David replied.

"What do you mean?" his mother asked.

"Humans are so combative by nature and so tribal. There's been wars and fighting throughout human history. I don't think there will ever be a time when humans are not fighting with each other. It is what it is," David said.

David felt a little guilty that he hadn't seen his family more during the past five years even though the majority of his time spent stateside was on a military base. He was expecting his entire family to be at the airport when he got home, and he was excited to see his mother, father and brother. When he called his parents to let them know he was resigning after his current contract was up, David heard an excitement in their voice that he hadn't heard in a long time.

David did his best to stay in touch with them, but it was difficult because he couldn't always tell them what he was do-ing or where he was going. While he kept in touch with his family mainly by calling them, he kept in touch with his friends through social media although he rarely used it. David's friends back home would joke around about his social media presence and ask why he even was on Facebook if he was never going to post anything. While David would regularly check in to see how his friends were doing, he rarely commented or posted. He cared more about seeing what his friends post, so he knew they were doing good. As he sat there on the bench waiting to get picked up, David was hoping he could reconnect with some of his friends that he grew up with now that he was back home. He knew his best friend Michael became a pilot while he was in the Special Forces, fulfilling a lifelong dream and something Michael talked about from the first time they met back when they were five.

David and Michael grew up in the same neighborhood and lived within a half mile of each other. They were in the same grade, but went to separate schools because Michael went to a private school while David's parents sent him to public school. After school David would either go over to Michael's house if he didn't have practice, or Michael would come over to David's. Throughout the summer Michael would spend the night so often at David's that his parents joked that Michael was their adopted third son.

Michael was always the one that got David to explore new things, even when David was a little hesitant. One of the things David admired about Michael was how confident he was around women. Michael never seemed to hesitate to speak to the most attractive females, and seeing his friend's confidence often gave David more confidence of his own. Michael always managed to be the life of the party or at least so it seemed. Whenever Michael's parents went out of town, he would have parties and because he lived close it was very convenient for David. He met a lot of friends through Michael as well.

Besides his immediate family, David probably looked forward to seeing Michael the most. Obviously seeing his brother was David's top priority. Zander had just graduated high school and was about to leave for college in a month. David wanted to spend as much time with him as he could before Zander went off to school at Ohio University. Zander was going to be the first one in the family to attend college and had already decided he wanted to study law. David hated the idea of his brother becoming a lawyer as he trusted lawyers and politicians less than anyone. As David was thinking about his brother, he saw a familiar face he hadn't seen in over a year. David saw his brother and was so happy he didn't even notice he was the only one there. David dropped his pack when he got close and faked for a double leg takedown before embracing his little brother. "Don't let me get double underhooks little bro," David said with a smirk. The two smiled as they hugged for the first time since David left for his last deployment.

"Good to see you bro; glad you made it back safe. I'm sorry I couldn't help you move back home," Zander told his brother.

"Ah don't worry about it; between Mike, Dad and I, it was a breeze. Besides I wanted you to enjoy your vacation with Rachel and her family," David replied. He squeezed a little tighter before letting go and looking around. "Where's Mom and Dad?" he asked his little brother.

"Dad's still at work and Mom is home getting ready. They want to take you out to dinner tonight; she said you could pick where we go," Zander told David.

"Shit, we going to Benihana then," David said as they both laughed.

"Yeah, I figured you'd want to go there." Zander smiled.

"Frankie still work there?" David asked.

"No he moved to New York City," Zander replied.

"Poor bastard. You couldn't pay me to live in that shithole," David said. At first Zander was confused, but then he remembered how much his older brother hated big cities and preferred smaller towns and rural areas. Once they got in the car, David asked Zander, "How are things with you and Rachel?"

"Pretty good. She's going to be a cheerleader at OU next fall," Zander said.

"That's cool; does she know what she wants to study yet?" David asked.

"No, she's still undecided, although I think she will go into nursing or something similar. Kind of like her mom did," Zander told David.

"Yeah, that's cool you both get to go to college together. I'm sure it's easier not to get homesick if you've got your girlfriend with you at college," David said.

"Yeah, it'll be good for both of us," Zander replied.

"Wait, why are you turning right?" David asked, knowing they had to turn left after getting off the highway to go home. "Sorry bro," Zander said with a grin on his face. After the second right turn, David knew exactly where he was, where they were going, and what was happening.

"Ah you jackass," David said as they pulled into a lot full of cars at the local American Legion where they had their uncle's fiftieth birthday party. David was very familiar with what was happening because he helped his mother surprise his uncle years ago when he turned fifty, and his uncle didn't see it coming then either. David saw a huge sign over the front doors that read in big bold letters, *Welcome Home David!* "You do realize I have to kick your ass now," David told Zander.

"Blame Mom. She made me do it," Zander replied, still laughing. David recognized some of the cars there and started to get an idea of who all was invited. His parents most likely invited many of his friends that he played sports with and their parents, and then some of their parents' coworkers who knew David and Zander when they were younger as well.

When David got out of the car, he saw a lady take off running while yelling, "He's here! He's here!" David recognized the woman who worked with his mother, but couldn't remember her name. *Hopefully it comes to me by time I speak to her* David thought to himself. David was really good at recognizing people even if he had only met them once before and a long time ago; however he was horrible with names. Before he could even get into the building, David's mother came running up the stairs and quickly hugged her son with huge tears rolling down her face. Many of the other party goers had now gone outside and began clapping for the soldier returning home.

"Thank God you're home," David's mother whispered to him. After giving his mom a hug, David's father gave him a big hug as well. While his mom wiped tears off her face, David noticed his father's lip quiver a bit, and he could tell his father was holding back tears.

"Welcome home my number one son," David's father said.

"Thanks Dad. Feels good to be back," David replied. Next up was his best friend Michael.

"Come here ya handsome bastard!" Michael told David with a grin on his face.

"Glad to have you back buddy," Michael said.

"Thanks man, it's been a long five years. I've missed all you guys," David replied.

"Well I'm sure you learned some new things in the Army, but I hope you still remember how to run a beer pong table because we are having a tournament tonight. Gotta run the table like we used to in high school," Michael said confidently.

David could hear some friendly smack talk coming back from some of his other friends that showed up for his welcome home party. The voice that he heard over all of them, however, was his mother's, "Oh I don't want to hear that," David's mother said as she turned to walk back inside.

"Don't worry, ol' Johnny didn't buy him any booze until he was eighteen. Right, sir?" Michael said to David's father.

"Damn straight. Anyone who's old enough to serve their country should be able to drink a beer," David's father replied. David's mom just shook her head and walked back into the building to finish getting everything ready for David's return home party. David realized the last time he saw a lot of these people was at his graduation party after high school. *I'm sure my parents have kept in touch with them and told them all about how I was doing in the Army*, David thought to himself. Even then he wondered if any of them were curious regarding his whereabouts while he was in the Special Forces because he wasn't always able to communicate exactly where he was going with anyone, even his parents.

After everyone ate, David made his rounds saying *hello* to everyone who attended the party and thanking them for coming. Over and over he heard them say something along the lines of, "No. Thank you for your service." Some of the party goers asked David if he had any stories, but he tried to avoid talking about anything specific that he did or saw in Iraq or Afghanistan and instead focused on talking about some of the training he went through. A few people that attended made ignorant comments about the military or the war which David ignored because he didn't want to cause problems. He simply walked away from them and continued making his rounds to say hello to all those who showed up for his welcome home party.

David mainly wanted to play beer pong and hang out with his friends, but he knew he had to at least engage in conversation with as many people as possible to make his parents happy. After a few hours of chit chat with what felt like thousands of people, even though there was far fewer than one hundred people at the party, David was reminded of why he didn't like attending parties and gatherings when he came home. Several times when he was stateside, his friends would try to get him to go out to bars and go to parties with them, but he almost always had something else going on that was more important to him. Because he was used to waking up early, when he was stateside and not on base, he preferred going to bed early so he could get up and go hunt or fish instead of going to bars and being surrounded by strangers.

There was really only one time when he was stateside and decided to join his friends to party. He was invited to go to Panama City Beach for spring break with five of his closest friends and decided to go since he had just turned twenty one, and he figured he would probably never get to experience anything like that again because he would most likely be training or sent overseas. Just thinking about it made him remember how much fun he had on that trip. While he was in the military, David always thought about what could go wrong, but when he was on spring break with his friends—that was the only time he didn't worry about the bad things that could happen and just enjoyed the moment. Before David could think about the specifics of that trip, Michael and his other friends started setting up the beer pong table, and David knew it was time to go to work.

David and Michael dominated the beer pong table from the start and didn't really face any legit competition until Zander and his girlfriend Rachel played them. By the time it was their turn to face the champs, David already had a pretty good buzz and was consistently making his shots. He remembered how he always seemed to start slow and get better as the night went along. Michael, on the other hand, seemed to start off playing really well and then got worse the more he drank. Before their match against Zander and Rachel began, David felt pretty good and was hoping Michael was still at his peak as well because he knew if they were going to beat Zander and Rachel, they needed to both be able to make their shots. Zander seemed to be the only person that could beat David at beer pong. Considering he had never played against Zander's girlfriend, David wasn't sure if she was any good or not. Right from the beginning, David knew it was going to be a tough matchup because after Michael missed his first shot, Zander and Rachel both made theirs and brought it back. Rachel sunk her second shot and Zander's bounced off the same cup she made almost ending the game right then and there. "Damn kid, not even home twenty-four hours, and you're already trying to death cup me?" David said jokingly.

"I learned from the best," Zander replied with a smile.

As usual, David managed to carry the team late, and by the time they were down to their last cup, he had made seven and Michael had made two. Luckily, they didn't need to re-rack and David felt comfortable that he was close to making the last cup before Zander and Rachel could make the last two. They had re-racked earlier when they were down to four cups, and Zander sunk two of them making it much closer. Zander liked using the diamond formation just like David did, and when Zander was down four to one, David expected his brother to make that adjustment. The problem for Zander was that Rachel preferred a straight line when there were only two cups left, and now their setup was only benefitting Zander's preference. It was Michael's turn and he missed badly, the ball not even hitting the table, much less the last cup. "Damnit!" Michael said loudly. "I don't know how many more games I got left in me man," Michael told David.

"It's all good. Let's just end this game and then go chill by the fire or something," David replied.

"Oh what's the matter; you finally get some competition and you can't handle it?" Zander joked.

"Well, when you run the table all night, eventually the alcohol is going to kick in," David jokingly replied. They all four laughed as David almost made the last cup. "*Ooooo*, that was close," David said. He had a feeling as long as Zander and Rachel missed their next shot he would be able to finally sink the last one. They had traded back and forth several times now, and he always hated having to make the last cup. Michael was always pretty clutch at sinking the last one, but he wasn't exactly at his peak performance at this point in the night, so David really tried to focus on that last cup, so they could go sit down and relax. Zander let Rachel shoot first, and the ball didn't even come close, so David felt a little relieved. The feeling of relief was short lived because Zander sunk the front cup leaving only one more remaining and now tying it up.

"Alright. We didn't re-rack. Let's sink this and end it," David said to Michael who was swaying back and forth. Michael gave his best effort as his shot fell short and clipped the front end of the cup.

"Ah damn man, I thought I had it," said Michael. Without saying a word, David stared the final cup down and remembered what his instructor told him during his sniper training. Don't just focus on the target; focus on a specific mark on the target because chances are if you slightly miss that specific mark, you will still hit your target. David didn't just look at the cup; he looked at the back rim inside the cup, took a deep breath and exhaled slowly. At the end of the exhale, he shot, releasing the pong ball at a high point to get more arch on his shot and then . . . splash.

"Boom baby!" Michael said in his best Dick Vitale impression while David smiled and laughed. David immediately walked around the table extending his hand to Rachel and said, "Good game." Then he gave his brother a hug and said the same to Zander.

"Well you still got it," Zander told David.

"Yeah, some things never change. He was always the sniper," Michael said.

"I just wanted to end it so we could sit down," David joked. As David and Michael walked over to the fire pit where several others were sitting, he could see his parents and some of his other friends. He turned and noticed Zander and Rachel walking back inside. "Hey, can you grab a couple beers?" David asked his brother.

Eventually most of the party left and it was just David, his parents, Zander, Rachel and Michael sitting around the fire. After the party cleared out, David asked Zander, "Bow season opens in about a week; you want to go to West Spoon Lake and hunt with me?"

"Hell no," Zander replied.

"Why not?" David asked.

"Because last time I was there someone tried to follow us, and who knows what their intent was. Besides there's been a bunch of people that went missing at that damn place," Zander explained. David sat there remembering the encounter they had while hunting years ago when a random man was following them. With his training and combat experience, David wasn't concerned if he crossed paths with the stranger again. Still, he understood his younger brother's hesitation considering how young Zander was when it happened.

"No one will mess with us. I won't let anything happen to you," David told Zander.

"I don't doubt that. I just don't want to take a chance," Zander replied. He and Rachel left after helping David's parents clean up inside. Rachel had to work the next morning, and Zander was already pretty drunk and ready for bed. Once it was just David, his parents and Michael around the fire pit, his parents started asking questions that David had preferred they wait until later to ask.

"So what are you going to do now that you're out of the Army?" David's mother asked him.

"I'm not sure yet," David replied.

"Is there anything in particular that you're looking at?" his father said.

"There's a few things I'm interested in; still haven't made up my mind," David replied.

"You could always fly planes with me," Michael joked.

"Hell I'm used to jumping out of planes. Not sure if I could fly one," David laughed. His mom shook her head because she hated the thought of her son jumping out of planes and started to realize no matter what David decided to pursue, it was probably going to be something dangerous and risky that she didn't approve of.

"Why don't you come work with me," David's mother said.

"I'm not a stock broker," David replied.

"Yeah, but you can always learn," his mom said.

"Mom, no offense, but I have no interest or desire to do anything related to the stock market. Most of your clients would hate me because I'm not going to sugarcoat anything," David replied.

"What about law enforcement," David's father asked.

"Hell no," David said quickly.

"Why not?" David's mother asked.

"Because I've already worked in a thankless career, and I'm not about to jump into another one; besides with the rioting, protests and shit all over the place, I'm not dealing with that mess," David explained.

"Well I was thinking maybe something more along the lines of like a conservation officer or game warden," David's father said.

"Oh yeah, that'd be perfect for you," Michael said. That did intrigue David a little bit. He always had a love for hunting and the outdoors; problem was he always had a negative opinion of conservation officers because the hunting community made jokes about them, and he felt like there was generally a stigma toward conservation officers.

"Ah, I don't know if I can be a nark," David said. Michael's and David's father laughed, and David's mother asked what a nark is making all of them laugh even more.

"I just found a home. I'm going to focus on getting settled in before I decide on a new career. Besides if Bitcoin prices keep rising, I may not have to find another job with what I have invested in that right now," David told them.

"What the hell is Bitcoin?" asked David's father.

David laughed and said, "I'll have to explain that another time; if I tried to explain Bitcoin to you guys right now, it would take all night."

Chapter 3

The man who was following David and Zander in the woods was asleep in his mobile home on the outskirts of West Spoon Lake State Park. He lived alone now after the tragic events that took his entire family when he was younger. In his dream he is taken back to the day his father passed away after battling cancer for two years. His father was diagnosed with lung cancer when the man was in seventh grade and passed away shortly before he started high school. High school without a father was very difficult for him, and the tragic turn of events all began around this time.

While his father was alive, his mom didn't work; she was a stay at home mom that raised himself and his younger sister Haley. She was four years younger and extremely spoiled as the youngest of the family. His father worked as a dentist in the small town outside the state park. As the only dentist in the area, business was pretty good, although he started to lose customers because of his severe smoking habits. His father would smoke between patients and some would complain about his hands smelling like cigarettes even after washing them thoroughly and wearing latex gloves.

When his father started chemo, it made matters even worse as the treatments took a financial toll on the family with only one parent employed. While in middle school, he remembered his parents constantly fighting over the fact his mother didn't work and his dad was the only one bringing home any income despite literally dying from cancer. One of the last things his father talked to him about was asking if he could do some yard work around the neighborhood to help out. He started cutting grass and doing other landscaping jobs to help his father financially. Most of the money he earned paid for groceries for the family. It was a foreshadowing of what he would have to do in the future to provide for the family when his father was gone.

He was in his father's hospital room with his mom and sister. The doctor came in and said, "I am very sorry. There is nothing more we can do at this point. We don't expect him to make it through the night." His mother and sister were hugging each other, crying and unresponsive. He just looked at the doctor and then put his head down, knowing how difficult his life was going to become without his father around. His father had always provided for the family, and his father was the one who taught him a good work ethic. Now, not only was his role model gone, but he was going to have to really help provide for his mother and sister. At age fourteen he felt overwhelmed by the task he was about to take on.

"I'll let you all say your goodbyes; we have grief counselors if you'd like to speak with them. Take as much time as you need," the doctor told the family as he walked out of the room. His mom didn't take much time or say a whole lot. She was speaking quietly as she usually did, so he couldn't even hear her. His father was heavily sedated. When she finished whispering in his father's ear, she lightly kissed him on the forehead and then walked out of the room.

His sister walked over, put one hand on his father's hand and said, "I love you Daddy. I'll miss you." Then she kissed her father on the forehead and walked out. As he sat alone next to his dying father, he was at a loss for words. His father had always been there for him to give guidance and advice even though he worked extremely hard and wasn't home as often as his mother. The relationship his mother and father had was unstable at times, and sometimes he got the impression that his father only stayed with his mother for him and his sister. He looked around the room just to make sure he was alone; then he stood up from the chair and slowly walked over to the bed where his father was lying. As he sat in the chair closer to his father's bedside, he grabbed his father's right hand with both his hands and said, "Dad, thank you for everything. Thank you for all your selfless sacrifices you made for our family. I'm sorry you had to go through this. I hope that you soon find peace." He began to tear up and almost choked trying to speak again. As he cleared his throat he finished, "Goodbye Dad. I love you."

Immediately he woke up and he was alone in his mobile home. *Son of a bitch,* he thought to himself. He could feel his entire body aching with stiffness. As he rolled over to look at his alarm clock, he realized he woke up about a half hour before his alarm even went off. *I can just go back to sleep* he thought to himself. Unfortunately, he played this game one too many times and ended up late for work several times over the years. He worked for an independent auto body and repair shop as a mechanic. Even though the shop specialized in body repairs, he was known to fix many engine problems as well.

His boss was getting older, and the two had agreed to a simple contract rather than fill out a bunch of official paperwork. The shop owner basically told him he had to work forty hours a week, and he could come in and work those hours however he wanted. He could work weekdays, weekends, early mornings or late evenings. It didn't matter to the owner. Even though he had a lot of flexibility with his work schedule, he always felt bad if he was late and made the old man open up shop by himself. They usually weren't that busy around 8 a.m. when they were officially open, but he liked being there on time, so he could get in the habit of leaving right at 4 p.m. and staying on a consistent schedule. After breakfast, changing his clothes and brushing his teeth, he loaded up his rusty Ford Ranger pickup and headed to work. As he was driving along the backroad to work, he saw corn to his right and soybeans on his left as the sun was rising from the east. The drive to work was about fifteen minutes away from his mobile home, and he had driven this route so many times he found himself daydreaming, picking up where he left off with his dream from the night before.

After his father passed away, his mother started dating another man named Stephen. He was a part-time bartender and drug dealer who got his mom addicted to heroin and meth. Stephen met her in the bar he worked at shortly after his father passed, and her drug use started with alcohol, marijuana and cocaine, and then just spiraled out of control from there. His mother experimented with just about anything she could get her hands on including psychedelics, but heroin was what hit her the hardest. The combination of her drug addiction and his father's medical bills caused the family to lose their house and forced them to move in with Stephen in his mobile home. The move was extremely hard for Samuel considering how much smaller the mobile home was and the fact that he no longer had his own room. Instead of once having his own bed, when his family moved in with Stephen, he had to sleep on the couch in the living room/kitchen.

The mobile home only had two bedrooms, which were very small, one for his mother and Stephen and then his sister got the other one. They also had to share one bathroom, but the worst part of it all was the ridicule and embarrassment he received at school. He didn't attend a private school or live in the wealthiest of school districts. Living in a mobile home within a trailer park made him the brunt of many jokes beginning his freshman year and that carried on throughout high school. This led to many fights, suspensions and eventually got him kicked off the wrestling team. Even though he had more time to study because he didn't have to practice anymore, his grades started to slip. His daydream took him to his first time spent with his mom's new boyfriend Stephen, just the two of them. It was shortly after he got kicked off the wrestling team; all four of them were sitting in the living room of Stephen's mobile home watching TV. They were watching a show where the main characters went hunting, which sparked his interest. "You ever hunted before?" he asked Stephen.

"Hell boy, I've killed more deer than I can count," Stephen replied.

"Sammy, you don't need to worry about hunting; you need to focus on getting your grades up and get back on the wrestling team," his mom chimed in. Samuel had pretty much given up on his dream of a wrestling scholarship. He knew that with his family's financial situation, the only way he was going to college was through wrestling, and considering he got kicked off the team as a freshman, most colleges were not going to be interested in someone who got kicked off the team and was academically ineligible.

His father had taken him fishing when he was young, and they made a point to go fishing at least once a month during the spring and summer. Samuel always wanted to try hunting though. Most of his friends that he grew up with and played sports with always talked about hunting with their family and friends. Samuel had always dreamed of getting a big buck like the other boys he went to school with. "Think you could take me hunting with you sometime?" Samuel asked Stephen.

"You really want to get a deer?" Stephen replied.

"I'd like to get a buck, maybe learn how to hunt other game as well, turkeys, rabbits, squirrels, whatever else you can hunt," Samuel said.

"Well, let me grab my rifle and keys," Stephen told him.

"Wait, we are going right now?" Samuel asked in confusion.

"Honey, it's dark. Just wait until tomorrow. Is it even deer season yet?" Samuel's mother asked.

"Nah, that doesn't matter," Stephen replied. Samuel stood up from the couch and looked at his mom confused and then looked toward the bedroom where Stephen walked out with a long, black rifle he had never seen before. It looked more like something used in the military than something used for hunting.

"What's that?" Samuel asked.

"This, boy is a Smith and Wesson M&P 15. We gonna spot deer and drop 'em with this mofo," Stephen said.

"Spot?" Samuel asked.

"Just get your shit and get in the damn truck," Stephen said sternly.

"Honey, you've been drinking, and it's getting late. Can't it wait until tomorrow?" Samuel's mom asked Stephen.

"I'll be alright. We gotta go now. Deer should be moving since it's a full moon tonight," Stephen said. Samuel grabbed a hoody and followed Stephen to his truck. While driving toward the state park, Samuel recognized where they were going. Most of the state park was closed after sunset, but one park entrance stayed open so people who lived in a neighborhood along the park could have access to the neighborhood. It didn't give park goers the typical access the rest of the entrances did, but there were still some open fields where deer liked to roam, especially at night.

"Here's how this works kid, when we get to the field, there's probably gonna be deer moving around. I can't promise you there will be any bucks, but does are dumb enough to stand in the middle of the field pretty much any time. When we get there, I'll shine the light on 'em, and you shoot the one you want. I'm only putting one in the chamber, so make it count. If we shoot more than once, it'll attract attention and a fucking park ranger might come along. If it runs away, just let it go. I'm not tracking a deer this late at night and before the season opens. Hopefully you drop it and we can clean it out quick and get it in the truck."

Samuel sat in the passenger seat, wondering how much of this plan was legal or not. Considering how upside down his life has been recently, he didn't care. *What else could go wrong in my life?* Samuel thought to himself. At first Samuel was tempted to ask Stephen if this was legal or not; he decided not to because he already knew the answer, and he was at the point where he really didn't care. He also knew Stephen didn't care about the law, so he just assumed all of this was illegal.

As they approached the large field between two heavily wooded areas that were on a hill, Samuel noticed dark objects scattered all over the place. *There must be over a dozen deer in this field,* Samuel thought to himself. "Alright, looks like you got plenty to choose from," said Stephen. Stephen handed the rifle to Samuel and then grabbed a large, heavy duty flashlight from underneath his back seat and started to shine the light across the field.

"Just say *stop* when you see the one you want," he told Samuel as he started scanning the field with the light. Samuel looked for a buck, but only saw does.

"I don't see any bucks," said Samuel.

"Damn kid. I can't control what deer show up. Just shoot one, so we can get out of here before we get caught. The longer we spot, the bigger the risk." Samuel was disappointed there were no bucks, but he also agreed with Stephen that he needed to shoot quickly.

"Alright stop. I see the one I want," Samuel told Stephen. Stephen had a red, infrared laser mounted on his rifle that made it somewhat easier to see the deer at night. Samuel was nervous as he lifted the rifle. He decided to use the hood of the truck to stabilize the rifle as he lined up his shot. "Any tips on shooting a deer?" asked Samuel.

"Yeah, aim slightly behind the front leg if you have a broadside shot, exhale and squeeze the trigger," Stephen told him. Almost immediately after Stephen stopped talking, *Bang!* Samuel shot, and the deer he was aiming at dropped right where it once stood. The other deer in the field stared at the lights being shined on them, and then scattered in all directions.

"Nice shot! Let's go clean it and drag that bitch back to the truck," Stephen told Samuel. The doe was about fifty yards away from the truck. Once they reached the doe, Stephen quickly went to work field dressing it.

"I should make you clean this damn thing, but we ain't got time and I don't want to get caught," Stephen said.

"Yeah, maybe next time you can teach me," replied Samuel.

"Just watch and learn kid; if you pay attention, you should be able to handle it yourself next time," Stephen told him. Samuel stood over Stephen with the flashlight and tried his best to observe what Stephen was doing. First, he noticed Stephen make a cut down the middle of the deer's chest all the way to its back legs and beyond. Stephen pulled a hammer out of his tool belt and used the knife and hammer to sever a bone by the deer's back legs. Samuel could hear a cracking noise along with Stephen's grunts as the legs widened. Stephen then cut up through the breast plate and ribs all the way to the deer's throat. When Stephen reached the windpipe, he cut it with his knife and then began to cut what looked like skin away from the deer's rib cage. Stephen reached up into the deer's chest cavity with one hand and then started pulling. As the organs started moving with the deer's throat, Stephen reached in and grabbed the rest with his other hand.

"Hold the deer and don't let it move," Stephen said as he continued pulling. Samuel couldn't believe how essentially every organ and body part inside the deer came out as Stephen pulled. When Stephen pulled the gut pile out of the doe, he left it in the field.

"Should we move that somewhere else to remove evidence?" Samuel asked.

"Hell no, coyotes or something will get to it before anyone

notices anyway," Stephen replied. After Stephen finished up, they each grabbed a leg and started pulling. It didn't take them long to reach the truck as the deer wasn't very big to begin with, and the deer was significantly lighter with its internal organs removed. After they loaded the deer into the truck, they both got in and Stephen drove away heading toward the park exit. Samuel felt a sense of pride and joy that he hadn't felt since before his father told him he had cancer. His life had been such a mess since that day, and it felt like everything was getting worse and worse as time went on. Even though it was before the deer season officially opened and they illegally poached a deer, Samuel was happy.

"You gonna skin it and do the rest of the work, boy," Stephen told Samuel.

"I don't know what I'm doing. Can you at least walk me through it?" Samuel replied.

"Just use my hunting book; that thing shows how to field dress and butcher every damn animal in North America," Stephen said. "When we get back, I'm gonna bang your mom and go to bed, so just keep it down when you're butchering that deer." *Fucking asshole,* Samuel thought to himself. Just like that, Samuel's brief moment of joy was ruined by the toxic individual that had crept into his family's lives.

Chapter 4

A week had passed since David's return, and as he was unpacking, he found a photo of him and his friend Danny. Before his permanent return home, he flew to El Paso for Danny's funeral. His best friend in the Army was killed in combat while they were on deployment in Afghanistan. David was Danny's best man in his wedding before their first tour in Afghanistan, and over the years, he felt like he became part of Danny's family, so he wanted to say goodbye to his friend one last time before coming home. Instead of hanging the photo on the wall somewhere, David decided to put the photo on his dresser, so he could see his friend every day. After he resigned from the Army, David found a three bedroom house on about ten acres of land outside of the suburbs where he grew up. While he wanted to find even more land, so he could hunt more often, David wasn't exactly sure where he wanted to live or what exactly he wanted to do after the military, so he found a nice quiet spot to live in the meantime.

Most of his possessions were back at Fort Bragg, so before

he left for Danny's funeral, David rented a U-Haul to get the rest of his belongings on base. Michael and his father helped him pack up and move to his new home. Now that he had a home, his next step was furnishing it, so the first couple weeks he was home, David took some time picking out furniture. Luckily his black Toyota Tundra had enough space to haul most of the new furniture he bought, and it saved him a lot of money on delivery fees. Whenever he needed a hand moving something, Michael and Zander were there to help.

"You got a couple extra bedrooms. You need a roommate?" Michael jokingly asked David.

"Nah, I'm going to turn one of the spare bedroom into an office. Besides I don't really want a roommate, no offense," David replied. Even though Michael was his best friend, David sometimes worried that if he lived with someone he was really close to and things didn't work out, it could possibly ruin the friendship.

"I'll make one of the spare bedrooms a guest room though, so you can stay there occasionally, but I promise you don't want to live with me," David told his friend.

"What makes you say that?" Michael asked.

"Because I'll put you to work," David replied. "Anyone that wants to live with me is going to help clean and take care of this place. There's more work to be done here than just a normal house or apartment," he continued.

"Yeah that's true; besides you'll probably wake everyone up at the crack of dawn," Michael said.

"Damn straight, no sleeping in here," David said.

One of David's top priorities besides finishing up furnishing his home was finding a range, so he could keep his skills intact. He visited a few indoor ranges around the city, but he didn't like indoor ranges because he was limited to how he could move and also didn't like how many random people would use them with very little training. David always felt like the chance of getting shot by someone who didn't know what they were doing was much higher at an indoor range. While buying ammo one day, he saw a flyer inside the store that was inviting new members to an outdoor range north of West Spoon State Park. "Bullseye Shooting Center," the flyer read. He decided to drive over and check it out. David met the owner of the range, a man named Jim. He explained to David that he was a retired marine, and he opened the range about a decade ago with his wife who was also a retired marine. Jim told David that even though they wanted to increase their membership, they were still hesitant as to who they would allow to join.

"I'm basically only allowing members who are current or former military, law enforcement or have their concealed carry weapon permit. I don't want members who lack firearm safety and training," Jim explained to David.

"I understand. I respect that," David replied. He was impressed with the layout of the range. They had a one hundred yard rifle range with about half a dozen or more lanes; they had a separate range area where you could move around and use rifles, shotguns and handguns. Then they had about half a dozen pistol only ranges with several different setups and targets. Members were allowed to bring their own targets or to use the steel targets the range had set up. David was focused on preparing for bow season; yet he still wanted to shoot at the range at least once a week as well.

Besides going to the range weekly, David was also interested in finding a gym to work out and stay in shape. He really wanted to find a mixed martial arts gym. Ever since his training in the Army, he became intrigued by hand-to-hand combat and the different disciplines of martial arts. When he was younger, David was a huge fan of boxing; yet he never had any formal training outside of wrestling until one of his platoon commanders in the Army, a former golden glove competitor, showed him some basic techniques.

Another one of his platoon leaders was a Gracie Jiu Jitsu black belt, so he became obsessed with Brazilian Jiu Jitsu while in the Army. The problem was when he was state side, he moved around a lot and was having a hard time finding a gym to continue his training. It wasn't until one day at the range that David hit the gold mine and found a spot to train. While sighting in his Mossberg .450 Bushmaster at the range one day, he noticed another man a few lanes down from him wearing a shirt that said, "Eastside MMA & Fitness."

"Excuse me sir, do you train there?" David asked as he pointed to the logo on the man's shirt.

The man chuckled and said, "Yeah, but I spend more time coaching than actually training these days." David held out his hand and introduced himself, "Hi, I'm David."

"Greg, nice to meet you," the man replied as he shook David's hand.

"What all do you teach there," David asked.

"I'm one of the striking coaches," Greg replied. "I coach Muay Thai and Kickboxing," he continued.

"Oh wow, that's cool. Do you guys have any grappling coaches there?" David asked.

"Yeah we have several wrestling coaches, one judo coach, and one jiu jitsu coach," Greg explained. "You interested in training there?" Greg asked David.

"Yeah, I learned some boxing and jiu jitsu from guys I served with in the special forces, and I've been looking for somewhere to continue training," David explained to Greg.

"Hell yeah man; just come in whenever and check it out. We'd love to have you train with us," Greg said as he handed him a business card with an address, phone number and email address.

David finished glancing at the business card and said, "Thanks man. I appreciate it."

"No problem," Greg replied. "I teach classes 5-6:30 p.m. Monday and Wednesdays. Hope to see you there," Greg continued as he packed up and headed out. David nodded and started packing up himself.

The next day David wanted to walk around West Spoon and look for signs of deer. He knew to look for rubs, scrapes, frequently traveled deer routes and of course, deer scat. Unfortunately, when David woke up, it was raining and he still had some stuff to unpack and some new furniture to build and install. David was waiting for a rainy day to complete some indoor tasks anyway, so after breakfast he started working on building his new dresser. It didn't take him long to build the dresser, and he immediately filled it with clothes that he typically wore on a daily basis. He had all his clothes in boxes and even after filling up the dresser, there were still a few boxes of clothes, most of which were hunting clothes or clothes he wore to work out. David decided to use the space in his closet for his nicer shirts and hunting gear. He realized he probably had enough room in his closet for all his clothes, but he mainly bought the dresser so he had a spot to put his TV against the wall across from the foot of his bed.

He liked to watch TV as he fell asleep. Throughout most of his life, he had an easier time falling asleep if there was music playing or a TV on. During his time in the Army, David didn't always have that luxury, so he wanted to make sure that now he was on his own, he could set up his bedroom exactly how he wanted it. Once he got all his clothes put away, he wanted to get started on building a desk for his office in the spare bedroom. The desk took longer to build, but David knew getting that installed would help, so he would have more space to put some of his belongings instead of just leaving everything in boxes.

David's parents had decided to get some new furniture, so he did get some older stuff from them. One of the items they gave him was their old kitchen table that seated four people and fit perfectly in his dining room/kitchen. While eating lunch at the kitchen table, David decided to do some research on what his brother Zander mentioned—that several people had gone missing at West Spoon State Park. After doing a simple Google search, David found several articles from local news that covered reports of people who had gone missing while visiting West Spoon State Park. David discovered that the oldest report was a high school couple who had gone missing two years before David and Zander encountered the man following them while hunting that day. The search team never found their bodies.

A year after David and Zander's encounter with the stranger, a park ranger went missing and was never found either. Little more than a year after the park ranger's disappearance, a group of four teenage boys went missing. A fisherman found one of their cell phones near the edge of the lake, but their bodies were never found. The final disappearance was a man whose motorcycle was discovered unattended in a parking lot near the state park.

Probably the most controversial case was the double murder that happened right along the boundary of the park. A man and his son were found dead after being shot several times on the backside of their property that was right next to the state park boundary. The man's wife said they both left the house to hunt that morning, and she later found them dead. It didn't take her long to find them because their dogs were barking near where she found the bodies. The forensics team had determined that both the father and son were killed on their property before their bodies were dragged across their property and into the state park. Both men were found with one 9mm hollow point round in their head, as well as at least one .12 gauge slug shot into them. The father was shot in the chest, and his son was shot in the upper back.

After reading about all the murders and people that had gone missing at the state park, David started to wonder if it was just a series of random killings, or if one person was responsible for it all. "Jesus Christ" David said to himself out loud as he finished reading while eating his lunch.

He continued organizing his new apartment, thinking about the murders at West Spoon Lake the entire time. At first he thought about what was going through each person's mind before they were killed. Then he began to wonder who could have done it and how exactly each murder happened. The news reports were vague, and there didn't appear to be much follow up investigation. Most of the victims' bodies were not found, so David knew it was going to take authorities longer to find the culprit. The authorities never caught anyone, and to David's knowledge from the news reports, they didn't have any leads either.

Whoever was responsible for all the killings was very careful about leaving a trail or evidence behind. David wondered why there were so many cases where the bodies were never found, and then there was one case where the authorities did find the bodies of a father and son that were out hunting. It didn't take long for David to wonder if the man who stalked him and Zander that one day was the one responsible for all the murders at West Spoon Lake. David didn't sleep much that night as his mind kept wondering about all the news reports of the murders. He decided to drive to the mixed martial arts gym Greg told him about just to see where it was and if he could take his mind off all the murders around West Spoon Lake.

Since David lived closer to the south side of the lake, and the gym was on the north side, it took him about twenty minutes to drive around the lake and find the gym. The lot was empty, and the building looked more like a warehouse than a gym. He wasn't even sure where the main entrance was. After looking around for a couple of minutes, he decided to head back home and check it out tomorrow when it was open.

When he pulled up to the parking lot the next morning, there weren't many places to park, and there were no signs to help him locate exactly which building was the gym. David noticed only two doors by the building where the address was located. One door was open, so he decided to head that way. As he got closer, he could see inside and hear loud music and some weight lifting equipment.

It didn't take long for David to realize he found the place; as he walked through the front where the weight lifting equipment was, he could hear people talking inside, and he noticed a smell he recognized very well. Blood and sweat. As he rounded the corner, he noticed a sign in sheet by a desk. David looked at the sheet and wondered if he needed to sign in yet or not. "Hey! You need some help?" asked a large man standing in a caged area.

"Yeah, I'm interested in taking classes. Just need to know who I should talk to," David replied as he walked over to the cage. The man stepped out of the cage and started to walk toward him.

"I'm Ray; I'm a co-owner of the gym," the large man said as he reached out his hand. David shook his hand and introduced himself.

"There's a class schedule over there by the sign in sheet; we offer classes in the morning and evening. The class schedule is subject to change depending on what the coaches schedules are like, but you're more than welcome to attend any class or come in and train whenever you want. The gym is pretty much open 24/7, and we got plenty of active pro and amateur fighters to work with," Ray told David.

"Awesome. That sounds great. When can I start?" David asked.

"Well you'll need to talk to Mark about fees. I don't deal with the finances. Not sure what he's charging new members these days to be honest. Once you get that sorted out, you can start whenever you want," Ray replied.

"Ok, any idea when he might be here?" David asked.

"He should be here any minute; we do have a wrestling class starting in about five minutes if you want to hang around and watch," Ray said.

"Would you mind if I participated? I promise I'll pay once Mark gets here," David said.

"We do offer a free trial class, so feel free to start today if you want. I'd just recommend finding Mark and sorting things out with him before you leave today," Ray replied.

"Ok, sounds good," David said. He already had on most of the gear that he needed for wrestling practice. He sat on a bench facing the caged area where other fighters were getting ready to start warming up. He opened his gym bag and thought about putting his wrestling shoes on, and then he noticed the rest of the fighters were not wearing shoes and he opted not to wear them. *Maybe this is more of an MMA-oriented wrestling class,* he thought to himself. Ray taught the class and they started by shadow wrestling. David hadn't shadow wrestled since he was in high school. He drilled plenty of take-downs while he was in the Army, but he always hated shadow wrestling. David understood the importance of shadow wrestling though; it was a great way to warm up and use similar movements he would likely use later during class whether it was drilling a technique or even during sparring. Ray had the class drill some basic techniques before they partnered up with someone of similar size to spar. David could feel Ray watching him closely and eventually Ray said, "I like what I see Rambo." David just smiled and kept working. After class ended and everyone was packing up to leave, David heard someone say, "Who's the new guy?"

"This is David," Ray replied.

"You must be Mark," David said as he extended his hand.

Mark shook his hand and said, "Greg told me you might swing by; former Special Forces right?"

"Yes sir," David replied.

"Usually I charge one hundred per month, unlimited access to the gym. Since you're former military, I'll let you train here for seventy-five, military discount," Mark told David.

"Thanks, I appreciate that," David replied. *Seventy-five dollars per month for unlimited access to all the classes was a great deal*, David thought to himself.

"Some of our coaches offer private classes. You'll have to get with them and see what they charge though. I leave that up to them," Mark told David who nodded and then walked toward the desk to grab a class schedule before heading out.

The next day David decided to go to West Spoon Lake to scout for the upcoming bow season. Considering squirrel season was open, he decided to print out his small game license along with a park map and he loaded his Remington .22 Long rifle into his truck to do some squirrel hunting while he was scouting for deer. Usually he was in the woods before sunrise to get settled in before the deer started moving. David knew he didn't have to worry about that with squirrels, so he got to sleep in a little bit before heading out. He decided to hike along the same path he took with his brother the last time he was at West Spoon.

Part of him wanted to come across the same guy who stalked him and his brother all those years ago. David had his concealed weapon permit and decided to bring his Sig Sauer P320 along with him as well. If he did cross paths with a stalker and potentially a murderer, David wanted to be armed with more than just a .22 long rifle. As David was walking along the trail toward the legal hunting area, he noticed several squirrels running around, but knew he shouldn't shoot in a no hunting zone.

David had hunted at West Spoon many times and never saw a park ranger. *But knowing my luck, I'll cross paths with one as soon as I pull that trigger,* David thought to himself. He saw park rangers driving around all the time; he just never saw one in the woods. David thought that might be why they couldn't find the person responsible for all the killings. David eventually made his way into an oak grove where he saw plenty of signs that deer were moving around in that area.

He found about half a dozen rubs and scrapes and a heavily traveled deer path that ran directly into the oak grove across from a steep hillside next to a creek. Because the hill was very steep, David assumed deer traveled directly through the oak grove before moving toward the deer trail and into another heavily wooded area. The only problem was this area was right beyond the illegal hunting zone, and he worried that if he shot at a deer in this area, it would run off into the no hunting zone. David was aware that deer don't understand boundary lines; the problem was a park ranger or conservation officer might assume he was hunting in an illegal hunting area. It was a shame because David did find a really good spot that he could use to set up a climber or a blind. As he was looking around, he noticed a large fox squirrel bouncing around on the ground and noticed him pick up a hickory nut before climbing a tree and then sitting on a branch that extended out about twenty feet off the ground. David lined up his shot and put the crosshairs right on the squirrel's ear. *Poor bastard,* David thought to himself just before pulling the trigger. *Bang!*

The .22 wasn't very loud; still the complete silence of the woods that morning made it sound a little louder than normal. David saw the fox squirrel drop directly below the branch he was once sitting on. David knew he hit it and slowly started walking up toward it. Along the way he picked up a long, skinny branch and poked the squirrel just to make sure it was dead. Although it had never happened to him, David did hear stories of hunters who were bitten by wounded squirrels because they picked them up thinking the squirrel was already dead. David had field dressed enough squirrels to notice how big their front teeth were, and he had no desire to get bit by one regardless if it was wounded or not.

The rest of the day, David didn't have as much luck finding signs of deer. He walked up and down hills through plenty of thorn bushes and thick briar patches. He cut his legs up pretty bad; yet he still managed to fill his daily bag limit within a couple hours of being out. Carrying around the squirrels all morning weighed on him more than he expected, and as he started to get hungry, David decided to head back. On the way back he came across a couple walking their dog, and they asked him if he "caught" anything. He laughed and said, "Yeah, hit my bag limit. Just heading home to finish cleaning them now." It always annoyed David a little when people asked if he "caught" anything. *You don't freaking catch them like they are a damn fish!* David thought to himself every time a non-hunter asked him that question. Shortly after running into the couple walking their dog, David came across a park ranger.

"Morning!" the ranger said as they approached each other along the hiking trail.

"Good morning, or afternoon I guess I should say," David replied.

"Yeah, I guess so," replied the ranger. "How'd you do?"

"Filled my daily limit sir," David told him. David noticed the ranger's last name was Durham from the name tag on his uniform.

"Good for you; mind if I take a look at your license?" asked the ranger.

David reached into his back pocket where he kept his wallet and hunting license. As he pulled out the small game license, he said, "Here ya go, Officer Durham." David's parents taught him to be as respectful as possible toward cops and law enforcement officers. He hoped if the ranger noticed that he at least took the time to learn the ranger's name, the ranger would be polite and let David go on his way. David didn't do anything wrong and had nothing to worry about; he just knew that some park rangers were always looking to cause problems for park goers.

"Well, we got calls from a couple about someone doing some shooting out here walking their dog, and I was just sent over to check it out. I'm sure you were in the legal hunting zone. I just gotta do my job," Officer Durham told David. *Those fucking assholes,* David thought to himself as he remembered the couple he passed. They were probably the ones that called the cops on me David assumed considering he hadn't seen anyone else out in the woods all day.

"I understand sir," David replied.

"Everything here looks good; just be careful out there," the ranger told David as he handed the hunting license back to him. *I wonder why he made that comment,* David thought to himself. Almost immediately it hit him.

"Excuse me sir, but do you know anything about the disappearances that have happened around here the past couple years?" David asked.

"Why do you ask?" the ranger replied.

"Well, I've been in the Army the past five years, and it's been a while since I've been here. I tried to get my brother to come hunt with me today, and he seemed afraid to step foot in this park after what's happened in recent years," David told the ranger. David chose not to mention the run-in they both had with the stranger who stalked them the one night while they were returning from hunting.

"I can't blame him," the ranger replied. "There's been at

least ten people killed or gone missing at this park in the past seven or eight years," the ranger continued.

"Holy shit. You guys got any leads?" David asked.

"Hell no. The park rangers don't have the funding, and the local police department is too busy dealing with drug dealers in this area to put together a legitimate investigation," the ranger told David.

"What're they pushing," David asked.

"Mostly heroin and meth; there's been a couple of busts at local bars or the trailer park, but it's still not really making a dent in solving the problem," the ranger explained.

"How long have you been a park ranger?" David asked.

"Be twenty years in about four months," Officer Durham replied.

"Did you know the ranger that went missing?" David asked.

"Yeah, Roger was a good guy. Married with two daughters; one just graduated high school and was about to start college and then the other was a sophomore. He didn't have much longer until retirement either," the ranger told David.

"Ah shit man. I'm sorry to hear that," David replied.

"Yeah, I bet you know a thing or two about losing someone you serve with though, huh?" the ranger said quietly.

"Yeah, we lost some good men over there. Men much better than me," David said.

"That just means we gotta honor those we lost, live our lives the way they'd want us to," the ranger told David.

"Yes sir," David replied as he nodded his head.

"Have a good evening; hope to see you around more often," Officer Durham told David.

"You too," David said as he walked back to his truck. After he got done putting his gear back in his truck, David reached into his pocket to check his phone and realized he got a text from his friend Michael. "Want to meet up later and grab a few brewskis?" the text read.

"Sure, what time you thinking?" David sent back. Hunting and sparring had worn David out physically; trying to figure out who was behind all the murders at West Spoon was starting to wear David out mentally. When he got back to his apartment, he checked his phone again and saw Michael wanted to meet at 8 p.m. After showering and changing his clothes, he made himself dinner and then ordered an Uber, so he could meet Michael and some of their friends. They decided to meet at a bar called the Oasis that was closer to his parents' house and was somewhat known for having great pizza. David started to regret eating before he came out because Michael and his girlfriend ordered a pizza that looked delicious. This was the first time David was meeting Michael's new girlfriend, Avery. David noticed Michael was always either in a relationship or looking for one. When David left for basic, Michael was dating a girl named April who Michael swore up and down he would marry one day. They dated for about two years in college before Michael found out she was cheating on him.

David remembered trying to warn Michael not to date a girl who lived so far away. "Just because you went to high school together doesn't mean she's going to be loyal in college. If you were both going to the same school, it'd probably work, but when you're not around, you don't know what she's doing," David tried to warn Michael. David still remembered getting the phone call from Michael when he went up to visit April at Toledo, and her roommate warned him that she had started seeing some other guy. Michael eventually confronted April about the other guy, and she claimed they were just friends.

David had heard that before and knew what that meant. April actually broke up with Michael before he realized what was going on and almost immediately after their break up, she was dating that other guy. Because of Michael's experience trying to date someone long distance, David had no desire to date anyone while he was in the Army.

"Now that you're home, you gonna find yourself a girl-friend?" Michael asked David.

"I don't know man. I'm still just getting settled into civilian life," David replied.

"Yeah, but that won't take you long. You adapt pretty well," Michael said.

"I guess so. I'm just focused on finishing up with my house and finding a job," David told Michael.

"You see Josie is dating some guy she met in college?" Michael asked David.

"I'm not surprised. She's got an awesome personality and she's beautiful. I'm happy for her," David said. David had become close with Josie who he met through Michael and some other friends of his. They knew each other a little bit in high school, but they really hit it off their senior year and the summer before David went off to the Army and Josie went off to college. They went on multiple dates and discussed trying to date even if it was a long distance relationship. David explained to her that their relationship wouldn't just be a long distance relationship; he knew it would be even harder because he would have limited ability to communicate with her.

"Yeah, we all kinda fell out of touch with her when she went to OSU. Apparently she's moving back home though," Michael told David. "Wonder if she will bring her boyfriend back with her," Michael continued.

"No idea," David said hoping Michael would change the subject.

"You know, I have a lot of single friends who would love to go out with a marine," Avery told David.

David laughed and said, "I'm not a marine."

"He was in the Army Special Forces," Michael told Avery.

"Oh, I'm sorry," Avery replied.

"No worries. Next time, feel free to invite whoever you want though. I'm always down to meet new people," David told her.

David and Michael played a couple games of Golden Tee. Michael won the first game, and then David won the second. After David beat Michael, Michael got very competitive because apparently he played Golden Tee a lot and David had just learned how to play the game. David hated golf; he understood the game; he just didn't have the patience to get really good at it. Golden Tee came much easier to David, and he started to enjoy it. About midway through their third game, Michael started to get really frustrated because he was down by two strokes. David decided to purposefully start screwing up to let Michael win. David started to notice how drunk Avery was getting because she had gone up to the bar about half a dozen times while David and Michael were playing Golden Tee, and she kept ordering shots. Avery also kept coming up to Michael and asking if they were done playing yet. Michael was starting to get annoyed, and David felt it was best to just let Michael win so they could all get an Uber ride home before Michael and Avery started arguing at the bar. When David needed to use the restroom, he decided to let Avery play for him which he figured would be all he needed to let Michael win.

"Common man, why are you letting her play for you? I'll just wait until you get back," Michael told David.

"It's ok; just let her play one or two holes. It's cool," David said. "Giggity," Michael replied as David laughed and walked to the restroom.

David's plan worked; when he came back, Michael had a five stroke lead, and there were only three holes left. After they finished their third round of Golden Tee, they decided to order an Uber. David and Michael walked outside so Michael could smoke while Avery closed her tab and said goodbye to a few of her friends that she ran into while they were at the bar. While David and Michael were outside, David decided to ask Michael if he had heard anything about the people that had gone missing at West Spoon, "Hey man, did you hear about all those people that went missing and the murders at West Spoon?"

"What?" replied Michael.

"Zander told me a bunch of people went missing over the past few years and then when I looked into it, I saw a bunch of articles online. Apparently there was a high school couple that went missing; then a park ranger; there was also a group of high school kids that vanished; a biker went missing and then a father and son were found murdered with several gunshot wounds," David explained to Michael.

"Holy shit, no wonder Zander didn't want to go hunting there. I'd stay the fuck away from that place too," Michael replied.

David laughed and then said, "Well I went hunting there today and actually ran into a park ranger. I asked him if he knew anything about the murders and the people that went missing. The only thing he told me was that he knew the park ranger that went missing. Basically the park rangers don't have the funding, and the local PD is too busy with drug busts."

"Yeah, that place is like heaven for heroin addicts. I guess a bunch of meth is coming from the trailer parks out that way too," Michael replied.

"You ever go out that way?" David asked.

"There's a small airport about ten minutes west of the state park, but beyond that I don't usually go out there for any reason. Definitely going to stay the fuck away from that place now. I heard about the park ranger going missing, but I think a lot of people just assumed he committed suicide or something out there. They never found his body or anything, and that place is huge, so who knows what happened to him. Now hearing about all the other murders and stuff, there's no way I'm going out there. You're fucking crazy for going hunting out there by yourself," Michael told David.

David laughed and replied, "I've put myself in far worse danger than that."

"Well yeah, I'm sure you have. But you were serving your country and getting paid while you were in the Army. No sense in risking your life out there at that fucking place," Michael said.

"My training will keep me safe. I'm not worried about it," David replied. He started to tell Michael about the time Zander and he went hunting years ago and were followed back to his truck before the stalker split and went in a different direction. David realized he had never told anyone about that night, and Zander was too scared to talk to anyone about it.

"Jesus Christ man, do you think the same guy that followed you two is the one out there killing all those people?" Michael asked David.

"I'm not sure; it was definitely a sketchy situation, but I never even saw the guy's face, so there's no way I could identify him even if they had any suspects. I barely heard him speak, and I doubt I would recognize his voice if I ever heard it again," David explained.

"Dude, promise me you won't go out there looking for that lunatic," Michael said.

"Come on you know me better than that. I'm always hunting," David smiled as their Uber driver pulled up.

Chapter 5

After a long day of work, Samuel decided to go to a small bar near the trailer park. It was a pool bar called The Last Call, and a woman named Lyndsey, who Samuel had been seeing frequently, often showed up there to drink after she got off work as a waitress. Samuel had always had a crush on Lyndsey although she didn't always reciprocate the same feelings. It was pretty well known that she got around, and it seemed like whenever she was officially single, she would spend more time with Samuel, but before he knew it, she would be with a new guy out of nowhere. When Samuel walked through the front doors, he walked up to the bar and ordered a Budweiser; then he looked around to see if he could find Lyndsey. It was still a little earlier than when she usually showed up, and he didn't see her.

"She's not here yet, sweetheart," the female bartender told him. Samuel had met her several times, but couldn't remember the bartender's name. She must have been a new hire because Samuel knew pretty much everyone else that worked there.

"Ok, thanks," he replied. *Nosy bitch,* Samuel thought to himself. He decided to text Lyndsey to see if she was coming to the bar later. "Hey, what's up," he sent to her. As he was sitting at the bar finishing his beer, he noticed she saw his text and she didn't respond. Usually if she wanted to see him, she would reply right away and seem excited. *She's probably with some other guy right now,* Samuel thought to himself. He was tired, but he decided to stick around in case she showed up.

Samuel was partially hoping she would show up with some guy, so he could confront him and fight the guy so he would leave her alone in the future. Samuel had fought several guys in the parking lot or behind the bar over Lyndsey and even though she would always tell him not to fight, he started to think she enjoyed it because once the fight started, she never tried to break it up. Several times after Samuel fought some guy hitting on her, she would go back to Samuel's trailer, and they would have passionate sex. Sometimes Samuel felt like she would sleep with him as a reward for fighting for her.

A couple of hours had passed, and Lyndsey never showed up. Instead, a few guys that Samuel went to high school with showed up. They were always arrogant and mean to him, so he decided to close his bar tab and leave. He was tired and didn't expect to see Lyndsey that night, so he went home. When he got home he rolled a joint and went outside to smoke. Once he was high, Samuel reheated some pizza; then watched some porn and went to bed.

Once Samuel drifted off to sleep, he had a similar nightmare, the nightmare that destroyed the rest of his family. It was Samuel's junior year of high school, and he got home late after school one day. He decided to go smoke weed with some friends at a skate park, then walk to his friend Jay's house and watch TV until his high wore off. Samuel didn't have a car, so he had to walk home from Jay's, and it took him about fifteen minutes even though he knew a few shortcuts. As he walked through the door of Stephen's mobile home, he didn't hear anyone inside. "Hello?" he called out.

"In here," Haley responded quietly from her room. Samuel walked over and looked in to see her in bed reading a book.

"What's up, sis?" he asked.

"Just reading for class," Haley replied.

"What book are you reading," Samuel asked.

"*To Kill A Mockingbird*," Haley said.

"Oh nice. That's a great book. Have you seen Mom?" Samuel asked Haley.

"I think she's in her room," Haley told him. Samuel walked over to Stephen's and his mother's bedroom and saw her passed out, which had become a common theme for her the past couple years. Stephen's drug dealing had severely contributed to Samuel's mother's drug addiction. Stephen provided her with whatever she wanted, and she had almost overdosed on heroin several times in the past few months. Samuel walked over and placed his hand on her neck to check for a pulse. He found one, but it was much slower than normal.

Samuel looked over on the nightstand and found a needle. "Fuck," he said under his breath. *She must have injected not too long ago,* he thought to himself. Since he had some homework to do, and Stephen was nowhere to be found, he grabbed his backpack and decided to do his homework in this room, so he could keep an eye on his mom and make sure she kept breathing. As much as he wanted to take her to get help, he was afraid that exposing her drug addiction would get Stephen in trouble, and then they would have nowhere to live.

About two hours later he heard a knock on their door. *That's odd* he thought to himself, Stephen never knocked, and it was a little late for any of his or Haley's friends to just stop by. Samuel was always embarrassed to admit to his friends that he lived in a trailer park, so he never invited his friends over anyway and only a few knew where he lived. Samuel decided to look out the bedroom window where he could see the front porch of the trailer and see who was at the door. Two cops were standing there, and he was immediately concerned because his mom was still coming down from the heroin. Samuel opened the drawer by the night stand to hide the needle, and as soon as he opened it, he noticed a bunch of small baggies containing several different substances. "Oh fuck," he said to himself. Just then he looked down the hallway and saw Haley at the door ready to open it. "*Wait!*" Samuel said sternly trying not to make too much noise. It was too late. Haley opened the door and she immediately had a concerned look on her face as she saw two tall cops standing in front of her.

"We have a warrant to search the home," the taller blonde cop said as he opened the screen door and walked into the mobile home holding up a piece of paper. Haley backed up and looked over at her older brother visibly scared of what might happen next. Samuel closed the bedroom door behind him where his mother Sandy was still passed out from the heroin she injected. "Is the homeowner here?" the other cop asked. He was short and bald.

"No," Samuel replied.

"Do you know where he or she is and when they might be here?" the blonde cop asked Samuel.

"Stephen owns this dump. I don't know where he is or when he will be back," Samuel responded.

"Ok, I'm going to need both of you to sit down on the couch please and keep your hands where we can see them," the cop told Samuel and Haley. "I'm going to ask you a few questions while Officer Munson looks around." The shorter, bald cop started searching through the kitchen and then made his way down the hallway and looked into the bathroom and Haley's room. Samuel was more concerned about his mother's health than the possible drug charge Stephen may face when the cops inevitably found all the drugs in his trailer. It was going to be difficult finding another place to live. However, he hated it where they currently lived, so it couldn't get much worse.

"Do you know why we are here?" the bald cop asked.

"I have no idea," Samuel replied.

"We have several reports of drug dealing and suspicious activity coming in and out of this home," the cop told them.

"It's a fucking trailer. It's not a home," Samuel said sternly.

"Ok, well we've been sent to search this *trailer* for drugs and illegal substances. Is Stephen your father?" the cop asked.

"Hell no, he's my mom's piece of shit boyfriend."

"Ok, do you have his number?" the cop asked Samuel.

"No," Samuel lied.

"You know lying to an officer is obstruction, right?" the cop asked Samuel.

"*Oh shit!* Call the paramedics!" the bald cop said from the bedroom.

"What is it?" the blonde cop asked as he stood up and looked down the hallway toward the bedroom.

"We might have an OD here," the bald cop replied. Samuel started to get up off the couch before the blonde cop sternly told him to sit back down. Samuel looked over and noticed Haley started crying.

"Stay right where you are!" the blonde cop said as his partner radioed in for an ambulance. Shortly afterward another cop car showed up and two more officers got out of the car. After waiting for a little while, the blonde cop walked over and asked, "Where does Stephen work?"

"At Tony's Bar and Grill," Samuel replied.

"Ok go pick him up," the blonde cop radioed to someone else. Haley and Samuel sat on the couch for about another five or ten minutes although it felt like an hour for them. Once the paramedics got there, they carried their mom out of the trailer and put her on a stretcher, and they loaded her up into the ambulance. "We are going to take your mom to the hospital; we can give both of you a ride there, and you can wait for her in the waiting room. They are going to treat her for opiates," the blonde cop told Samuel and Haley.

"Then why are they handcuffing her to the stretcher?" Samuel asked the cop.

"She's a suspect right now, and it's standard procedure," the blonde cop replied.

"That's fucking bullshit. Stephen is the one you're looking for," Samuel said.

"We will figure that out when we find him and question both of them," the cop told Samuel.

Samuel and Haley were in the waiting room at the hospital for over two hours before they were able to see their mother. Before they could go back to see her, they saw two cops escort Stephen back to her room. As Stephen passed them, he briefly looked over and smirked at them. Samuel had a bad feeling and didn't trust what Stephen was going to do next. While Stephen was in their mother's room, the two police officers that came to the trailer came out to speak with Samuel and Haley.

"Your mother is being charged with possession of an illegal substance. We still have our suspicions about her boyfriend, Stephen, but we couldn't prove anything. He didn't have anything on him when we picked him up; nor did he have anything in his vehicle. The only drugs we found were in your mother's bedroom when he wasn't even home. If convicted she could face up to eighteen months in prison considering the amount she had on her. It is my understanding that your father passed away, and your mother is your sole parent/guardian. Stephen has offered to become legal guardian to both of you while your mother is in prison as long as she agrees to it. With good behavior and considering she has no priors, there's a good chance she will be out in a year," the cop told Samuel and Haley.

"I don't want to live with that asshole," Samuel said.

"I understand. The problem is if your only legal guardian is in prison, then you and your sister will go into foster care, and there is no guarantee the two of you won't be split up. We are trying to do what's best for you *and* your sister," the cop replied.

"Please. I don't want to live in a foster home," Haley told Samuel as she began to cry. Samuel reached over to give his sister a hug.

"Ok, I won't let them separate us," Samuel whispered to his sister.

The cop let them embrace for a moment and then said, "Alright, we got some paperwork to fill out and legal stuff to take care of. Once everything is sorted out, we will let you go back and see your mom, and then Stephen is going to take you home. I'm sorry you two have to go through this. Here's a card in case either of you need to speak to a therapist." He handed the business card to Samuel as he walked out the front door of the hospital. Samuel watched him leave and then crumbled up the card and threw it on the floor. Samuel woke up briefly to use the restroom, but quickly fell back asleep and his nightmare continued.

A year later Samuel's mom was released from jail. Stephen was still dealing drugs, although the authorities never seemed to be able to catch him. Samuel was a few months away from graduating, and he was staying after school trying to catch up on his academics because his GPA had slipped over the years. He was trying to do extra credit work and get some tutoring, so he could finish strong and graduate. What happened to his family ever since his father passed had embarrassed him enough; the last thing he wanted to do was fail his senior year and not be able to graduate with his friends. He was also worried the stress of him failing to graduate might cause his mother to relapse. She had gone through a tough rehab while in prison, and Samuel was hoping she would find a job to keep her busy and avoid using again.

His sister was doing well in school although she seemed unhappy and sad. She used to talk about her friends a lot and hangout with them in her free time, but now she just went to school and came home. Haley spent most of her spare time in her room studying and watching TV. Samuel thought having their mother come home might brighten her spirits, but it seemed like nothing could cheer Haley up anymore. Before his mother came home, Samuel decided to ask Stephen to keep the drugs away from her, "Hey, when Mom gets back, can you please keep your stash away from her? At least keep them out of the trailer, so it's not easy access for her?"

"Mind your fucking business you little punk," Stephen replied.

"Look man my mom almost died because of that shit and instead of you being held accountable for dealing, she went to prison for a year!" Samuel yelled back at Stephen.

"Watch your fucking mouth or you can find a new home," Stephen snapped back at Samuel as he turned his back and started to walk away. Frustrated by Stephen's lack of empathy and disrespect, Samuel shoved him in the back as hard as he could and sent Stephen stumbling against the wall. Stephen was able to brace himself and immediately turned around to punch Samuel in the face sending him crashing to the ground. The loud noise from Samuel hitting the floor woke Haley and she quickly came out of her room to the sight of Stephen standing over her brother repeatedly punching him in the head as Samuel desperately covered up.

She ran over to help her brother, and as she started pulling on Stephen's shirt trying to get him off of Samuel, Stephen whipped around and slapped Haley across the face as hard as he could with the back of his hand sending her to the floor as well. Seeing his sister fall to the ground sent Samuel into a fit of rage, and he desperately began to fight Stephen. For a split second Samuel felt like he was getting the upper hand as they wrestled to the ground, and he ended up on top of Stephen. They both fell down near Haley on the floor. Samuel had his hands around Stephen's neck and began choking him. As he gasped for air, Stephen looked over and saw Haley crying as she sat up against the couch. Stephen kicked her in the face as hard as he could with his steel toed boots and immediately split her chin open. Hearing his sister whimper after she had been kicked, Samuel looked over at her, and then Stephen was able to push Samuel off of him and get back on top of Samuel.

Stephen punched Samuel over and over until Samuel was

knocked unconscious; then Stephen hit him a couple more times after that. As Haley lay on the floor bleeding and Samuel lay on the floor unconscious, Stephen walked to the kitchen and grabbed duct tape out of a cabinet. Stephen picked up Samuel and strapped him to a chair with duct tape. Stephen wrapped the duct tape around Samuel's mouth as well before going over to Haley to do the same. As Stephen grabbed Haley by the arm, she objected, "Please don't hurt me."

"Shut the fuck up or I'll slit your brother's throat and make you watch before I do the same to you!" Stephen snapped back. Haley tried to stop the bleeding on her chin as Stephen taped her to another chair in the kitchen. She sat in the chair crying as her brother was still unconscious; then Stephen walked into the kitchen and grabbed a knife. Once Samuel regained consciousness, he looked around the room confused. Samuel first saw Stephen on the couch staring at him and then glanced over to see his sister crying as blood was dripping down her chin onto her shirt. Immediately he remembered what happened and feared Stephen was about to kill both of them. Stephen stood up off the couch and approached them.

"If either of you two try that shit again or ever mouth off to me in my home, I'll kill both of you while your mother watches. I won't have to worry about killing her because that stupid fucking junkie is going to end up killing herself anyway. Mark my words, when she gets out, it won't be long before she ends up back in prison or ends up killing herself from an over-dose. Once that happens you two piss ants are on your own," Stephen told them. He then pulled his knife out and cut Haley loose right before he slapped her across the face again. Haley whimpered and Samuel grunted as he tried to break free of his restraints.

"What did I just fucking tell you?" Stephen asked Samuel as he pushed the knife blade against his throat. Haley looked over with tears rolling down her face, and Stephen continued, "Don't forget who owns this place. Now look at me . . . do you understand?" Samuel reluctantly nodded slowly.

"Good. You cut him loose," Stephen said to Haley right before he slapped Samuel across the face one more time and then walked out of the trailer slamming the door behind him.

From that point on Samuel noticed Stephen would keep a gun on him at all times and he always locked the bedroom door even when Samuel's mother got out of prison. When Samuel's mother got out, both he and his sister had visible bruising and wounds from their fight with Stephen. Before she was released Stephen warned Samuel and his sister that if they told their mother the truth, they were all going to get kicked out. Samuel's wounds were far worse, so he decided to tell his mother he was jumped on the way home from school one day, and Haley told her mother that she slipped and busted her chin open.

Unfortunately, Stephen was right about their mother, and shortly after Samuel graduated high school, she started using again. It started when she decided to have some friends over to celebrate Samuel's graduation. Sandy began drinking heavily and smoking marijuana often. Samuel had a hard time telling her to stop because he was drinking and smoking a lot as well. It wasn't until she started coming home with mushrooms and other psychedelics that Samuel started to get worried. He also noticed pills in plastic baggies around the trailer, and when he confronted his mother about them, she just said they were Stephen's. Samuel was afraid to say anything to Stephen. Every time Haley would ask their mother to stop using, Sandy would just pretend like she wasn't doing anything wrong or that she was just having fun. The lies only made Haley's depression worse.

Samuel started working at the auto body and repair shop right after high school. It was much better money than working landscaping. Without his knowledge, Samuel's mother made Stephen the legal guardian for Haley. Samuel was eighteen so Sandy wanted to make sure Haley had a place to live if anything ever happened to her, and she didn't want to make Samuel responsible for his sister. About two months after Samuel graduated high school, he came home from work and found his mother unresponsive on the couch. He checked for a pulse, but there wasn't one to be found.

Samuel knew what happened and was devastated. Distraught with grief he locked the front door and went into his mother's bedroom trying to find the source. He found needles all over her nightstand and realized she overdosed from heroin. Stephen was still dealing anything and everything he could get his hands on, and Samuel held him responsible for his mother's death because she never had any substance abuse issues until she met Stephen. Samuel franticly searched the mobile home for any weapon he could find. As he searched the mobile home up and down, he found the gun cases where Stephen would keep his rifles and handguns. Everything was locked up and he had no idea where Stephen kept the key. Stephen's truck was gone, and he was likely either at work or making some runs.

Samuel wondered where his sister was because she usually got home from school before he got home from work, so he expected Haley to be home with their mom. While he was hesitant to call Haley because he wasn't ready to tell her about what happened, he needed to find her and make sure she was ok. Samuel sat at the kitchen table across from his mother's body and couldn't decide if he should call his sister first or 9-1-1. When he picked up his cell phone, his hand was shaking and he decided to call his sister first.

The phone rang several times before she answered, "Hello?"

"Haley, where are you?" Samuel asked.

"I went to the park for a while," Haley replied.

"Anyone with you?" Samuel asked.

"No, I decided to go by myself," Haley said.

"Why did you do that? You know that's dangerous," Samuel told his sister.

"Mom started using again and I tried to get her to stop, but she just ignored me, so I didn't want to be around her while she was getting high. I figured I'd leave for a few hours and wait for it to wear off," Haley told her brother.

Samuel hesitated for a moment and then said, "You won't have to worry about that anymore. Mom's gone." Samuel waited for Haley's response, but all he could hear was her crying in the background. She knew what happened. "Stay where you are sis. I'll come get you," Samuel told Haley. Samuel didn't want his younger sister to see their mom dead on the couch, so he left the door open and on his way to meet his sister at the park, he called 9-1-1 and reported what happened. He was hoping that when the authorities got to the mobile home, maybe Stephen would show up with something on him and get caught. After a short walk to the park, Samuel could see his sister on the swings all alone with her head down. As Samuel walked up to her, he could hear her sobbing. Eventually, she noticed his shadow and looked up with tears rolling down her face. She ran toward him and jumped into his arms.

As Samuel held his sister, she began crying even harder, and her pain made Samuel start to tear up. While embracing his little sister, Samuel started to think about his father and how his father would want him to handle this. Samuel knew they had to get away from Stephen. He pulled his sister back, so he could hold her by the face and said, "Look at me Haley. Look at me." Haley's eyes were focused downward before she looked up at her brother.

"I promise you I will do everything in my power to get us away from Stephen. I know we don't have the money right now, but just be patient and let me save up. I will get us a place of our own," Samuel told his little sister.

"Mom made him my guardian," Haley said crying.

"What?" Samuel replied.

"When she got out of prison, she told me she was going to make Stephen a legal guardian in case she got caught again. I asked her not to because you would be eighteen, but she said she didn't want to put that kind of pressure on you and that you wouldn't be able to afford a place for both of us while I was in high school," Haley explained.

"Ok, here's what we do then. We live with Stephen while you finish up high school. Living with that piece of shit will help me save up so that when you graduate, we can both work and support ourselves. We will find our own place and probably find a place a lot nicer than Stephen's dump that we are in now. You've only got three more years of school left, and that should give me more than enough time to make some good money so we can find our own place," Samuel told his sister.

"I don't think I can live with him for three more years," Haley cried.

"I know it's going to be hard. I don't want to live with him either, but it's going to be a lot easier for both of us if we stay with him temporarily while we save up to get our own place. We just gotta be strong and take care of each other. I promise I'll protect you from him. You trust me right?" Samuel said. Haley nodded and then fell into her brother as he held her.

Despite Samuel's hopes that the authorities would finally catch Stephen, they still didn't arrest him because of Sandy's past record with drug use and her arrest. Because they could not prove Stephen was the source or supplier, they just assumed that Samuel's mother got the drugs on her own and began abusing them again. After their mother's death, Stephen told Samuel that he had to start paying rent if he wanted to live with him. Stephen explained that legally he was now Haley's guardian and she did not have to pay rent, but that he would find another way for her to pitch in.

At first Haley asked Samuel if she should get a part-time job to pitch in and try to help save up money so they could move out when she finished high school. Samuel told her not to worry about it because Stephen would just take a lot of her income, and he knew how hard it was to get good grades while working in high school. For the next two and a half years Samuel spent most of his time working and saving up money. Samuel would lie to Stephen about how much he was making, so that Stephen wouldn't charge him as much for rent. The only real hobby Samuel enjoyed during his free time was hunting. Samuel hunted with Stephen before his mother's arrest, and Stephen taught Samuel many unethical hunting practices. While he enjoyed hunting a lot, Samuel did hunt less, so he had more time to work and save money.

Samuel was determined to provide a better home for himself and his sister. He had his eyes on a two bedroom apartment not too far from where he worked and near many places where his sister could look for a job or go to community college. Samuel knew if his sister found a job right out of high school, it would help them afford a better apartment than the mobile home they were currently living in, but at the same time he wanted his sister to get a better education, hoping in the long run she might make even more money and be able to afford a house of her own. Samuel always thought his sister was very smart; he believed she could probably become a dentist like their father and earn a steady income.

The years they lived with Stephen after their mother's death were the hardest on Haley. Even though Samuel was working full time and trying to take the financial burden completely away from Haley, her grades were still slipping. At first Samuel expected her grades to fall a bit after their mother passed away. Eventually, her GPA steadily declined, and Samuel was worried if she would even graduate because she was struggling to finish high school just as much as he did. Samuel did everything he could to help her study and prepare, but she still was failing many tests and classes. It got to the point where Haley would hardly speak to him anymore, and his once bright, friendly sister was so despondent, she wouldn't even make eye contact with him. Every time he tried to talk to Haley, she would just say, "I'm fine." Samuel wanted to help her see a therapist, but he knew he couldn't afford it, and there was no way Stephen would help pay for it.

One day Samuel came home during his lunch break because he did not pack a lunch for work, and he walked in on Stephen raping his sister. The front door was unlocked, and he could hear that the TV was on, so he walked in trying to be as quiet as possible in case Stephen was home sleeping. Samuel usually did everything he could to avoid speaking or even seeing Stephen.

When he walked inside the mobile home, he could hear grunting, and he looked down the hall toward his sister's room and saw her door was cracked open. As he slowly walked closer to her door, he got out his pocket knife and could hear the grunting getting louder. Samuel peaked into his sister's room and saw Stephen on top of Haley thrusting into her. Stephen was pinning her down with his right arm and had his left hand around her neck to prevent her from screaming. Samuel could see Haley's face, and she was looking at him with hopeless eyes. For a split second his heart sank because he realized what was happening to his sister all along. Samuel quietly walked into Haley's room, sneaking up behind Stephen. While Samuel moved in on Stephen, Haley closed her eyes. Samuel raised the knife above his head and slammed it as hard as he could into the side of Stephen's neck.

As Stephen let out a blood curdling scream, he whipped around and shoved Samuel away from him. With the knife still stuck in his neck, Stephen dropped to his knees in pain clutching at the knife. Samuel quickly got back up and ran into the kitchen to get another knife or any weapon he could find. He noticed he left his hammer from work on the kitchen table and grabbed it. As he headed back toward Haley's room, he saw Stephen crawling out into the hallway with blood dripping down his body. Stephen was on all fours when Samuel approached him again. Samuel raised the hammer and yelled, *"Aaaaaaaahhhhhh,"* as he slammed the hammer down into Stephen's skull as hard as he could. Stephen's body immediately went limp and fell to the floor. Blood had splattered up against the walls, and more blood was dripping from Stephen's neck. Samuel pulled the knife out of Stephen's neck and blood came gushing out. Samuel left the hammer in the back of Stephen's head, but grabbed a towel and wiped down the handle of the hammer to remove any prints.

Samuel looked over at his sister who was naked and hugging her own knees while sitting in her bed. As he walked over to her, he grabbed a blanket and placed it around her and covered her body. Samuel put his arm around Haley, caught his breath and said, "I am so sorry. I didn't know."

Haley was shaking and crying. Eventually she stuttered, "I-I wanted to-to t-t-tell you. He-He said h-h-he'd kill me."

"How long has he been doing that to you?" Samuel asked.

"S-since M-M-Mom d-died," Haley struggled to reply.

"He can't hurt you anymore," Samuel said.

Samuel and Haley decided to tell the authorities they came home and found Stephen's dead body. They told the authorities Stephen owed massive debt to other drug dealers. To help cover it up, Samuel burned all the clothes he was wearing when he killed Stephen to hide any DNA and he threw the pocket knife he used to stab Stephen in West Spoon Lake after pouring bleach all over it removing any blood and DNA. After the authorities found all the heroin and meth in the mobile home as well as drugs in Stephen's truck, they realized Stephen was one of the biggest drug dealers in the area, and they failed to catch him multiple times. Since there were several other major drug dealers in the area, they didn't question Samuel and Haley's story. Shortly after remembering how he killed Stephen, Samuel awoke from the nightmare.

Samuel looked over at his alarm clock and realized he slept in until noon. Luckily it was Saturday, and he didn't have to work. Samuel was usually off on the weekends unless he chose not to work one day during the week; then he would usually try to make up those hours he missed. Samuel woke with a terrible hangover and noticed an empty bottle of Jack Daniels next to his alarm. Samuel just remembered he had taken several shots when he got home from the bar. Whenever he was depressed from Lyndsey letting him down, he would drink as much as possible because he had a hard time sleeping. The combination of the beer, liquor and weed allowed him to sleep for well over ten hours straight which became an extreme rarity for him as he got older. Every day it seemed like he would think about losing his family or the terrible things he'd done; the only time he felt at peace was when he was drunk or with Lindsey.

Samuel struggled to get out of bed, but eventually made his way to the kitchen to make a cup of coffee. Once his coffee was ready, he headed over to the couch and sat down to light up a cigarette while he watched college football. As he sat on the couch, he checked his cell and saw that Lyndsey finally replied to him. She didn't respond until long after he went to bed the night before and she had one of her typical lame excuses. Lyndsey told him that she couldn't make it out because she couldn't get a ride. Lyndsey had epilepsy and couldn't drive, but he knew if she wanted to see him, that didn't stop her in the past. Samuel just assumed she was with another guy; yet he invited her over to watch football with him anyway. After waiting for about half an hour, Lyndsey told him she had to work, so he offered to pick her up and give her a ride. Lyndsey politely declined and claimed she already had a ride to work. Usually when this happened, that meant she had spent the night at some other guy's house because she lived with her parents and whenever she needed a ride to work, Samuel would pick her up from their place.

Frustrated and let down by Lyndsey blowing him off and most likely hooking up with another man, Samuel decided to start drinking again. Samuel took a few Advil with his morning coffee, but he still had a slight headache and figured if he started drinking and smoking again, it might go away. Samuel decided to roll a few joints while eating cereal; then he passed out on the couch after smoking and downing a six pack. As he drifted off to sleep, the worst part of his nightmare continued.

Samuel had worked extremely hard to find a new place for Haley and him to live, and after Stephen's death, they had thirty days to find a new home. For the next week or two, both of them checked out a few apartments. While Samuel was thrilled to get away from the mobile home, Haley didn't show any excitement or emotion at all. Samuel was getting worried, and every time they viewed an apartment, he would ask her what she thought, and she would often just shrug her shoulders and give him very short, vague responses. After work one day Samuel had come home early because they had one last apartment to view before they made a decision. To his surprise Haley was not home, and after he checked the mobile home, Samuel called her. She didn't answer. Samuel was worried; his sister *always* answered when he called. He waited a couple minutes and then texted her. No response. Not wanting to miss their scheduled appointment to view the apartment, he called the agent that was going to show them the apartment and notified the agent that they would be a little late. If he could not find his sister, Samuel was afraid they would have to reschedule and prolong their search even longer as time was running out before they would be kicked out of Stephen's mobile home. Besides, Samuel had no desire to live there anymore after everything that happened.

Samuel texted a few of Haley's friends, and the ones that responded told him they had hardly seen or heard from her at all. Her friends told Samuel that she was acting very weird and avoiding everyone, and that she had not spoken to anyone in over a week. Growing more concerned, he walked out of the trailer and started walking around the trailer park hoping to find her. As he did a lap around the trailer park, Samuel started to wonder if maybe she went to the park. Haley enjoyed going to the park to get away from things, and it was a nice day, so he thought maybe she just wanted to enjoy the sunset. Samuel walked through the narrow path in the woods that led from the trailer park to the small park where children from the suburbs and the trailer park often played.

While Samuel was in high school, the park became overrun with drug and gang activity, so typically later in the day the park cleared out. Once he got through the woods and headed over the hill, he looked around and saw the park was empty. Samuel glanced over toward the swings where he met his sister after their mother's death and noticed the swings looked different. From a distance it almost looked like they added a swing, but it didn't make sense because it looked like they placed a swing on top of a swing. Samuel was walking down the hill when it hit him. "Oh my god," Samuel cried out as he took off running toward the swings. Samuel sprinted across the playground to the back of the park where the swings were.

"No, no, no, no . . ." he said as he came upon his sister. Haley was hanging from the swing set above the same swing she always sat upon. Samuel fell to his knees and began crying uncontrollably. After all the pain and suffering he had been through since his father's passing, nothing hurt him as bad as losing his sister. He loved her more than anyone, and he had worked so hard to get her away from Stephen and into a safe home. Samuel was so close to providing that for her, but the heinous acts committed by Stephen made life unbearable for his sister.

"Somebody help me! Please!" Samuel screamed over and over until neighbors came and called 9-1-1. The fire department and paramedics eventually came, and they brought a ladder to cut his sister down. Once they got her body down, he held her for several minutes before they placed her in a body bag.

Samuel felt his body shake as tears rolled down his face. His tears made it so that he could barely see, and yet as he looked at her dead body, he noticed her facial expression. Even after all her pain and suffering, her face after death seemed somehow peaceful. Samuel felt terrible that he failed to protect his sister after the promise he made. Then Samuel was woken up by a loud knocking at his door. "Who the fuck could this be," he said to himself as he got up off the couch and slowly made his way to the front door. It was Lyndsey. She had finally shown up.

Chapter 6

Now that David felt pretty comfortable in his new home and had finished setting up his furniture, he wanted to start looking for a job. However, he still had some work to do on his property, so during the day he spent his time outside. There were a few trees he wanted to remove, so he could have better access to the pond on the far side of his property, plus with the winter approaching, he figured it wouldn't hurt having some firewood. David's father offered to let him borrow his lawn mower to cut the grass, but David wanted to have his own equipment. His yard was much larger than his parents' yard, and he figured it would be beneficial to get a riding lawn mower to speed things up a bit and free his time for other chores.

After a trip to Home Depot and bringing home a new riding lawn mower, he decided to grill some burgers while he worked on his new law mower to make sure it would work the next time he needed to cut the grass. Later that night as he was getting ready for bed, he decided to get online and search for jobs.

The majority of places that were hiring were offering entry level positions for less than optimal wages. Compared to what he was making in the Army, if he took these jobs, he would be taking a significant pay cut. Getting frustrated, he decided to go to bed and continue the job search later.

The next day David woke up and saw that it was sunny outside. As usual he checked his phone's weather app to see what weather the day would bring. "Fuck," David muttered. The forecast was calling for rain around noon. He quickly packed up his rifle and handgun along with his range bag filled with the equipment he needed to go shooting. David had planned on going to the gym, but he wanted to get some range time before the rain came, so he decided to go to the gym afterward and participate in one of the later classes. While he was making a quick breakfast, he glanced at the gym's schedule and noticed there was a Brazilian Jiu Jitsu class that started a half hour later than the wrestling class. *Perfect,* he thought to himself. Then he ran upstairs to get his gym bag with a change of clothes and quickly packed up the rest of his gear for the day ahead. Instead of sitting down at the table to eat, David decided he would eat his meal on the way to the range to save time.

When he got to the range, the parking lot was empty. He decided to go to the area where he was allowed to use both rifles and handguns, so he could practice with both while moving around, reloading, etc. After about an hour of drilling, he noticed the clouds were getting darker around him and figured it was time to pack up and head to the gym. As he was walking up the hill to the entrance/exit of the range, he could feel a few rain drops, and he realized the range was probably empty because no one wanted to come shoot in the rain. *Timed it perfectly,* David thought to himself.

As David was pulling up to the gym, he noticed a lot more cars than the last time he was there and figured he would have to park on the street. He still had a hard time finding a spot and he had to circle the block a second time to find a parking spot. By the time he got to the gym, it was raining pretty hard, and he realized he had a pretty long way to walk to the front door of the gym. On his way to the front door, he noticed some guy running from his car to the front door trying not to get wet. David didn't speed up his pace at all; after spending all that time in Afghanistan and Iraq, he didn't mind a little bit of rain.

The front door was propped open, and there were many people inside getting ready for class. Besides the number of individuals that showed up for Jiu Jitsu class, David also noticed something else. The wrestling class was mainly filled with middle-aged males who were pretty built. The Brazilian Jiu Jitsu class had a much wider variety of individuals. David noticed some with a more muscular build, some with a tall and lanky build kind of like they were swimmers or basketball players. He also noticed that some were older; some were younger and there were even women and children getting ready for the class. While he was somewhat surprised, he was thrilled to see so many people interested in learning martial arts. *This is great,* David thought to himself.

After David changed his clothes and walked out of the bathroom, he saw Mark and Ray talking to a man with a large build and thick beard. The man was wearing Gi pants and a T-shirt and David started to wonder if he needed to bring a Gi or not. As he approached the three men, Ray spoke up first. "Hey David, good to see you again. This is our jiu jitsu coach Terrance Adams. We call him TA."

"Nice to meet you, sir," David said as he shook Terrance's

hand. David noticed Terrance's handshake was very strong.

"Been hearing a lot about you. You interested in competing?" Terrance asked.

"Maybe. I just moved back home, so I'm getting settled in right now. I am currently looking for a job as well. I just wanted to find something to challenge myself and help keep me in shape," David explained.

"For sure. Well you came to the right place," Terrance responded. He patted David on the back and then walked over to the center of the mats to get class started. As Terrance called out what line drill they were to do next; three students led the line drills, and the rest of the group followed what they did. Since it was his first class, David went to the back of the line and tried his best to observe what they were doing. Luckily he remembered some of the informal jiu jitsu training he got while overseas. The first drill the class did was called "shrimping" or hip escapes. After shrimps they did another variation of hip escapes before practicing forward rolls. Terrance called out for the class to do "backward rolls" and "sideway rolls" and then "sit throughs." After about a half dozen line drills, the class finally got to one of David's favorites; they worked on their "shot." A "shot" is a simple technique that can be applied when shooting for a single- or double-leg takedown and one that David was very familiar with considering his wrestling background. David had practiced a power double so many times that it became second nature to him. It was a favorite and most effective wrestling technique that he utilized quite often. After line drills Terrance had them partner up with someone of similar size.

As he looked around the room, David noticed a few guys his age and close to his size that would probably be good drilling partners, but since he did not know any of them, he was hesitant to approach them. The three people leading the line drills were similar in size to David, so he figured whoever was the odd man out, he would likely partner up with. The two taller guys decided to partner up and drill together. The short and stocky built man walked over to David and introduced himself, "What's up man? I'm Evan."

"David," David replied as the two shook hands. For some reason this man looked familiar, but David always felt bad asking people how he knew them if he could not remember their name.

Partner drills were more challenging than line drills. At first Terrance had the class do "Knee on Belly" switches. While one person lay on their back flat on the mat, the other person would place their knee on the stomach of the person lying down. The person on top would step over the bottom person's head and switch their other knee down on the stomach as they brought the opposite leg around to the outside of the person lying down. Basically, the person on top was applying direct pressure with their kneecap to the person lying down for five minutes straight. The only time when the pressure was slightly relieved was while the person on top was switching and shifting their weight from one knee to the other. The person on bottom really needed to control and time their breathing during this drill, and David could hear several people in the class grunting and struggling to breathe during knee on belly drill.

Since he had never done this drill before, David let Evan go first, and he started to wonder how much Evan weighed. When it was David's turn to do the knee on belly switches, Terrance came over and helped show him how to shift his weight as he stepped over and switched from one leg to the other. At first it was challenging, and David felt he needed to use Evan's knees to help keep balance. Like most of the class, while David was doing his knee on belly switches, he noticed Evan grimacing and struggling a bit to breathe. When the timer went off, Evan said, "Damn, I need to work on my abs."

David laughed and replied, "Yeah, me too."

Next, Terrance had the class do swimming guard passes which was much easier on their bodies. While one person lay on their back similar to the "knee on belly" drill, the other person had their hands on one knee cap each. The purpose of the drill was for the person standing to use one arm as an anchor to move their body from side to side of the person lying on the ground. After swimming guard passes, each person had to do ten kick-overs and then ten chair passes. David remembered doing kick overs when he wrestled in high school, so knocking out ten of them wasn't too bad for him. Chair passes, on the other hand, were a bit more challenging simply because he had never done them before, and Evan was clearly heavier than him. Evan went first and told David to keep his guard closed tight, and then to wrap his arms around Evan as he lifted David up from the grounded position. David decided to do five extra after he finished his ten chair passes since his legs were feeling pretty good.

After partner drills, Terrance told the class to get a drink and use the restroom if needed, and then he had the class gather around to cover some techniques. The first technique he showed was a basic guard break from full guard. Terrance taught the class how to keep one arm centered under the opponent's breast plate while placing the opposite arm inside their hip. Terrance explained how to break down the opponents guard by getting them to separate their legs. From there, he showed a few different options on how to pass the guard and end up in side control.

While each option clearly was effective, David seemed to prefer a simple knee slide into the nearest side after breaking apart the opponent's guard. Terrance let everyone partner back up and then drill the technique he showed for about fifteen minutes while he walked around the class and helped anyone who was confused or struggling. After a few reps Evan asked, "Damn, did you wrestle or something before?"

David laughed and said, "Yeah, why do you ask?"

"Because you're strong as a fucking ox," Evan replied.

"Thanks man," David laughed. "Yeah, I started wrestling when I was twelve, and I wrestled throughout high school," he continued.

"You know, you look kind of familiar," Evan told him.

"I was thinking the same thing. You from around here?" David asked.

"Yeah, I went to Nagel High School," Evan told him.

"Hmm, I went to Newtown. What year did you graduate?" David asked.

"09" Evan said. Before David could say another word, Evan continued, "Wait David Stoneking?"

"Yeah, how'd you know?" David asked.

"Son of a bitch," Evan said. "I used to play football against you. I had to key on you every year it seemed like," Evan said.

"Oh shit," David started to say.

Before David and Evan could continue their conversation, Terrance had the class gather around again to show them another technique. This time Terrance decided to show the class a basic sweep. Starting from full guard, Terrance showed what he called a hip-bump sweep. Terrance demonstrated that it was best to set up this sweep by getting the opponent to put their hands on the mat, and he did this by circling his hands inside of the opponent's hands that were on him. As Terrance circled his hands and separated the opponent's grip, he pulled the opponent into his body with his legs. He was basically doing a crunch while controlling the opponent's body. Once Terrance got the opponent's hands on the mat, he used his legs to push the opponent away just enough to create some space. When Terrance created enough space, he reached across his opponent's body with one arm and grabbed the back of his opponent's arm. Terrance showed how to sit up into the opponent and use the opposite arm as a bridge so that he could set up the sweep. Terrance explained to drop the leg that was on the same side as the arm being attacked, so the opponent's leg was trapped and their base would be completely taken away. Then Terrace completed the sweep, *"Boom!"*

The person Terrance was demonstrating the sweep with landed hard on the mat, and Terrance ended up on top of the individual in full mount. David was impressed. David had an extensive background in wrestling and even studied a little bit of judo as he got older, but he was always intrigued by any grappling mechanism and effective martial arts technique. David learned some basic submissions while he was on deployment, but sweeps were relatively new to him, and from the first demonstration by Terrance, he could tell he found a great instructor. Terrance demonstrated the sweep a few more times and asked the class if anyone had questions before letting the group split up into partners again so they could drill the sweep on their own.

David and Evan took turns drilling the sweep and switched every five times, so each of them could get some reps. After they both got about two dozen or so reps in, Evan continued their previous conversation, "Man, I used to fucking hate playing against you guys. You beat us every year, and you always ran all over us. You were the only running back that could hit triple digits in rushing yards on our defense."

"Yeah, you guys always gave us some tough games though," David replied. While David was at Newtown, their football team always managed to just barely beat their cross town rivals. David remembered playing them his senior year when it was pouring down rain, and it was the last game on their old home field before they got rid of the grass and installed a field turf game field.

"You remember playing in the mud bowl?" Evan asked David.

"Oh yeah, those kids at Newtown now are spoiled," David joked.

"Yeah, football just isn't the same sport anymore. So what have you been up to since high school?" Evan asked David.

"Well I joined the Army Special Forces, and I've spent most of my time the past four or five years either training or overseas on deployment," David replied.

"Holy shit," Evan said sounding shocked. "You're a Green Beret?"

"I was, yeah," David said.

"No wonder why you're so damn strong; you're probably going to kick my ass when we spar," Evan told David.

David began to laugh and then replied, "Nah, this is my first legitimate jiu jitsu class. I don't expect to submit anyone my first day."

"Trust me, with your wrestling background and your military training, you will pick this up quick," Evan said.

Once everyone had started to move around and finish up getting their reps, Terrance told the class once again to get water and use the restroom if needed and get ready to spar. While David was taking a sip of water from his bottle, he noticed several students from the class grabbing a mouthpiece. I wonder if I should get one, David thought to himself. The last thing he wanted was getting a tooth knocked out by accident while sparring. Terrance told the class to keep the same partners for the first round of sparring, and then he would pair people up for the rest of the rounds later on. Terrance also wanted everyone to start on the ground and not from a standing position because there were so many people on the mats that he didn't want people accidentally running into each other.

David was slightly bummed. He knew his wrestling was one of his major advantages, and removing his takedown ability just made it easier for the opponent. Before they started, Evan held out his hand like he wanted to shake hands, so David grabbed it and started to shake his hand. When David let go, he noticed Evan's hand was now in the shape of a fist. David was confused and Evan started laughing, "Here let me show you what we do here. Before the roll starts, you slap hands, fist bump and then begin."

"Oh ok," David said as they tried again. During his first "roll" with Evan, David quickly got top position because Evan pulled guard. Immediately, David could tell Evan had more jiu jitsu knowledge and knew more techniques. David attempted the guard pass that Terrance showed earlier in class, but Evan shut it down pretty easily because he was expecting David to try it. Despite Evan's superior jiu jitsu knowledge, David was able to keep Evan from establishing any real submission attempts or sweeps.

About halfway through the round when both men were beginning to get a little impatient, Evan started opening his guard a little bit more and attempting more and more submission attempts. David was aware that he didn't really know the proper defense to stop Evan from submitting him; David simply relied on his strength and grappling instincts. With about a minute left in the round and after a wild scramble, David managed to take Evan's back. While on deployment David did learn some basic submissions from one of his platoon commanders, and the very first submission he ever learned was the Rear Naked Choke. Immediately once David had his hooks in, he went for it. At first Evan made it very hard and was hand fighting very well, stifling all of David's attempts.

Eventually, David's endurance and repetitive attempts to get one arm under Evan's chin paid off. David had it locked in tight and slowly began to squeeze. Even though David was beginning to like and respect Evan, he also wanted to at least be able to say he submitted one person during sparring at his first class. With about twenty seconds left, David squeezed as hard as he could and Evan tapped. They both looked at the timer and realized they didn't have much time to start over, so they just shook hands and Evan said, "Nice job man; that was a hell of a scramble."

"Thanks. You sure as hell didn't make it easy," David replied. He was eventually paired with three other people during sparring, and each one ended up somewhat similar to what happened with Evan. At the beginning of the round, David spent a lot of time trying to pass their guard; his opponent would start attempting submissions off their back and then eventually start hitting some sweeps. It seemed the last guy David rolled with kept using the same technique.

Somehow David's opponent was able to trap his arm between the two of them, and then David no longer had a way to use his arm as a base when his opponent went to sweep him. *I'm going to have to figure out what this technique is after class,* David thought to himself. After the last round of sparring, David walked over to the guy who kept sweeping him with the same technique and after introducing himself, he asked, "Hey what was that sweep you kept using against me?"

The man named Ethan replied, "It's called a pendulum sweep."

"Ok, cool. Think you can show me that sweep sometime?" David asked.

"I can show you," Terrance replied over his shoulder.

"Oh, ok. Want me to come in before class or something next time?" David asked Terrance.

"What are you doing Sunday?" Terrance said.

"Don't have any plans so far," David replied.

"Alright, come in around noon. I'll give you a private," Terrance told him.

"Ok cool. How much does a private cost?" David asked.

"Don't worry about it," Terrance said. "Just don't tell anyone," he continued.

"Works for me," David said. As he was getting ready to leave, David wanted to go over and say bye to Evan. "Thanks for the roll and drilling with me," David told Evan. "I also wanted to come over and ask what you've been up to since high school. I was about to ask you earlier, but I got busy with drilling," David continued.

"Oh no worries man. I get it," Evan said. "After high school I got a football scholarship to Bowling Green, but I blew out my knee before the first game, so my freshman year, I spent most of the time going through rehab. And then they picked up a walk on outside linebacker that kinda replaced me. The coaches felt bad because they knew the injury was out of my control, but they only had so many scholarships, so they gave the walk on a scholarship my sophomore year before I was able to come back fully. The knee didn't fully heal, and it still gives me some problems every now and then. I decided not to play football after that, and it was probably the right move," Evan explained to David.

"So instead, you come here and learn to rip people's limbs off?" David jokingly replied.

Evan laughed and then said, "Yeah, well I figured it would be a good skill to learn as a cop. I studied criminal justice at Bowling Green and joined the Henderson Township PD after graduation." Immediately David was intrigued. Henderson Township was the area that surrounded West Spoon Lake, and David was tempted to ask Evan about the people that went missing over the past couple years. Before David could mention anything, Evan looked down at his watch and said, "Shit, I gotta get home for dinner, or my fiancé is going to kill me."

"Alright man. I'll let you get going," David replied.

"For sure; hey are you coming to Gi class tomorrow night?" Evan asked David.

"I wasn't planning on it. I don't even have a Gi. I should probably get one," David said.

"Oh yeah, the Gi helps a lot man. Makes you way more technical," Evan said.

"How so?" David asked as Evan finished packing up his bag.

"Well there's a lot to explain, but basically everything you can do in no Gi you can do in Gi, but not everything you can do *with* a Gi on, can you do without one. If that makes any sense," Evan explained.

"Yeah, a little bit," David replied.

"I'd go online and try to find a Gi. There's all kinds of brands and places where you can order one for a decent price," Evan said.

"Ok, cool. Still doesn't really help me tomorrow night though," David said.

"Well, I'll check and see if I have one you can borrow; if not I'm sure Terrance might have one around here somewhere you can use," Evan told David.

"Ok thanks, I'll see ya tomorrow," David said.

"For sure brother, have a good one," Evan replied as he came over and gave David a hug.

When David got home he was pretty sore. More so than he had been in a while. His biceps were bothering him more than anything, and he figured it was from fighting off armbars all night during sparring. Couldn't hurt to take an ice bath, David thought to himself. As he got ready to go to sleep, he got out his laptop, so he could look online for a Gi. Once he looked around for about an hour, he decided to buy a black Gi. Every time he saw photos or videos of people practicing martial arts with a Gi on, he noticed most of them were wearing a white Gi, and he wanted to get something that didn't follow the crowd. Even though his body was sore and he felt physically tired, it took David a while to fall asleep because he still felt a little adrenaline from sparring earlier, and he was excited to get back on the mats.

The next day David decided to relax a little bit and rest. He spent most of the day searching for jobs online and eventually decided to look into what he would have to do to become a conservation officer. David was struggling to find something that interested him, and he thought back to the conversation he had with his parents and Michael at his party when he came home. After doing some research, he decided he would look into it more later, but he was optimistic about his potential future career.

That night David decided to leave a little early for Gi class hoping Evan would be there with a Gi for him, or he could find Terrance to see if there was one around the gym he could use. Luckily David found Evan almost immediately and Evan did remember to bring a Gi for him. After he got dressed in the restroom, David realized the pants were a little short, but the top fit pretty well. David suddenly realized he didn't even have a belt. As he walked over to the mats, he approached Evan, "Hey man, I don't even have a belt yet."

"Oh don't worry about it. I'm sure Terrance has one somewhere," Evan replied. Shortly afterward as everyone was gathering around the edge of the mats to start line drills, David noticed Terrance and asked, "Do you have a belt I can use?"

"Oh yeah, let me grab you one. Go ahead and start line drills. I'll be right back," Terrance told the class. He walked into an office and came back with a folded white belt that looked brand new. "Here ya go. Do you know how to tie it?" Terrance asked David.

"Not this kind of belt," David replied.

"Alright I'll show you," Terrance said laughing. He walked over to his gym bag and put his top on and then reached into his bag and pulled out a very worn, black belt. *Damn,* David thought to himself. *I wonder how long it took him to get that.* After learning the proper way to tie his belt for his Gi, David joined the class as they were about halfway through line drills.

Even though he was a little behind, David still wanted to start with hip escapes simply because he wanted to get more reps and get better at it. One thing David remembered Terrance explaining during the first class was how important hip escapes were. David had been a perfectionist all his life, and he wanted to develop the perfect technique no matter what that technique was.

The Gi class was structured much like the no Gi class the day before. The main difference David noticed was the techniques taught and the fact there were far fewer people at the Gi class. While he did recognize a few faces, there were some others that he didn't see at the no Gi class. After learning a few different grip breaks, Terrance showed the class a basic Gi choke that he explained could be applied from any position, but for the sake of demonstration, he showed the class how to apply it from full mount. David wasn't sure if it was just because it was the first Gi submission he learned or what, but from that day on, the Ezekiel choke became one of his favorite chokes and one of his go to techniques, especially whenever he had the Gi on. David partnered up with Ethan for the Gi class in hopes that Ethan might teach him the pendulum sweep that Ethan was able to hit on David so often during their roll at the end of the no Gi class.

David also noticed Ethan was a brown belt and wanted to partner up with someone who was a higher rank. Looking around, David noticed most of the class was white or blue belts, with a couple of purple belts while Ethan was the only brown belt, and Terrance was the only black belt. David saw that Evan was a blue belt although his belt seemed a darker shade of blue than some of the other blue belts. David wondered if that was because Evan had more recently been promoted to blue belt compared to a few of the others in the class. David did get submitted a few times during sparring for Gi class, and while he remained respectful toward his sparring partner, he was visibly frustrated. Mainly frustrated at himself because David hated to lose.

After class, Evan invited him to grab something to eat, "Hey man, you wanna get some food? My fiancé has yoga class tonight, so I'm on my own."

"Yeah sure. Where were you thinking?" David asked.

"There's a bar and grill about ten minutes from my place called Rudy's Sports Bar that has some of the best burgers in town. My fiancé is a vegetarian, so I gotta eat meat every chance I can when she isn't around," Evan explained. "Here, give me your phone. I'll give you my number, so you can text me when you get there," Evan said.

David laughed and said, "Yeah that sounds good man. I need to shower and change first though. Meet there in about an hour?"

"Yeah that works," Evan replied. When David got back home, he noticed he had a text from Michael and decided not to reply because Michael was trying to get him to go out drinking with a big group of people. David was focused on meeting with Evan and trying to see if he knew anything about the missing people at West Spoon Lake. *I'll just text Michael back tomorrow morning,* David thought to himself right before he showered and changed clothes to go back out and meet Evan.

David pulled into the parking lot, and after he turned his truck off, he sent Evan a text, "Hey man. I'm here."

"Alright, come on in. I got us a table," Evan replied. David walked inside, and a young waitress at the front desk asked him how many would be joining him.

"I'm just meeting my friend. I think I see him actually," David said.

"Oh ok, well enjoy your meal," the waitress said as David walked by.

"Thank you," David responded. He did a quick scan of the restaurant and found Evan sitting in a booth by a window in the back of the room. *Perfect,* David thought to himself. David preferred to sit in the back of the room and with his back against a wall, so he could see people coming and going and have better awareness in case there was ever a threat. Situational awareness was something instilled in him during his time in the Army, and that mindset never left David. He and Evan sat and talked briefly before another waitress came and took their order. After Evan ordered a cheeseburger with fries, David said, "I'll try the blackened Mahi Mahi sandwich with a side of fries, and is there any way I can add bacon to that?"

"Yeah sure," the waitress replied.

"Oh damn that sounds good. You're not getting a burger though?" Evan asked David.

"I was going to until I saw the blackened Mahi Mahi sandwich. No way I was passing that up. Blackened Mahi Mahi is without a doubt my favorite type of fish. Hard to find around here too," David explained.

"Good point. I guess you'll have to try a burger next time," Evan said. Throughout the rest of the night, the two mainly talked about Jiu Jitsu, and David discovered that Evan had been training for about three years and recently got his blue belt. Evan explained that he started training Jiu Jitsu in college and then found the gym when he moved back to Henderson township and bought a house with his fiancé. David also found out that Evan's fiancé was a teacher and that they met while in college.

Evan asked David a few generic questions about the military and what David planned on doing now that he was no longer in the Army. David was getting tired of everyone asking him this question because at the moment he didn't have an answer for it. Nevertheless, David mentioned possibly becoming a conservation officer which sparked a conversation about hunting. Evan explained that he had two beagles and that he really loved to rabbit hunt. The two agreed to go rabbit hunting once the season started. Their only obstacle would be finding property they could hunt on. Evan told David he didn't want to take his dogs hunting on public land. Toward the end of the night, David decided to ask Evan about the people that went missing at West Spoon Lake, "Hey do you know anything about the disappearances at West Spoon?"

"How did you know about that? Evan replied.

"When I came home, my brother mentioned it to me, and then I did some research online, but couldn't really find anything. Stories from the local media were pretty vague," David said.

"Yeah, there's been some really sketchy cases around that area the past couple years," Evan told David.

"Do they have any suspects?" David asked.

"As of right now, they have no suspects, and the only evidence that's been found was the motorcycle from one of the guys that went missing. They also found a single cigarette that was found near two bodies, a father and his son who were murdered on their property and then dragged onto the state park," Evan explained.

"The cigarette didn't have any DNA on it?" David asked.

"No it hadn't even been touched yet. Must have slipped out of the package or something," Evan said.

"Do you know what brand of cigarette it was?" David asked.

"I can't remember. I'd have to look at the report," Evan replied. "I was actually one of the first officers on the scene back when that happened," Evan continued.

"Oh really?" David said.

"Yeah, that was a rough one. We got the call from the wife. She was hysterical. I guess her husband and son went hunting one morning, and she heard gunshots near their house which didn't make sense to her because they were hunting during bow season, so she knew they didn't have rifles on them or anything. When she went out to see what happened, she yelled out to them a few times and got no response, so she walked to the back of their property toward the tree stands that were set up and noticed her husband and son were not in them. She looked around a little bit and then found their dogs barking near the bodies on the other side of their property. Whoever killed them dragged their bodies onto the state park for whatever reason," Evan told David.

"Do you think the killer was trying to hide the bodies and was afraid the wife would catch him in the act, so whoever killed them just took off?" David asked.

"I have no idea. That makes sense though," Evan replied.

"So what about the other people that went missing at West Spoon?" David asked Evan.

"To tell you the truth, I'm not as familiar with those cases because I was still in college when most of them went missing, or I wasn't on the force yet. The double murder was the most recent case related to West Spoon," Evan told David.

"Any chance you can look into the files related to those other cases?" David asked.

"Why are you so curious about all this?" Evan responded.

"It just seems weird that there would be so many murders and disappearances in one area without authorities finding out who is responsible," David said, explaining his curiosity.

"Well our department is short staffed, and even the county sheriff doesn't have enough man power or resources to really do a thorough investigation," Evan said.

"Gotcha, do you have access to files for those other cases though?" David asked again.

"I could probably check them while at the station, but there's no way I can let a civilian look at them without proper clearance. Sorry. I'd get fired," Evan told David.

"Just make copies," David said smiling.

"That would still get me in a lot of trouble," Evan laughed. David was still curious about what happened to all those people that went missing and were murdered. He was hoping Evan would look into it and then get back to him if any new information was found in the official reports and investigations. As Evan changed the subject and started talking about hunting again, David found himself having a hard time focusing on the conversation because he was so determined to find the truth. When he got home, David even did more research online, but he couldn't find any new information. Slightly frustrated and somewhat exhausted, David decided to go to bed as he hoped Evan would soon have some new, useful information for him.

Chapter 7

Samuel was lying in bed after a long night. As he rolled over, he saw Lyndsey facing him fast asleep. The night before the two of them went to The Last Call for some drinks and to play pool. Samuel had to work late and told Lyndsey he would have to meet her at the bar. When Samuel first got there, he walked back to the room where the pool tables were and found Lyndsey sitting on some guy's lap. Before Samuel could say anything, Lyndsey jumped up and ran over to give Samuel a hug. Samuel was angered that Lyndsey was flirting with another man, but this was nothing new, and Samuel had to deal with this type of behavior all the time. *If this guy hangs around too long, I'm going to have to fight him,* Samuel thought to himself. When Lyndsey tried to introduce the two of them, the other man named Chris held his hand out to shake Samuel's hand, but Samuel kept his hands in his pockets and just stared at him.

"Come on Sammy," Lyndsey started to say. Sensing the obvious tension between the two, Lyndsey suggested they play a game of pool. Samuel and Lyndsey partnered up and played against the man and his friend. Samuel was clearly the best pool player at the bar that night, and he quickly won the game even though Lyndsey only knocked in one ball. When the game was over, Samuel walked away to grab two more beers, and when he got back, the two men he just beat were gone, and another couple was getting ready to play against him and Lyndsey. Samuel was relieved when the two men left. He wanted to focus on playing pool and spending time with Lyndsey. Nights like these started to remind Samuel of when he first started seeing Lyndsey after his sister died.

After Haley's passing, Samuel became severely depressed which eventually turned into anger. Samuel developed a short temper, and it seemed like anything and everything annoyed him. The only person who could really get through to him was Lyndsey even though she wasn't always there for him. After Haley's funeral, Samuel moved out of Stephen's trailer and bought his own mobile home that was in the very back of the trailer park near the boundary of West Spoon State Park. Samuel was hoping to get a two bedroom apartment for him and his sister, but after her suicide, Samuel was worried he wouldn't be able to afford an apartment on his own. There was a lot available in the trailer park, and he had enough saved up to buy a nicer mobile home. Samuel liked the new location because even though he still lived in the same trailer park, he now had more room and easy access to go hunt at West Spoon. All he had to do was simply walk out the back of his mobile home and into the woods; before long he was bound to find a trail that would help navigate through the heavily wooded area where he could hunt.

To help him keep his mind off losing his sister, Samuel

worked as many hours at the shop as he could. He wanted to work as much overtime as possible, so he could save up and buy some new hunting equipment before the season started. Samuel also started spending more time with Lyndsey. She and her mom seemed to argue and fight a lot, so whenever they would get into it with each other, Lyndsey would text Samuel and ask if she could come over. Samuel was very lonely and didn't like going out much because he didn't want to run into anyone he knew, and he wanted to save money. Samuel was afraid they would ask him about his mother or sister, and he hated talking about them after everything that happened.

While Samuel enjoyed Lyndsey's company and was grateful she would often spend the night with him, he hated that she smoked cigarettes and stayed up really late. Samuel thought Lyndsey was such a beautiful woman, and he saw what smoking did to his father, so whenever they were together, Samuel would always give Lyndsey a hard time for smoking and try to convince her to quit. Lyndsey's response was always the same: "I know. I'm working on quitting." When Samuel and Lyndsey first met, she didn't really drink much because she had epilepsy, and the alcohol didn't mix well with her medication. Samuel was the one that drank more often, and he even had to show her how to tap a keg because when they were at a keg party one night, she kept pouring foam into her cup.

As Samuel spent more time with Lyndsey, he noticed she was drinking a lot more, and eventually it got to the point where Samuel began to smoke cigarettes and marijuana with her as well. Many times after they had sex, Lyndsey would go outside to smoke, and it bothered Samuel because he just wanted to cuddle with her or go to sleep. Instead of waiting for her to return, Samuel started going outside and smoking with her. As long as I just have a cigarette or two after sex, it won't hurt anything, Samuel thought to himself. To avoid developing a habit, Samuel would only smoke cigarettes when Lyndsey was around, and he refused to buy them. He wasn't even sure if there were other brands that he would like better or not. Lyndsey ended up staying with Samuel for almost a month straight, and the more they saw each other, the more Samuel started noticing what a slob she was. Every day when he came home from work, he would find cigarette packs all over his place, and he wondered why Lyndsey would keep buying more and more packs if she wasn't finished with them. When Samuel asked her about it, she told him that she was used to buying one pack per day on her lunch break, and she just kept them around until she finished the pack.

The more time Samuel spent with Lyndsey, and the longer she lived with him, the less money he had. Before she started spending the night all the time, he had saved up quite a bit to buy more hunting gear, but with the season right around the corner, Samuel checked his savings and realized it was almost depleted. Samuel started to wonder where all his money was going and then it hit him. Lyndsey had lived with him for months without helping out at all with rent, food, utilities, etc. When Samuel confronted her about it, at first he tried to remain calm and polite, but when Lyndsey used the excuse that she didn't work many hours, he was furious. He yelled at her, "Then get off your ass and work more!"

Lyndsey packed up her clothes and moved back in with her parents the next day. While she never officially moved in with Samuel, he felt like they had broken up after his flare up. Samuel would try to hang out with Lyndsey after work, and most of the time she would say she was busy or blow him off completely not even responding to his texts. Meanwhile, he would see her snapchat story and notice she was out at a bar or hanging out with some other guy at his place. *She is a nomad, going from guy to guy as long as she has a place to stay* Samuel thought to himself.

Samuel was bothered by Lyndsey leaving at first, but before long he got over it because hunting season was about to begin and when he wasn't at work, he wanted to be out in the woods. In the beginning of squirrel season, Samuel was having a lot of success. He was harvesting so many squirrels that often times, he would still go over his daily limit. Samuel knew he should get a hunting license for small game; he just didn't want to spend the money, so he would simply go kill as many squirrels as he could before bow season started. Eventually he started seeing fewer squirrels and decided to shift his focus to finding some spots where he could set up a blind or climber for the bow season. While squirrel hunting he even made a few make shift blinds for deer season, some of which were near trails and in areas where it wasn't legal to hunt. Samuel decided to hunt these areas anyway because he would often find large rubs or scrapes and he knew deer were moving around in that particular location.

During the first month of bow season, Samuel was hunting every morning when he got the chance. The more he hunted and didn't harvest a deer, the more frustrated he would get. Samuel had even seen several does over the past few weeks while hunting. A couple times the deer busted him and took off running away. Samuel eventually shot at three separate does and missed all three of them badly. When he walked off to see how far away the does were, he realized he was shooting way too far out of his crossbow's range. Samuel was growing impatient and rushing his shots. Late afternoon one day after Samuel had been hunting all morning in one of his favorite spots, he overheard voices approaching.

At first he couldn't really hear what they were saying, but as they walked along the trail and were getting closer, he could hear their conversation much clearer. *Samuel realized it was a boy and a girl, probably teenager's* he thought to himself. Samuel was in one of his makeshift blinds and hoping the two teenagers would either keep walking or turn around and head back to wherever they came from. If they remained in the same area where he was, Samuel was certain no deer would come through because they were being way too loud. "Would you two shut the fuck up?" Samuel whispered to himself. After about fifteen minutes of listening to them laugh and giggle, Samuel was fed up. He grabbed his crossbow and started walking toward where he could hear them while trying to be as quiet and stealthy as he possibly could.

"Come on; you promised you would do it," the teenage boy told his girlfriend.

"Yeah, but I'm not sure I want to do this here anymore," she replied.

"Ok. We made a bet and you lost the bet, so you have to follow through," the boy said.

"Yeah. I said I'd give you a blowjob anywhere you wanted, but why did you have to pick the woods?" she asked.

"Because we are out in the wilderness and can enjoy the fresh air; there's no one around that's going to hear or see us," the boy explained. He leaned forward to give his girlfriend a kiss and then unbuckled his pants and pulled them down. As the teenage girl tried to get comfortable on the blanket they had laid down on the ground, she began sucking on her boyfriend's penis. After a few minutes, she heard a twig snap and quickly reacted, "Oh my god! What was that?"

"What was what?" the teenage boy replied.

"I just heard something," she told him.

"Yeah, probably a squirrel or something," the boy told her.

"No, Damien, I think someone is out there for real," she explained sounding concerned.

"Oh, you're just trying to get out of the bet," the boy said laughing.

"I'm serious. I feel like we are being watched," she said.

"You know the quicker you get me to finish, the quicker we can get out of here," the boy said with a smile.

"Ok," the girl replied. As she continued, she could feel her boyfriend holding her hair back so it wasn't in the way. Not long after she felt his legs start to twitch a bit like he usually did when she gave him fellatio and she thought to herself: *Thank goodness he's done.* Once she was finished, she looked up and saw another man in full camouflage standing over her boyfriend with his hand grasping Damien's hair. She immediately saw a knife in the man's other hand covered in blood. Frightened, she glanced back toward Damien and saw blood rushing down his neck towards his shirt, "Oh my God! Nooooooo!" she yelled out right before she took off running. Sprinting as fast as she could to get away from the man in camouflage, suddenly she heard a *thwap* noise as she felt a piercing and burning sensation in her back. It knocked her down. The girl desperately tried to get back to her feet and even though in her mind she wanted to run away, her legs stopped working. The girl began to panic and was starting to crawl away using just her arms as fast as she could. She could hear the footsteps of the man approaching her, and she turned around to face him. "Please don't hurt me," she pleaded. "Somebody help me!" she screamed.

As the teenage girl had her mouth open screaming for help, Samuel kicked her in the face as hard as he could and then said, "Shut your fucking mouth whore." The teenager reminded him of the girls that used to make fun of him and his sister when they moved to the trailer park to live with Stephen after their father passed away. Samuel specifically remembered watching his sister walk home from school one day when a group of girls from one of the private coed schools began to make fun of her. He couldn't hear everything they said, but he did remember one of them hollering out, "Trailer trash!" The uniform this teenager was wearing looked exactly like the uniform worn by the girl that bullied his sister.

After Samuel kicked her in the face, she brought her hands up to her mouth and began to cry hysterically. Samuel then bent down beside the girl grabbing her hair with his left hand. She looked right at him wide eyed just before he drove his right knee into her stomach and then ran the blade of his knife across her throat as fast and hard as he could slicing a deep wound all the way across. Blood began to pour down her neck and instead of covering her mouth, she moved her hands to her neck. The girl began to kick and roll around on the ground. Samuel sat beside her as she bled out. He thought about stabbing her again to speed things up, but he didn't want to make too much of a mess and get her blood all over his clothes.

After he killed the two teenagers, he carried their bodies over to his makeshift blind so he could conceal them. Samuel followed the trail back to his trailer and grabbed a shovel, a can of gasoline and some matches. Once it got dark, he walked back into the woods and retraced his steps to head back to his makeshift blind. Not wanting to dispose of the bodies too close to his blind, he moved them again, this time choosing a spot that was heavily covered by trees, bushes and thickets. He also wanted to dispose of them far enough away from the hiking trail so that they would be harder to find. Samuel dug a large, wide hole big enough for both bodies and then he dragged them into the hole. He walked around gathering fallen sticks and logs to put on top of the bodies.

Once he had their bodies completely covered by firewood, he doused the firewood and the bodies in gasoline. After Samuel lit a match, he lit a cigarette and then threw the match on top of the firewood, and the gasoline immediately caught fire. Samuel sat on a downed tree as he pulled a flask out of his jacket and took a big swig of bourbon whiskey while the fire continued to burn. Samuel continued to drink his bourbon while the fire burned for about two more hours. He waited until enough embers were built up. He wanted to make sure the bodies were burning. Before he left, Samuel decided to throw more firewood on top of the fire to make sure it would burn a little longer during the night. The next morning Samuel woke up early, so he could go check on the bodies. When he found the fire pit, all he could see was ashes. Samuel grabbed his shovel and covered the fire pit area with the dirt he removed the night before hoping it would cover any tracks or evidence. After he replaced the dirt and filled the hole, he grabbed sticks and foliage to cover the fresh dirt and conceal the area a little bit more. Confident that he had successfully disposed of the bodies and any evidence of the murders, Samuel walked back to his trailer and lit a cigarette. Once he got back, he saw a familiar face waiting for him on his front porch. Lyndsey had returned again.

"Where have you been?" Lyndsey asked.

"Had to take care of some things," Samuel replied. "I've been texting you. Why haven't you responded?" Samuel continued.

"I was still a little upset I guess," Lyndsey told him.

"Yeah I understand. Listen I'm sorry. It's just that money is tight right now, and I would appreciate it if you helped out a little more if you're going to be living with me all the time," Samuel explained.

"Can we talk inside? I'm cold," Lyndsey asked.

"Yeah sure," Samuel replied. Lyndsey sat down on the couch after they entered his trailer.

"I don't really have much money either," Lyndsey started to tell Samuel. "You make way more than I do because I work about half the amount of hours you do, and you probably make more than me per hour anyway," she continued.

"I understand," Samuel said.

"If we decide to make things official and I move in, then of course I wouldn't mind helping pay some bills," Lyndsey explained. Samuel could tell she wanted him to invite her to live with him. Samuel just didn't trust her enough to let her move in yet.

"Well I'm not ready for a roommate or a relationship right now, so let's do this. You can come and go as you please; all I ask is that when you are staying here, you bring or buy your own food. That would help me out a lot," Samuel told Lyndsey.

Lyndsey hesitated and then said, "Yeah I can do that. Seems fair."

"Alright cool. I'm going to shower and then get ready for work. Do you need a ride?" Samuel asked Lyndsey.

"Yeah sure," Lyndsey replied. "Wait, before you take a shower, you got time for a quickie?" Lyndsey asked with a smile.

"Fuck, yeah," Samuel replied as Lyndsey took his hand and led him to his bedroom.

Chapter 8

David was continuing his job search and after talking to Evan about becoming a Conservation Officer, David realized he would need a degree in Criminal Justice in order to become a CO in Ohio. While he had college credits from some of his training and courses in the Army, he would still have to go to college to finish the rest of his credits to get a degree. David despised the idea of going to college after being in the Army for the past five years. Instead of enrolling and going to a college the "traditional" way, David started to look into the possibility of enrolling in a smaller college and trying to take online classes, so he could finish his coursework from home and never have to step foot on a college campus.

Luckily, David was able to find a local college that was much smaller than most universities and did offer many online classes. He would be able to finish most of the classes he needed for a degree online with only a few classes he would need to attend in person. For the online classes, he could do his coursework pretty much whenever he wanted; his assignments and tests just needed to be completed by a certain date and time. For the classes he would need to attend in person, he tried to take them as early in the day as possible. He was determined to get those classes over with, and then he also didn't want to take classes mid-day or too late in the afternoon which would get in the way of his training at the gym.

While David was working on finishing up the required classes he needed, he was still spending time looking into the murders and disappearances at West Spoon. Evan provided a little more detail into the cases that interested David. Several times after Jiu Jitsu classes in the evenings, David and Evan would meet in the parking lot by the gym and discuss recent findings. The first bit of information that Evan could provide was related to the biker that went missing.

"So I found the report on the biker. Apparently his name was Winston Morrow; he was thirty-five and had a pretty long rap sheet of drug-related charges as well as some speeding tickets, traffic violations and other misdemeanors," Evan began. "The last time he was seen was at a pool bar called The Last Call; that's out east of West Spoon, about ten minutes away from the state park," Evan continued.

"Was he from around here?" David asked.

"No, I don't think so. His only local affiliation was with a motorcycle club called the Venomous Riders," Evan replied.

"There's a motorcycle club in this area?" David asked sounding confused.

"Eh kinda. I think they are based out further east, but they come through this way sometimes. A lot of guys at the department are convinced they are running drugs into town and stuff like that. They might be the source of all the heroin and meth," Evan explained.

"Do you guys have proof of that?" David asked.

"Well, we've heard many reports about them bringing in all kinds of stuff. A couple of their members do have drug-related charges. The problem is our police chief knows the club president somehow, and they rarely get convicted of anything," Evan explained.

"Good lord, no wonder no one prosecutes them," David said.

"Yeah," Evan agreed.

"Did you guys interview anyone from the club for more information about that guy's disappearance?" David asked.

"We tried, but those guys won't talk to cops," Evan replied.

"Hmm," David responded. He wondered if there was any chance he would come across members from the club if he went to The Last Call. Knowing there was no way he could get any information if he went with a cop, he decided to check it out alone. "Alright, I'm going to go home and do some homework. I'll see ya at class tomorrow," David told Evan as he got into his truck and drove away.

When David got home, he knew he didn't have a lot of time to waste, so he decided to cook a Red Baron pizza in the oven while he was in the shower. When he got out of the shower, he quickly dried off and got dressed. While he was getting dressed, he fired up his laptop, so he could check to see if he had assignments due in his online classes. By the time he went downstairs, his pizza was ready, so he checked his assignments while he scarfed down his dinner. David felt guilty for eating pizza just after he worked out at the gym for over two hours, but he was hungry and didn't have time to make a healthier meal.

He noticed he had an assignment due by noon the next day, and he decided to work on it while he was in class the next morning instead of completing it that night. He knew his 8 a.m. class would be a lecture, and he could finish the assignment while pretending to take notes. After he finished eating, he put the address for The Last Call into his phone and headed out. On the way to the bar, David started thinking to himself. He was wondering if it would be better to talk to multiple members of the club or to try to single out only one of them, so he didn't attract too much attention to himself. David wasn't even sure there would be members from the club at the bar that night. As he was pulling up to the parking lot, he didn't see any motorcycles at first. Trying to get a better look at the terrain and perimeter, David decided to take a lap and drive around the entire parking lot just looking out for anything that might be useful. While he was scoping out the bar, David noticed there were only security cameras by the back door facing the back of the parking lot, but not the front or the side where they had a patio. David decided to park near an entrance and near a light. Even though he drove a manual and was confident no one would steal his truck, David always felt more comfortable parking near street lights or well-lit areas to deter thieves from breaking into his truck and trying to steal something.

The bar was pretty crowded, and as David walked toward the entrance, he could hear a band playing. When he walked inside David had a hard time finding a table or booth that wasn't occupied, so he decided to grab a seat by the bar. He ordered a Budweiser and turned around in his chair to take a look around the bar. The middle of the bar was filled with booths and tables; there was a small stage to the left and then a separate room that was open all the way in the back right where David could see a couple of pool tables. Between the room and the stage, there were large, glass windows on the opposite side of the bar. In the middle of the windows was a glass door that led to a patio.

While the band was playing, most of the patrons stayed inside, and whenever the band took a break, many patrons would go outside to smoke or chat. David wanted to walk over to the pool table to take a look around, but he was hesitant to leave his spot because he didn't want to lose his seat. After about an hour, David noticed a man walk outside to the patio. He was wearing a black leather cut. When the man turned toward the door, David noticed a large patch on the back of the cut that read *"Venomous"* on the top of the vest and *"Riders"* on the bottom in large, red print. David ordered another beer and then followed the man out to the patio.

Since the band had just taken a break, the patio was pretty full, and there weren't many places to sit much less stand. David looked to his left and noticed the man in the cut over in the corner smoking by himself. As David walked over toward the man, he could smell what the man was smoking and realized he wasn't smoking a cigarette. There was only one bar stool empty in the corner of the patio, so David sat down and then took a look around the parking lot trying to spot a motorcycle that the man in the cut might have ridden in on. David failed to find one and started to wonder how the man got to the bar without a ride.

"What's up man? You smoke?" the tall skinny man in the cut asked David.

"Oh nah I'm good, appreciate it though," David replied. The other man nodded as he took another puff of the joint. "Where's your bike?" David asked him.

The man looked at David with a confused look before David said, "I noticed the cut; I just figured your motorcycle was around here somewhere, but I didn't see one when I pulled in," David explained.

"Oh, I parked down the street at my buddy's place, and then I walked here. He should be here any minute; I'm in town for a couple nights, and I figured I'd hangout with him before I head back," the man said.

"Ah gotcha, I'm Dave," David said as he extended his hand.

"Marcus," the man replied shaking David's hand.

"Nice to meet you," David replied.

"You too; do you ride?" Marcus asked David.

"Yeah, sometimes. I have a Kawasaki Ninja that I've had for a few years, but I'm considering getting something bigger that I can take on longer trips," David said.

"Oh yeah, get rid of that crotch rocket. Get you a Harley," Marcus replied. David laughed and then replied, "Yeah that's the plan; anything in particular you'd recommend?"

"Well I have a Super Glide Sport, but if you want to go on longer trips, you might want to get a Road King," Marcus said.

"Ok, I'll look into that. Thanks," David replied.

"No problem," Marcus said right before he took another hit from his joint.

"Hey, I read an article a while back about a member of your club disappearing at West Spoon; sorry to hear about that," David said. Marcus exhaled and then replied, "Yeah that was fucked up man."

"Do they have any leads on what might have happened?" David asked.

"Nah, cops around here are a fucking joke. They don't know shit. In fact, the last time we saw Winston was at this damn bar," Marcus said.

"Holy shit! Were you here the night he went missing?"

"Yeah, we had over a dozen members here that night," Marcus replied.

"And none of you saw him get into it with anyone or anything?" David asked.

"Nah, Winston was playing pool all night. He was running a table, and when we all bounced, he decided to stay because he was kicking ass. Fucker loved to play pool," Marcus told David. "He must have gotten into it with someone eventually though; we just didn't see it. Winston would fight at the drop of a hat, man. Whoever killed Winston probably had to shoot him because that fucker could crack," Marcus said.

"Yeah, that's weird how his motorcycle was found at West Spoon, but they still haven't found anything else," David said.

"Well we found his cut the next morning. It was hanging in a tree out in the back of the parking lot here," Marcus replied.

"Oh really? You think a rival club killed him or something?" David asked.

"Nah, we don't have any rivals around here," Marcus said.

"Did you guys turn the cut in, so they could check it for prints or anything?" David asked Marcus.

"Hell no, we ain't giving the cops Winston's cut. We gave it to his mom. If they found his body, we would have buried it with him," Marcus explained.

"Ah gotcha. Well I hope you guys find out what happened to him, and again I'm sorry to hear about your friend," David told Marcus.

"Yeah I hope we find him too; we're gonna fuck that dude up," Marcus said. "Oh shit! My boy's here. I'll catch you later," Marcus said as he patted David on the shoulder and headed back inside.

David finished drinking his beer and then walked inside

toward the bar hoping his spot would still be there. As David got closer to the bar, he saw someone else sitting in his spot, but he noticed another open bar stool at the end of the bar. As David sat down, the middle-aged brunette behind the bar walked over to him and said, "Another Budweiser honey?" David wanted to stick around for a little longer, but didn't want to keep drinking because he planned on driving home. Instead of ordering another beer, he asked for a water.

David decided to stay and listen to the band play for a bit as he looked around trying to find any clues that might help him find the killer. David wondered if whoever was responsible for the murder of Winston would ever show up at the bar again. Eventually, the band stopped playing, and the bar cleared out a bit. When David was one of the last remaining patrons at the bar, the brunette bartender started talking to him a little more and more. David started to wonder if she was flirting with him and figured he could use her attraction toward him to his advantage. After the band left, it was much easier to hear, and David overheard someone else call the bartender "Betty."

"Hey Betty, I think I'll take one more beer," David said trying to get her attention.

"Sure thing sweetheart," she replied. Betty quickly brought David another Budweiser and then went back to helping other patrons. When she got a break in the action, Betty walked to the end of the bar near David who figured this was a perfect time to speak up, "Hey Betty, how long have you been working here?" David asked.

"Probably about seven or eight years. Why do you ask?" Betty replied.

"Well, I just recently moved here, and a buddy of mine was telling me about some guy that went missing at West Spoon.

I guess the last time he was seen was at this bar. I was just wondering if you knew what happened," David said.

"Yeah, I was working the night that guy went missing. Apparently him and some other guy were arguing after playing pool, but we were closing, so we told them to take it outside," Betty said.

"Do you know who the other guy was?" David asked.

"No. I didn't really see them arguing. I was cleaning up. I could hear them bitching at each other, and I was about to say something, but one of our bouncers just yelled at them to take it outside, or we were going to call the cops," Betty explained.

"Oh gotcha, do you know if the bouncer saw who it was?" David wondered.

"I don't know. Tony was busy putting up chairs and trying to keep people from coming back in as we were waiting for everyone to leave," Betty replied. "The cops came and talked to all of us, but no one really saw what happened. We did install a security camera afterwards out back though. Apparently whoever killed him left his cut in one of the trees," Betty continued.

"Wow. That's pretty ballsy, coming back here after what happened," David said.

"Yeah," Betty said before she went to help other patrons. David checked his watch and noticed it was getting pretty late, so he decided to close his tab. Betty actually offered to give him a ride home, but he respectfully declined. David told her he had to wake up pretty early which he did for his class, but he also did not want to leave his truck in the parking lot overnight. As he went to sign his name to his bill, he noticed that Betty left her number on the bill. David wondered how often she had done that in the past. Before he left, he overheard Betty say, "Have a goodnight sweetie!"

"Thanks, you too," David replied as he walked out the door and headed to his truck. Driving home David took his time and made sure to go the speed limit. Even though he didn't feel drunk; he didn't want to take a chance of getting pulled over for speeding and possibly get a DUI. He was pretty sure he would pass a sobriety test if he had to; he just didn't want to deal with it. He was tired and wanted to go to bed. The next morning when he woke up, he was still tired. He didn't feel hungover because he didn't drink that much. David was more physically tired from all the sparring he had been doing lately and felt a little sleep deprived. He remembered how sleep deprived he felt on some of his deployments and knew this was nothing compared to what he had experienced in the past. *Still, I need to find this guy before I lose even more sleep,* David thought to himself as he got ready for class.

While David was in class listening to a boring lecture from his professor, he began working on his assignment which was due that day at noon. He had to write an essay and turn it in online. After doing some research the weekend before, he had a pretty good idea of how he wanted to format his essay, so he spent most of the class typing away appearing as though he was actually taking notes. Tuning out the professor, David was able to complete most of the essay before the class ended. He decided to go to a student center to finish up his essay and figured the Internet on campus would be better for him to turn in his assignment anyway.

Back at his home it seemed the Internet was slower, and David had planned to talk to someone about getting faster Internet at his house; he just hadn't gotten around to it yet because he would use the Internet on campus to turn in his assignments most the time. After class he decided to get some more ammunition because he planned to go to the range later in the week.

David preferred to get his ammunition and supplies from a locally owned gun store called Camo and Ammo. It was owned by a former marine. David always tried to support small businesses and especially veterans. When he walked through the front door, he noticed the store was rather busy compared to normal. He walked around looking at different types of ammunition and the prices. While he was specifically looking for 9mm and 5.56 ammunition, he was having a hard time finding any 9mm rounds. After grabbing a few boxes of 5.56, he walked up to the counter to check out and saw the store owner Charles behind the register. "Hey, Charles, good to see you again," David said.

"David! How've you been?" Charles replied.

"Pretty good, just staying busy," David told Charles.

"Yeah that's good for you," Charles said.

"I guess so; hey do you know when you'll be getting in any nine millimeter ammo?" David asked.

Charles smiled and said, "Here. Come back to my office." David followed Charles back to his office, and Charles had a small stack of ammunition sitting on his desk.

"I only got a few left that I wanted to hang on to for my more loyal customers," Charles said as he tossed David two boxes of 9mm ammunition.

"Oh ok. Thanks man. I appreciate it," David responded. "Any particular reason why nine millimeter has been so hard to find lately?" David asked.

"Ah, the fucking democrats have been ramping up their gun control talk again because of the most recent school shooting. Every time they talk about banning guns or some shit, people freak out and buy up as much ammo as possible," Charles explained.

"Ah gotcha," David said.

"Yeah it's annoying, but at the same time, they are the best salesmen for guns and ammo," Charles said with a shrug and a smile.

"Yeah I guess so," David laughed as they walked back to the counter. As David was checking out, he wondered how many employees Charles had and if he could use some help.

"Hey Charles, are you hiring?" David asked.

"Yeah, I could use a couple extra hands. Why? Are you looking for a job?" Charles replied.

"Well, I'm currently taking a few classes trying to become a conservation officer, but I could use some extra income as well," David explained to Charles.

"Hell man. You don't even have to ask or apply. You know I always got room for a war hero," Charles told David.

David hated the idea of others calling him a hero. Still he appreciated the respect Charles had for him. "Ok great. When can I start?" David asked.

"Just email me your contact information and what you would like your schedule to look like, and I can work with that," Charles replied. "I don't know what your class schedule is like or anything, but you can basically work as often or as little as you'd like," Charles continued.

"Ok perfect, sounds good," David said as he reached over the counter to shake Charles's hand. Then he grabbed his ammo and headed out.

Chapter 9

Acouple months after Samuel and Lyndsey were back together, she started working a little more often and picking up extra shifts when she could. Samuel was glad she was finally helping out a little bit with the finances, and he felt a little less pressure. Still, she would frequently go to bars in the evenings and often come home late after the bars had closed. Samuel preferred to wake up early to get to work and maintain the habit of not sleeping in too late because when the hunting season came around, he wanted to be used to getting up early. Samuel always felt he had more success hunting early in the morning than later in the evening. Besides, he was hunting on public land and that usually meant there was a chance of coming across other people in the woods. Very few hikers, horseback riders, etc. were going out into the woods before the sun came up, so the early morning hunts were typically the most successful for Samuel. If he was struggling to harvest a deer, Samuel would resort to spotting them at night, but he tried to avoid this because he didn't want to get caught. After Samuel killed Stephen, he tried to stay under the radar. While it seemed everyone else was using social media and other apps on their phone, Samuel refused to add Facebook, Twitter and Instagram. The only reason he used Snapchat was so he could keep an eye on Lyndsey. Samuel still didn't fully trust her.

Samuel woke up early on a Saturday morning to someone knocking on his front door. It was a soft knock, but at such an early hour, he was suspicious of who it might be, so he grabbed his pistol out of his night stand and slowly walked toward the front door. As he tried to peek out the window to see who was standing on his porch, he realized his blinds were closed, and he could only see a shadow of whoever was on his porch. "*Bang! Bang! Bang!*" Whoever was on his porch knocked again, this time much louder. Samuel kept his pistol behind his back with his left hand as he slowly turned the knob to open the front door with his right. Samuel breathed a sigh of relief when he saw it was Lyndsey. It was the first time in over a month that Lyndsey didn't spend the night with Samuel; he was not used to having to wake up early to let her in, and he suspected a cop may be at the front door looking for him after all the recent murders. Even though he was taking precautions to not get caught, Samuel often wondered if there was any way the murders could fall back on him—if authorities ever found any evidence.

"Good morning sunshine," Lyndsey said as she walked through the front door.

"Eh morning," a tired Samuel replied. "Have fun last night?" Samuel asked Lyndsey.

"Yeah, I had a good time. Ran into some friends," Lyndsey replied.

"Who all did you see?" Samuel asked, expecting Lyndsey saw some guy she knew and possibly hooked up with him the night before. As Lyndsey rattled off a bunch of names that Samuel didn't know. He noticed that she only mentioned females she saw at the bars the night before.

"Weren't any guys there?" Samuel asked.

"Yeah there were a few guys I knew; most of them have girlfriends or left early," Lyndsey said.

"So where did you stay last night?" Samuel asked.

"I went back to my parents' house. I needed to grab some clothes, and I figured you were already asleep, so I didn't want to wake you," she explained.

"I'd rather you wake me up and spend the night here than spend the night at some other guy's place," Samuel replied.

"I didn't sleep with anyone last night," Lyndsey said sounding defensive.

"I never said you did," Samuel told Lyndsey.

Samuel walked back into the bedroom and returned the pistol in the drawer in the nightstand by his bed. As he lay in bed drifting off to sleep, Samuel remembered the last time he used that pistol. It was a little over a year and after he had killed the two teenagers engaging in oral sex in the woods. Samuel was out bow hunting at West Spoon after the gun and muzzleloader season had ended. Typically this time of year, Samuel had no luck harvesting deer since many had already been harvested, and by this time the deer were spooked and on high alert. For whatever reason, Samuel was having an extremely hard time hunting this year, and he was starting to get very frustrated. Even during the gun season, he had gone out at night trying to spot a large buck, but had no luck finding one. Samuel wasn't sure if he was just too busy with work or if the deer herd had been wiped out by some disease, but he decided to try one of his more promising spots where he had often seen deer move later in the season.

The evening before, Samuel grabbed the climber he stole during gun season and headed out to set it up in the area he wanted to hunt. There were clear skies and no wind, so Samuel was very optimistic about the hunt that morning. Unfortunately, he could not get out to hunt right away because he had to drop Lyndsey off at work. After he dropped her off, Samuel went straight to West Spoon, so he could get set up. As he was walking along the trail toward his hunting spot, he could hear chatter and some laughter in the distance. He kept getting closer and closer to his climber, and the voices were getting louder. *You've got to be fucking kidding me*, Samuel thought to himself as he approached.

Through the trees he could see at least three teenage boys sitting around an old campsite, and it appeared they were smoking marijuana. It was pretty cold that day and from a distance, Samuel could see their breath, but instead of their breath disappearing, he could see a faint cloud of smoke above them every so often. Samuel quickly was aware that these teenagers were smoking almost right in the center of the area he was hoping to hunt that day. Samuel was frustrated that his hunt was not only delayed by having to take Lyndsey in to work, but now a bunch of kids were smoking and making noise in the one spot he was sure there would be deer. Samuel looked around for a path he could take to get closer to them.

The boys were sitting between several large oak trees. Samuel could see one boy sitting with his back up against the oak. Another boy was sitting on a downed log to the right of the boy sitting up against the oak. Samuel could see the outline of another boy through some thickets and briars, but couldn't tell if he was sitting on the ground or a stump. As Samuel started walking off the path and around the thick cover, he could hear a fourth voice; yet he couldn't tell where it was coming from. Now that he had walked all the way around the thick cover, Samuel decided to use it to his advantage. He realized he could keep walking around and have a clearer path toward the boys, but was also aware they might see him first. Samuel had to take a zigzag pattern through some thorn bushes and other thick vegetation to get closer. *These stupid fucks are stoned out of their minds*, Samuel thought to himself.

"Alright. Your turn Timmy," Samuel could hear a boy say.

"He's gonna be barbecued if he takes another hit," one said while giggling.

"I don't care. We need to finish this bowl before we head back," the boy up against the large oak tree said.

"Ah fuck! Alright," another voice reluctantly said.

Samuel could see three boys and knew the fourth was sitting on the ground up against another tree with his back turned toward Samuel. As the three other boys were focused on their friend smoking out of the bowl, Samuel raised his crossbow and aimed through the thick cover. With his crosshairs directly on the boy sitting up against the oak tree, Samuel pulled the trigger. Thwap!

"Whoa, what was that?" asked one of the teenage boys. As the others looked around, one of them glanced over at their friend who just had a bolt pierce his chest. The boy sitting up against the oak moved his hands to his chest and immediately slumped over.

"Yo what the fuck?" one of the teenage boys screamed. The boy sitting to the left of the one Samuel just shot reached over

to check on his friend. The boy sitting to the right of him stood and started to walk over as well.

"Curtis are you ok?" Samuel could hear one of them cry out. Samuel began walking closer to them, and as he made his way through a thick thorn bush, he saw the fourth boy peak out from behind the tree that was almost parallel with the boy Samuel had just shot. His eyes were wide as saucers when he saw Samuel approaching.

"Oh shit," the boy staring at Samuel said and took off running. This drew the attention of the other two teenage boys who were checking on their friend. By the time they turned around to see who was approaching, Samuel had his pistol out and began firing. *"Bang, bang, bang."* Samuel shot the boy who first checked on his friend. The boy dropped back to the ground as soon as he stood up. Just when the second teenage boy checked on his friend Curtis turned and started running, Samuel fired again, *"Bang, bang, bang . . . bang."* The first three shots hit the boy in the back and he fell. Samuel walked up to him and put the fourth shot in the back of his head killing him instantly. The last teenage boy took off running, and at first Samuel did not have a clear shot at him because he was running through some thicker cover. The frightened teenager ran toward the trail he took into the woods; unfortunately for him that trail had just been cleared, and it opened up shooting lanes for Samuel.

Even though Samuel could only see the boy's legs, it was still enough, *"Bang, bang, bang, bang, bang."* The boy fell to the ground and desperately clutched at his right leg that now had two bullet wounds. The third shot hit him in his hip; Samuel's fourth and fifth shots missed him entirely. Samuel looked over at the boy who ran and realized he wasn't going anywhere.

Then Samuel looked over at the first boy he shot with his pistol. The boy was holding his chest and still breathing. Since this boy was closer, Samuel walked over to him first. "Please don't kill me," the boy said right before Samuel put the barrel up to his forehead and pulled the trigger.

Unsure of how many rounds were left in his pistol magazine, Samuel reloaded as he walked over to the fourth boy who was now rolling around in agony. Despite being shot three times, he still cried out for help, *"Somebody help me! Please help me!"* Samuel approached the last teenage boy, and as he got within range, the boy desperately tried to kick Samuel with his left leg as he rolled over to his right. Samuel pointed the pistol at the boy who was laying on the ground crying. For a split second Samuel thought about putting several more rounds in him. As the boy lay on his right side with his face toward the dirt, Samuel shot him one more time. Samuel looked down at the large bullet wound on the side of the boy's head. Suddenly the woods were quiet. *Someone had to hear all that noise and commotion,* Samuel thought. As he looked around, Samuel wondered where it would be best to hide their bodies. Samuel had successfully hid two bodies over a year ago and briefly considered using the same method to dispose of the four teenagers until he realized how far away from his trailer he was and how far he would have to walk at night hoping no one would see him. Since Samuel had hunted at West Spoon quite often, he was relatively familiar with the landscape.

Samuel remembered that a creek nearby fed into the lake. Several times while he was out hunting, he had seen people on smaller boats come up the creek from the lake to fish. Samuel decided to drag the boys' bodies down a steep hill into the creek bed. One by one he moved them hoping not to make too much noise and get caught. The first boy he moved was the one that almost ran away. His body was near the hiking trail and would have been found first. After he moved the two other bodies, he approached the first boy he shot. Samuel's bolt hit the boy in the chest and went right through his heart killing him almost instantly. Samuel found the bolt covered in blood up against the tree. The broadhead had pieces of cloth stuck in it from the hoody the boy was wearing. Samuel was very exhausted after dragging three bodies even though he was moving them downhill. The first boy was clearly the heaviest, but this last one was the tallest, and Samuel struggled moving him. As he pushed the last body over a log and into the creek bed, the boy's cell phone fell out of his pocked unbeknownst to Samuel.

Samuel scanned the area for evidence. While he didn't see anything that would alert park rangers or authorities, there was quite a bit of blood in certain spots, so he gathered some small branches and leaves and tried to cover the spots where he saw blood. *After a few hard rains, this blood will wash away,* Samuel thought. By this point Samuel knew his hunt for deer was over for the day, so he decided to walk back to his truck and head home. As he was walking back to his truck, he called his boss.

"Hey Ron, it's Sam," Samuel said.

"Hey man what's up?" Ron replied.

"I need to ask you a favor," Samuel said

"Sure, how can I help?" Ron asked.

"Can I borrow your Jon boat tomorrow morning?" Samuel asked.

"Yeah sure. You going fishing tomorrow?" Ron asked.

"No I wanted to check out a spot across the lake that's

easier to access by boat instead of walking. Plus if I harvest a deer, I can just load it on the boat instead of dragging it out," Samuel explained.

"Oh ok, yeah. Of course you can use it. I keep telling you, you need to just buy it off me," Ron told Samuel.

Samuel laughed and said, "Yeah I know. I just don't have the money right now."

"You've been working for me long enough. I trust you'll pay it back," Ron said.

"Well even if I could afford it, I got nowhere to keep it right now," Samuel explained.

"Just keep it at the shop. When you get a place with more room, then you can move it," Ron suggested.

"Alright, well I'll swing by later," Samuel said.

"Ok. I'll probably leave here in the next hour or so, but I'll leave the key to the trailer by the mailbox and make sure you lock up," Ron told Samuel.

"Ok I will. Thanks again Ron," Samuel replied.

"No problem, Sammy boy. I'm just glad someone will use it. I'm getting too old to mess with that thing," Ron said.

Samuel laughed before replying, "Alright. Sounds good. I'll talk to you later."

Samuel stopped by his trailer first to grab a bite to eat. He remembered he had some leftovers in the fridge and wanted to heat something up quickly, so he could move the bodies before someone found them. Before he swung by the shop to pick up the boat, Samuel went to Lowe's and bought some cinder blocks and rope. Samuel drove to the shop after dark and hooked up the small Jon boat trailer to his truck. After he had the boat hooked up, he moved the cinder blocks and ropes into the boat. *I sure hope this motor still works,* Samuel thought to himself as he was packing everything up. After Samuel left the shop, he headed to the boat ramp on the side of the park that stayed open after dark because there was a neighborhood right next to the state park. When he got to the boat ramp, it was empty. Samuel backed the boat down into the water and made sure the motor worked before he took the boat off the trailer. Instead of moving his truck and trailer off the ramp, he kept it there so he could get out quickly when he came back. Samuel didn't expect anyone would try to use the boat ramp after dark. Besides, the only street light was over in the parking lot, and he didn't want any park rangers seeing his truck in the parking lot.

Under the cover of darkness Samuel headed across the lake toward the creek where he left the bodies. It was hard navigating after dark, and Samuel had to take his time when he reached the creek. Luckily the Jon boat was small enough that he could maneuver in relatively tight areas without bottoming out. Using his heavy duty flashlight, Samuel spotted the bodies he left along the creek bed and drove the boat on-shore. After loading up the bodies, he headed back out toward the middle of the lake. Depending on what part of the lake he was at, the depth varied greatly. Samuel wanted to sink the bodies in the deepest part of the lake hoping they would never be found.

When he got to where he thought was the center of the lake, he tied the rope around the bodies several times and then around the cinder blocks. Samuel used several cinder blocks for each body to make sure there was enough weight to keep them under water. One by one he tossed each body over the boat, followed up by the cinder blocks that sank them to the bottom. Samuel stuck around to make sure the bodies didn't resurface, and while he was waiting, he lit a cigarette. When he was finished with his smoke, he fired up the motor and headed back to his truck at the boat ramp. Samuel was relieved when he got back to the ramp and no one else was there. He quickly loaded the Jon boat back on the trailer and drove away. Realizing he would need to keep the boat during the next day, Samuel decided to leave the trailer on his truck at his mobile home instead of taking the boat back to the shop. When Samuel got back to his mobile home, Lyndsey was already there getting ready to go out that night.

"Hey how was your hunt?" Lyndsey asked Samuel.

"Eh didn't see anything," Samuel replied.

"You wanna go to Longitudes tonight?" Lyndsey asked. "I'm meeting some friends from work later," she continued.

"I'm exhausted," Samuel replied.

"Ok, that's fine," Lyndsey said.

"Who's all going to be there?" Samuel asked as he started to get undressed, so he could take a shower.

"Claire, Abby and Steph for sure. Maybe more. I just haven't heard from anyone else yet," Lyndsey explained.

"So there's no guys going?" Samuel asked.

"Well Turner said he could pick me up if I needed a ride," Lyndsey replied. *There it is,* Samuel thought to himself. Samuel knew there was no way there weren't going to be any guys she worked with at the bar. A while back before Lyndsey decided to move in with Samuel, he found out that she was spending a lot of time with this Turner guy she worked with and even found out she was staying at his place several times. Samuel overheard people at the bar talking about how they saw Turner and Lyndsey making out all the time, but when Samuel confronted Lyndsey about him, she would always tell Samuel that

Turner and her were just friends and nothing happened. Since Samuel didn't fully trust Lyndsey and definitely didn't trust this Turner guy, he changed his mind.

"Let me get a shower real quick and change first. Then we can head out to meet your friends," Samuel told Lyndsey as she was putting on her makeup.

"Ok great!" Lyndsey replied enthusiastically. She then pulled back the shower curtain and leaned over to kiss Samuel while he was in the shower. Just then Samuel woke up from his nap and realized Lyndsey was laying on top of him in his bed and had just kissed him.

"Do you have to work tomorrow?" Lyndsey asked.

"Nah, I'm off. How about you?" Samuel replied.

"I'm off tomorrow too. You want to go out to dinner tonight? Maybe grab drinks after?" Lyndsey asked Samuel. He hesitated for a moment before he realized he just got paid and would be able to afford to go out for dinner and get a couple drinks. Now that Lyndsey was working more and buying her own food, Samuel was doing a little better financially.

"Yeah sure, that sounds nice," Samuel replied with a smile.

Chapter 10

David was beginning to settle in to his new schedule. He was working at the gun store on most mornings, helping open up and move any new shipments of ammunition or equipment. In the evenings he was going to the gym and with his spare time, he was mostly studying or searching for more information about the individuals who went missing at West Spoon Lake. One Sunday as he was home watching football, David decided to get ahead on some homework and then get on Facebook to see if he could find out anything about the victims. As he compiled a list of the individuals that went missing, he also looked to see who their families were. Once he discovered the parents, relatives and friends of the victims, he did a quick search online to see where they all lived. Even though he did not have the authority to do so, he wanted to reach out to several of them and see if he could get more information.

David decided to start with the first two that went missing at West Spoon Lake. David had read an article about two teenagers that disappeared at West Spoon. Damien Young and Megan McKinley were both last seen leaving school when they were juniors in high school. Several of their friends had told authorities they were going to West Spoon after class and then they were never seen again. After David found each victim's home address, he decided to drive over to Damien's parents' house first since it was closer. David parked on the street and walked up their sidewalk to the front door. After knocking David waited for an answer. No one came to the door, so he knocked again. Eventually, a tall man with a beard opened the door and asked, "Can I help you?"

"Yes sir, my name is David Celanese," David lied. He was hesitant to give his real name. "I am doing some investigative work into several disappearances over the years at West Spoon Lake, and I was wondering if I could talk to you briefly about your son's disappearance," David continued.

"Fuck off," the man replied.

"Excuse me sir? I'm just trying to help," David said.

"We contacted the authorities every day for over two years after my son went missing, and they never responded to us. If you didn't care then, you don't care now," the man said sternly as he slammed the door in David's face. *Well that didn't go well,* David thought to himself. As he got back in his truck, he sat there for a moment and wondered if he should even bother trying to talk to the teenage girl's parents based on the way the boy's father handled his interest in the case. *It's worth a shot I guess,* David thought to himself as he started his truck and headed over to the girl's parents' house.

Luckily for David, Megan's family didn't live far from Damien's and it only took him a few minutes to drive to her parents' neighborhood. *This is a nice neighborhood,* David thought to himself as he drove down the street toward the cul de sac. David noticed the houses on this street were much bigger than the homes where Damien's family lived. *Hopefully this family is a little more open and friendly,* David was thinking. After he rang the doorbell a short, frail woman answered the door, "Hello, may I help you?"

"Yeah, my name is David Celanese, and I was wondering if I could ask you a few questions about your daughter's disappearance," David said.

"Jeremy! Come down here quick," the lady shouted. "Here come in please; have a seat," she continued as she led David to their kitchen table. David took a seat with his back to the wall and facing the front door. As he started to look around, he noticed a lot of pictures of the woman with whom he assumed was her husband and a younger daughter. David heard footsteps and the lady asked, "Would you like something to drink?"

"Yeah sure, I'll take a glass of water," David replied. As the lady was pouring water into a cup, Megan's father walked into the kitchen and introduced himself. "Hey, I'm Jeremy," the man said as he reached out to shake David's hand.

"David, nice to meet you," David replied.

"So are you with the police department?" Jeremy asked David.

"No sir. I am an independent investigator. There weren't many leads through the local police department, so I was asked to look into some of the specific cases around West Spoon Lake," David lied.

"Oh ok. Well how can we help you?" Jeremy said as he sat down. The lady that answered the door handed David his glass of water and David said, "Thank you."

"The reports I read suggested that your daughter and her

boyfriend were last seen heading toward West Spoon; is that correct?" David asked.

"Yeah, Megan's friends told us her and Damien were talking about going to West Spoon Lake after school," Jeremy said.

"Is that something she did often?" David asked.

"Not really. Damien played baseball and Megan ran track, but I guess since it was in the fall, they both had more free time," Jeremy explained.

"Ok. When was the last time you spoke to your daughter, and what did she say?" David asked the parents.

This time the mother spoke up. "She texted me and told me she was going to West Spoon after school to go hiking with some friends."

"So were there others with them, or was it just Damien and Megan?" David asked.

"No it was just Megan and Damien," Jeremy replied.

"Ok. Do you know if there were any problems between the two of them? Had they been arguing or fighting at all before they went missing?" David asked.

"Not that we know of. Damien lived pretty close, so he usually would come over here to hang out with Megan, and as long as one of us was home, we let them come and go as they pleased. Obviously I wanted my daughter to be safe and make good choices, but I didn't want to smother her either," Jeremy told David.

"I understand sir," David said. "Was she having any issues with anyone at school or around the neighborhood?" David asked.

"No. She was always very cheerful and friendly. I never heard her talk bad about anyone, and all the parents would tell me how sweet she is," the mother chimed in. While David was looking at the mother, he saw her eyes begin to tear up. "Please tell me you're going to find my daughter," the mother continued.

"I cannot make any promises. I will try my best," David replied. Megan's father leaned over to hug his wife. "Do you happen to know what part of the park they went to?" David asked.

"They found Damien's car in a parking lot on the west side of the lake," Jeremy replied. "It was off of Slate Road," he continued. *"Holy shit,"* David thought to himself as he realized that was the lot where he parked his truck when the stranger was following him and his brother. Naturally David began to wonder if the same man who stalked him and his brother was the one responsible for Damien and Megan's disappearance. David didn't know Damien or Megan, but he began to think the worst had happened and maybe the stranger had killed them. David dropped his head and thought about how lucky he and Zander were to make it out of there alive that night.

"Ok, I understand how difficult this must be for both of you. I really do appreciate your time," David said as he stood up and began to leave.

"Wait," the mother cried out. David turned around and saw her reach into a drawer below the kitchen cabinet. "Please take this with you," the mother said as she handed David a picture of Megan. "I pray you'll find my baby girl." The mother trembled with tears running down her face.

David placed the picture in his coat pocket and gave her a nod before he told her, "I will do everything I can." When he got back in his truck, he glanced over at their front door and noticed both parents were standing there looking at him. David started his truck and held his hand out toward them to wave. They both waved back to as he drove off and headed home.

When David got home, he put the picture of Megan next to his photo of his friend Danny who was killed in Afghanistan. It was starting to get dark, and David checked his phone as he sat down on his bed. He had several missed text messages. Both his parents had tried to call him; his best friend Michael had texted him several times; his brother was texting him about the football games, and Evan was texting him as well. Even though only one victims' family from the first disappearance was cooperative, David was determined to continue his search, so he got back on social media and began looking into the four teenage boys that went missing a little over a year after Damien and Megan went missing.

Reading the older news articles, David discovered the four boys' names were Timothy Reynolds, Logan Miles, Mark Blaser and Curtis Davis. All four boys disappeared on the same day and had never been seen again. The article David was reading didn't give many details beyond the boys' names, so he searched online for another article related to the case. David found an article that included a little bit more information, and he discovered that an SUV registered to Curtis Davis's parents was found later that day in a parking lot on the south side of West Spoon Lake. A park ranger had noticed it in the parking lot when he went to close the park gates and reported it. Shortly after, the parents of the four boys realized they were missing, and a search team was organized to find them. Unfortunately, none of the park rangers or authorities could find the boys. The only thing found was Curtis Davis's cell phone in a creek bed by a local fisherman.

David did a quick search on social media and found the names of the four boys' parents. The following day after work, David decided to go talk to Curtis Davis's parents since the car found at the park was registered in their name. The Davis family lived on the south side of the lake in a smaller neighborhood with homes that appeared a little older. The front yard looked like it needed some landscaping work, and the grass hadn't been maintained very well. When David knocked on the front door, he could hear a man inside yell, "Hey someone's at the door!"

Shortly afterward a tall, middle-aged woman answered the door. "Hello?"

"Hi, My name is David Celanese. I'm investigating the disappearance of your son and his friends," David said.

"Oh ok, come on in," the lady said as she opened the screen door. When David entered the house, he immediately could tell both parents were smokers as the entire house reeked of cigarettes. When he followed the woman into the kitchen, he glanced over to his right and saw a man sitting in a chair watching TV in the living room.

"Please have a seat," the woman told David. He noticed several chairs already had clothes or other items on them, so he sat on the one chair that wasn't a cluttered mess. As the woman was shuffling in the kitchen, David looked around and saw several family photos; each picture showed three children along with the mother and father.

"How can I help you?" the woman asked as she cleared off another chair to sit at the table with David.

"Mrs. Davis, when was the last time you saw or spoke to your son?" David asked.

"Please, call me Karen," the woman replied. "I saw him the morning before he left for school on the day he disappeared," she continued.

"Do you happen to know why Curtis and his friends went to West Spoon that day?" David asked.

"The teachers at school told us all four boys skipped their last class of the day. When they found my son's phone, the authorities told us all four boys were texting each other about going to West Spoon to smoke weed," she explained.

"Was this something that was common?" David asked.

"Eh kinda. Curtis began smoking weed and experimenting with other drugs when he was a sophomore in high school. He was the oldest of the four boys, so I think they wanted to hang out with him because they wanted to look cool. Curtis would come home late after school all the time, and it was pretty obvious he was high," Karen explained.

"That kid was a fucking punk." The man sitting on the chair said as he got up, walked through the kitchen and grabbed a beer.

"He is your son," Karen replied sternly.

"Yeah maybe; jury's still out on that one too," the man replied as he walked back to the living room. David was confused.

"Are your other children around?" David asked Karen.

"No, Connor is at his girlfriend's house and Carly is at cheerleading practice," Karen replied.

"Ok. Would you mind if I spoke to them later?" David asked.

"Sure that's fine. I don't know when they will be home," Karen said.

"Well I can always come back another time," David replied. "Before I leave I have one more question though. Where did they find the vehicle Curtis was driving?" he continued.

"I believe it was in a parking lot near the south entrance of the state park," Karen responded. The article David read was correct.

"Ok, thank you for your time. I will let you know if I find anything," David said. He was surprised to see that the three sets of parents who lost children were such polar opposites. The first family he tried to speak to wanted nothing to do with him. The second family was very outgoing and interested in finding out what happened to their child, and then the third family acted like nothing happened. *Curtis's father didn't even seem to care,* David thought to himself. While it was fresh on his mind, David wanted to speak to the parents of the other three boys that disappeared the same day as Curtis, so later in the week, he decided to skip the evening Jiu Jitsu class so he had more time to speak with the other three families.

Fortunately for David when he went to speak to Logan Miles' family, Mark Blaser's mother was there as well since the Miles family and the Blaser family were neighbors. David parked his truck on the street out in front of the Miles' house and saw a man mowing the lawn when he got out of his truck.

"Excuse me, are you Mr. Miles?" David asked the man.

"Yeah, can I help you?" the man replied.

"Hi, my name is David Celanese. Nice to meet you sir. I'm investigating the disappearance of your son and his friends," David explained.

"Oh shit! Hang on. Let me go get my wife," the man quickly replied as he almost sprinted to the front door. David was walking up the driveway toward their front porch when the man came back out followed by two women that almost looked like they could be sisters if it weren't for the fact that one was blonde and one was brunette.

"Hi, I'm Shirley Miles," the blonde woman said as she held out her hand.

"Nice to meet you. I'm David," he replied.

"Kate Blaser," the brunette said after David shook Shirley's hand.

"Nice to meet you," David said.

"Larry," the man who was mowing the lawn, said as he shook David's hand. "Here, let's go inside," he continued. All four of them went inside and David followed the two women into a dining room where they sat down. "Can we get you something to drink?" Shirley asked David.

"Yeah sure, water is fine," David replied.

"Ok. I'll bring some out for everyone," Larry said as he left the room.

"So did you guys find out what happened to our sons?" Kate asked David.

"Not yet ma'am. I need to ask you some questions to help with the search," David started to say.

"You guys need to take a good look into that damn Curtis kid," Kate interrupted.

"What do you mean?" David asked.

"Ever since our boys started hanging out with him, they were getting in trouble. Mark and Logan were honor students, played trumpet in the band, and never had any behavioral issues at school or home. When that Curtis kid came around, they started skipping class; their grades slipped, and we found paraphernalia in our basement," Shirley explained.

"Were Mark and Logan pretty close?" David asked.

"Absolutely; they were inseparable," Kate said. "They have been neighbors since they were born, attended the same church, and they were always hanging out together. If Logan wasn't at our house, he was at Mark's and vice versa," Kate continued.

"Ok, do you know why they started hanging out with Curtis?" David asked.

"Well they were both kinda shy. Not the most popular kids in school, and they did get bullied sometimes. I think Curtis was one of the more popular kids, and they wanted to fit in," Shirley explained. "We noticed Curtis was a bad kid the first time he spent the night and he stole jewelry from my vanity," she continued.

"You caught him in the act?" David asked.

"No. We caught the boys in our bedroom which they never go into, and I didn't notice the missing jewelry until after Curtis left. When I confronted his parents, they said they asked him about it, and he said he didn't take anything. After that I kept our bedroom door locked when he came over, and I kept an eye on him," Shirley explained. "He probably sold the jewelry for drugs," she continued.

"I see. When was the last time you saw or spoke to your sons before they went missing?" David asked.

"Right before they left for school," both women said at almost the exact same time.

"Ok. Well I did talk to Curtis's parents before I came here," David said. "To be honest they weren't very helpful," he continued.

"Yeah his dad doesn't give a shit about him, and his mom wasn't much of a disciplinarian," Kate said. "He probably killed them and then ran away," Kate stated. David was surprised. "Wait! You think Curtis killed your boys?" he asked.

"I wouldn't put it past him. That kid was a criminal," Shirley replied.

"If he killed the other three boys, how would he have gotten away? He went missing as well," David asked.

"Probably stole a car. He stole his teacher's car during lunch one day," Kate said.

"Wait. What?" David asked.

"Yeah, he was suspended for two weeks his sophomore

year because he stole a teacher's car keys and left school in her car. They found the car in a McDonald's parking lot near his house," Kate explained.

"How did they find out it was him?" David asked.

"Security cameras at the school caught him," Shirley said.

"Ok, so if you think Curtis killed the three boys and ran away, what did he do with the bodies?" David asked the two mothers.

"No clue," Shirley replied. "He could have buried them somewhere at West Spoon; that place is huge," she continued. "The search team they sent out was pathetic and didn't find anything," she added.

"So they did conduct a search at West Spoon for them?" David asked.

"Yeah, they had a few park rangers go out with dogs looking for them, but they didn't find anything. We organized a search party with other kids and families that knew our sons. Like I mentioned before, they weren't the most popular kids in school, so they didn't have many friends show up to help look for them," Shirley said.

"Yeah, or he could have loaded them into a stolen vehicle and taken them with him to bury them somewhere else and make it harder to find them," Kate said. David sat for a moment completely confused.

"Did Curtis ever fight with your sons? I mean what would be his motive for killing your boys?" David asked.

"He didn't really pick on them like the other bullies they dealt with at school did, but he just ordered them around all the time, and they followed along with whatever he said," Shirley replied. Before David could respond, his phone started ringing, and when he checked it, he saw his dad was calling him. David decided to ignore the call and get back to his father later.

"Sorry about that," David said. "So you don't think your sons' disappearances have anything to do with some of the other individuals that have gone missing at West Spoon?" David asked.

"What do you mean?" Kate asked.

"Well there's been almost a dozen people who have gone missing within the past decade at that state park," David explained.

"Oh wow. I didn't realize there was that many," Shirley replied. "Who else went missing there?" she asked.

"Well the first two were a teenage boy and girl that were apparently dating at the time. Damien Young and Megan McKinley," David said.

"Oh yeah those were the two that went missing from St. Michaels," Kate said.

"Yeah I don't think they had anything to do with our boys," Shirley said. "They were older and didn't even go to the same school," she added.

"Ok. There was a park ranger that went missing as well; then some guy who was associated with the Venomous Riders," David explained.

"Yeah, we heard about the park ranger; that was all over the news," Shirley said.

"Who are the Venomous Riders?" Kate asked.

"Apparently it's a motorcycle club; they ride into the area from time to time," David replied.

"Yeah our boys wouldn't have anything to do with that guy," Kate said. David paused for a moment and then said, "Yeah, I doubt your sons knew the guy from the motorcycle club."

"There was also the father and son who were killed near the park," David said.

"Yeah, but didn't that happen on their property? Like it was a hunting dispute or something," Kate said.

"Well they found the bodies in the state park, but they had been dragged from their property. Not sure why," David replied. "Obviously finding two bodies like that is concerning, but what bothers me more is all the people that have went missing at West Spoon the past decade," David continued.

"Yeah that place is dangerous," Kate stated.

"Do you think all these disappearances are related or separate incidents?" Shirley asked David.

"Well at first it appeared they were all separate incidents, and there really isn't much proof that they would be related. Looking into each specific case, none of the victims knew each other or were associated in any way. Obviously the first two victims knew each other and were dating, and then your sons and their two friends knew each other, but beyond that there's no connection. I doubt the park ranger that went missing knew the biker or all the teenagers that disappeared," David explained.

"So do you think there's a serial killer on the loose or something?" Shirley asked David.

"I don't know," David began. "If there is they know what they are doing because there is very little evidence to follow up on," he continued.

"Have you talked to Timmy's mom yet?" Shirley asked.

"No, that was my next stop," David replied.

"Here. I'll get her number and address for you," Shirley replied as she walked into the kitchen.

"His dad's not in the picture?" David asked Kate.

"He passed away when Timmy was younger," Kate replied.

"Oh damn. What happened?" David asked her.

"He was killed in Iraq; he was in the marines," Kate said. Even though hearing about Timmy's father hit a little close to home for David, he didn't want to blow his cover, so he tried to stay composed.

"Ah damn! That sucks," David said quietly.

"Yeah, it was pretty hard on the two of them," Kate replied. Shirley walked into the room and handed David a piece of notebook paper with a name, phone number and address.

"Thank you," David said. "I need to get going, but if you think of anything else, please let me know. If I find anything, I'll be sure to contact you," he continued. Both women stood as David did and Shirley walked over to give him a hug.

"No thank you. You have no idea how much this means to us," Shirley said. David nodded and turned toward Kate who hugged him as well.

"You have shown more interest in finding our boys than any of the other cops we spoke to," Kate said.

"Really?" David replied.

"Yeah, they were very cold and distant. Almost like it was a burden to them that we were looking for our boys and trying to find out what happened to them," Shirley said.

"Well I apologize that they treated you like that; that certainly isn't helpful," David said. As David was walking toward the front door, Larry walked back into the house to thank him and shook his hand before David left. When David got back in his truck, he called his father back.

"Hey, what's up," David asked.

"Hey man, haven't talked to you in a while. What have you been up to?" his father asked.

"Oh you know, just staying busy with online classes, work and training," David replied.

"Shit kid. I figured when you got out of the Army, you'd have more free time, and we'd see you more. Sounds like you're just as busy as you were before," his father said.

David laughed and then replied, "I can't sit still; you know that."

"Yeah, you've always been that way," his father said. "Your mom is making fajitas tonight. Why don't you swing by for dinner?" his father continued.

"Alright that sounds good. I'm starving," David replied. "What time you guys eating?" David asked his father.

"Your mom is cooking right now. Just come on over," his father said.

"Alright, I'm on my way," David replied.

Chapter 11

After they grabbed dinner, Samuel and Lyndsey went to Longitudes to get some drinks and like always Lyndsey managed to run into a bunch of other people she knew. Some of them were other men, which started to anger Samuel. Lyndsey was often very flirtatious around other men and would deny it even though it was blatantly obvious. After they ordered a round of beers, Lyndsey wanted to go outside to smoke, so Samuel followed her. By this point her smoking had worn on Samuel, and he started smoking as well. Most of the time the only reason Samuel would smoke was to make sure she wasn't flirting with other guys when he wasn't around. Even if Samuel was inside and she was outside, he would often see her flirting with other guys. Samuel figured if he was present, that would hopefully deter any other guys from engaging in her flirtatious behavior.

There were even several nights where one of the guys Lyndsey would flirt with would come up and ask Samuel if the two were dating. His response was always the same,

"Yeah, pretty much." Typically after that the guy would back off and leave Lyndsey alone. On the rare occasion the other guy would continue flirting, Samuel would usually get combative. Sometimes it led to Samuel and the other guy arguing with each other until they were separated, and sometimes they would literally go outside the bar and fight behind the bar or somewhere in the parking lot.

Luckily for Samuel, the guys who tried to fight him were not very good fighters. Using his wrestling background, Samuel was able to take them down and just beat them up from there. Samuel's rage would also kick in, and the frustration he built up from losing his family combined with Lyndsey's provocative behavior led him to do serious damage to the men he fought. Once Samuel got the other guy to the ground, it was almost a sure bet he was going to bust up their face to the point it was just a bloody mess. As Samuel and Lyndsey were outside, he noticed a heavy set man he once fought a while back. The man walked into the bar through the main entrance. *Fucking great*, Samuel thought to himself. At this point he wanted to leave, so he walked up to Lyndsey to tell her, "Hey, we gotta get outta here."

"What, why?" Lyndsey asked.

"That fat fuck I beat the shit out of a couple months ago just walked in," Samuel replied.

"Which one?" Lyndsey asked.

"The bald guy who said you'd look good in his new home once he divorced his wife," Samuel replied.

"Oh yeah, you beat his ass," Lyndsey laughed.

"I know, let's get out of here. If he notices me, he might start shit or report me to the cops," Samuel told Lyndsey.

"Oh, he wouldn't do anything," Lyndsey argued.

"Bullshit. If he's got as much money as he claimed he did, he could sue me for assault or something. You and I both know I can't afford that shit. Let's get out of here," Samuel told her.

"Oh alright. We are almost out of beer back home though; can we stop at a drive-through and pick up another case?" Lyndsey asked Samuel.

"Yeah sure, let me close my tab and we can leave," Samuel replied.

On the drive back with Lyndsey, Samuel started to think about another close call he had while he was hunting one day. He began to daydream about the time he killed the park ranger. During bow season one fall, Samuel decided to take his .22 long rifle with him, so he could hunt some squirrels while he was in his makeshift blind. The day before he had gone out and spent almost the entire day waiting for a deer, but all he saw were squirrels. Samuel realized if he decided to squirrel hunt, he could have filled his daily limit easily considering how many squirrels were running around in that area that day.

Samuel decided to hunt early in the morning in the same spot where he was the day before. He spent about five hours in the same spot and managed to shoot six squirrels before 1 p.m. He did miss a few shots, but the abundance of squirrels made it easy for him to fill his daily limit. As Samuel shot them, he would leave them where they fell until he harvested enough to satisfy himself. Once he was ready to leave, Samuel walked around to collect his harvest. It didn't take long for him to realize that he didn't miss as many shots as he originally thought, and he actually ended up harvesting two more squirrels than what was allowed for the daily limit. Still, he put them all in his backpack and started heading to his truck.

As expected he didn't see any deer that morning, but he

brought his crossbow with him as well just in case. Carrying a rifle while bow hunting was illegal at West Spoon, but Samuel did it anyway because he didn't care. During his walk back to his truck, Samuel came across an unexpected stranger on the hiking trail. Samuel had his Remington .22 long rifle over his shoulder on a sling, and he was carrying his crossbow in his hands. He also had his camouflaged backpack filled with the eight squirrels he harvested earlier that morning. He was walking up a hill getting ready to turn the corner and walk back down toward a small ravine that led into the creek nearby; just then he heard footsteps. Samuel hesitated for a moment and wondered if he should walk off the trail and hide, hoping the person walking wouldn't see him and would leave him be. Samuel figured it was just someone hiking who didn't know the hunting rules and regulations, so they would most likely leave him be. Standing atop the hill, Samuel looked down, and to his surprise realized the man walking toward him along the hiking trail was a park ranger. "Oh fuck," Samuel whispered to himself.

"Good afternoon," the park ranger said to Samuel.

"Afternoon sir," Samuel replied as he continued walking toward him.

"Got a call that some gunshots were heard over in this area," the park ranger said.

"Yeah I was sighting my scope in," Samuel lied.

"Ok. Are you aware it's illegal to carry a rifle with you while you are bow hunting?" the ranger asked Samuel.

"Oh is it?" Samuel replied pretending to be surprised.

"Yeah, you were also shooting in a no hunting zone," the ranger told Samuel.

"Oh my bad. I thought this was a legal hunting zone," Samuel lied again.

"Nope, the other side of the creek is a legal hunting zone; this side is illegal because it's too close to the horse trails," the ranger told Samuel. "Do me a favor. Slowly set down your crossbow and rifle over by that tree, and I'm going to need to see your hunting license," the ranger continued.

"Sure, no problem," Samuel replied. He sat his rifle up against the tree and then laid his crossbow down on the flat part of the ground with the arrow pointing away from them. With his backpack still on, Samuel reached into his back pocket to get his wallet. Then he found his hunting license and handed it over to the park ranger. The park ranger looked down at the license Samuel just handed him and started to say, "Ok. Well here's the deal Samuel . . ."

Bang! Bang! Samuel had his pistol concealed under his camouflaged hoody and pulled it out firing two quick shots at the park ranger's chest. The park ranger wore a bulletproof vest under his uniform, but he still was knocked backward on the ground. As he lay on his back gasping for air, he looked up at Samuel with a shocked look on his face. Before he could speak Samuel shot again, *Bang!* The third shot went right into the park ranger's forehead killing him instantly.

Samuel looked to see if anyone was around to hear what just happened. Before he moved the park ranger's body, Samuel looked around for the brass casings from the three bullets he just fired. Once he collected all the casings, he dragged the park ranger's body off the trail and into some thicker cover where he could temporarily hide the body in case someone else walked by. Samuel realized he was going to have to return later to dispose of the body, but he did not want someone to find a dead park ranger in the woods before he could return, so Samuel decided to strip the park ranger of his uniform and equipment and place them somewhere else that would be hard to find.

Before Samuel walked back to his truck, he peeked out of the wooded area and into the field to see if anyone else was around or if there were any cars in the parking lot. Samuel noticed there was a silver SUV in the parking lot along with his truck and the park ranger's SUV. As Samuel scanned the area, he could not see anyone else, but he assumed whoever called the park ranger was likely the one who drove the silver SUV. Samuel was hesitant to return to his truck because he was aware that if the person in the silver SUV did in fact call the park ranger, they were probably going to notice him return to his truck and assume the gunshots came from him. Samuel thought if the park ranger's body was going to be discovered, he would be the prime suspect, and if the person who parked the silver SUV was smart, they would take a picture of his license plates.

Samuel decided to wait in the wooded area for a while and hoped the other vehicle would leave, so he could head back to his truck unnoticed. After waiting for about an hour, a couple walking their dog returned to the silver SUV. The man looked over at the wooded area Samuel was sitting in for a brief moment, and then got in the SUV and drove off. Now that his path was clear, Samuel decided to walk back to his truck, but he did so rather quickly hoping no one else would show up.

After Samuel got back to his mobile home, he decided to field dress the squirrels he harvested before heading back into the woods to dispose of the park ranger's body. Even though field dressing squirrels was tough for Samuel at first, he got better at it using a tail pull method that helped allow him to remove almost the entire hide at once. Samuel would make an incision with his knife at the base of the squirrel's tail right above the anus and then using a block of wood, he would step on the squirrel's tail. Then he would grab the back legs and simply start pulling upwards. As long as Samuel didn't cut the tail too deep and made the incision at the right location, he would be able to pull the hide of the squirrel all the way up to the head. Once he got the hide around the squirrel's head and neck area, Samuel would simply cut the squirrels head off, and the entire hide would be removed. Then Samuel cut the squirrel open to remove its organs and insides. Samuel then cut off any fat and placed the squirrels in a cooler filled with water and a little bit of salt.

After he finished field dressing the squirrels, Samuel loaded up his truck with a shovel, an ax and a garbage bag. Samuel drove back to the state park, but this time decided to park in the parking lot by the boat ramp. Samuel was wary about returning to the parking lot from before because the park ranger's SUV was still there. It was beginning to get dark, so Samuel brought his lantern and head lamp with him.

It didn't take Samuel long to find the park ranger's body, and once he did, he dragged it even farther off the trail where he killed the ranger. Once he found a decent spot with a lot of cover, he dug a deep grave for the park ranger's body. Before burying the park ranger, Samuel cut off the hands and feet with the axe. Then he cut off the park ranger's head. Samuel buried the body in one location; then he buried the head in a different spot far away. Even if by some chance the park ranger's body was found, Samuel wanted to make it harder for the body to be identified. He placed the hands and feet in the black garbage bag he brought with him and then threw the park ranger's clothes and equipment inside as well. Samuel thought about burning the body like he did with the two teenagers he killed, but he didn't want to dispose of the body the same way he had in the past. Instead Samuel decided he would burn the bag with the ranger's clothes, equipment, hands and feet inside. Before Samuel headed back to his truck, he dug a shallow hole for a campfire and stacked up enough firewood to get a fire started. Once the bigger logs were burning, Samuel started burning the park ranger's clothes, one item at a time. Samuel then burned the hands and feet he'd chopped off. Samuel threw a couple more logs on the fire before he left and headed back to his truck.

As he was walking away, Samuel looked back and noticed he could still see the fire going. He started to wonder whether or not it was noticeable from the lot where he parked. Samuel started to worry that if there was smoke the next morning, someone may notice and investigate the area. As much as Samuel wanted to check on it, he knew he should avoid the area as much as possible because he was sure there would be a search for the park ranger once authorities realized he was missing. Samuel debated on whether or not he should go back and put the fire out. Instead, he decided to leave it be and hope the authorities would assume campers had a fire going the night before. The last thing he wanted was the park ranger's body to be found because it was near where he burned the park ranger's clothes and other body parts.

While he finished his walk back to his truck, Samuel decided to turn off his light so no one would notice him. He got back to his truck rather quickly and sped out of the parking lot, so he could get out of the park without getting caught. As Samuel was driving past the other parking lot, he noticed the SUV of the park ranger he killed was still there; only now there was also another park ranger vehicle parked there with lights on. "Oh fuck," Samuel said to himself as he sped up. Just before he reached the park exit, he looked in his rearview mirror to see if the other park ranger noticed him driving by and could possibly be following him. Samuel was pleased when he saw nothing. "These woods are mine," Samuel said to himself with a smile as he drove home.

Chapter 12

After David had spoken with Logan and Mark's parents, he was eager to speak with Timmy's mother. She was the only parent from the missing group of four that David had not yet spoke to. David kept the address that Shirley gave him in the glove box of his truck. The next day after he ate breakfast, David decided to go talk to Timmy's mother and see if he could get more information about the four teenage boys that went missing. When David pulled up to the address, he noticed three vehicles in the driveway and wondered who they could belong to considering Shirley and Kate told him that Timmy was an only child and his father had been killed in Iraq. David noticed the front door was open when he got to the front porch, and he could see through the main hallway into the kitchen. David didn't notice a doorbell, so he knocked instead. Within seconds of his knock, he saw an elderly couple walking down the hallway toward him.

"Hello, may we help you," the elderly woman asked.

"Yeah, my name is David Celanese. I was wondering if I

could speak with Debbie Reynolds," David replied.

"Oh, I'm sorry young man; she moved away," the lady replied.

"Oh really, do you happen to know where to?" David asked.

"We don't know exactly where she moved to, but when she sold the house, our realtor told us she was moving somewhere in Florida to live with her parents," the elderly man chimed in.

"Ok. Sorry to bother you. Thanks for your help," David said.

"You're welcome. Have a good day," the elderly woman replied.

"You too," David said as he turned and headed back to his truck.

David thought about trying to contact the realtor that sold the house, so he could maybe email or call Timmy's mother, but he wasn't sure if that was a conversation he wanted to have over the phone. David felt talking about her deceased son through email or over the phone was a little insensitive, plus if he spoke to her in person, David felt confident she would provide more information.

Before David drove back home, he got a text from Evan asking if he wanted to go rabbit hunting the next morning. "Hell yeah," David replied.

He decided to go to the gym later in the day to see if there was anyone else there that he could maybe get some rounds in with. David planned on staying at the gym for at least two hours, but when he got there, he was the only one there that fought. A couple others there were lifting weights in another room, but he didn't know them, and he wasn't sure if they had any martial arts training, so he decided to get some bag work in after jumping rope and shadowboxing. David had been working out for about an hour when a training partner finally showed up. David recognized Ryan as he walked through the front doors, "What's up man?" David said as Ryan sat down by the cage.

"Same old, same old, brother. You trying to get some rounds in?" Ryan asked shortly before David's round ended. David had set a timer to give him a minute break between rounds, so he walked over to Ryan between rounds to talk, "Yeah if you don't mind. I've been here for about an hour just trying to get some work in, mix things up," David replied.

"So do you want to do grappling rounds then?" Ryan asked.

"I'm cool with whatever, but I'd definitely prefer grappling or MMA rounds since I just did a bunch of bag work," David told Ryan.

"Yeah I got you. Let me change and get warmed up, and then we can drill some stuff and then spar a few rounds if that's cool," Ryan replied.

"Hell yeah, works for me," David said. As Ryan was changing clothes, David finished up one more round of bag work. He had been switching bags each round going from the traditional heavy bag to the banana bag, then the teardrop bag and ending with the uppercut bag. Changing which bag he was hitting each round allowed David to mix up what kind of strikes he was working on. After the round ended, David decided to rest a bit while Ryan was warming up. As he was stretching, a few more people walked in, and it looked like David was going to have several sparring partners to train with. David and Ryan warmed up and drilled some basic techniques while the four others warmed up as well. Before David and Ryan began sparring, Ryan asked the rest of the group, "Hey, everyone cool with getting some rounds in?" Everyone nodded and agreed.

"Ok cool. Since there are six of us here right now, let's just do five, five-minute rounds for now," Ryan said. "That cool with you?" Ryan asked David.

"Yeah I'm good with that," David replied.

"Ok, just checking. I know you've been in here working already. Just wanted to make sure it wasn't pushing you too much," Ryan explained. David laughed then replied, "It'll be good for me." The first round with Ryan was the toughest for David. Ryan had many years of experience in MMA and had wrestled all his life. David and Ryan were both top heavy grapplers, so the majority of the round was spent fighting for top position for each of them. It seemed like whenever Ryan would get a dominant position, David would immediately hit a sweep or escape to regain a neutral position. Once David got a neutral position, then he would go on the attack and manage to get Ryan on his back. Ryan had a very good guard, and his guard retention was stellar, so no matter how David was trying to pass, it was a struggle. David felt like he had attempted more submissions during their round sparring together, but he did spend a little more time on his back as well.

Neither man ended up getting a submission during the round, and afterward David wondered who would have won if the round had been scored. David had been watching a lot of MMA and jiu jitsu recently trying to understand the scoring a little more, but he wasn't sure if he had done enough during the round to win if they had been in a competition. David gave Ryan a quick hug before grabbing a sip of water and getting ready for his next opponent.

While David was waiting to see who he'd be rolling with next, he was thinking about how much he hated not knowing if he won the round. Before stepping back on the mats, David looked over at Ryan and saw how heavily he was breathing.

Even with the hour of bag work David had done before he sparred with Ryan, David felt his breathing was more controlled. *Well at least I wore him out,* David was thinking to himself. As he glanced over at Ryan, he also noticed Evan was there. *"How did I miss him earlier?"* David thought to himself. He bowed to the center of the mats right before he decided to walk over and say hi to his friend.

"What's up man?" David said to Evan as he walked across the mats.

"Oh hey, didn't want to disturb you while you were rolling with Ryan," Evan smiled.

"Yeah, I was zoned out. I didn't even see you come in."

"All good man, no worries," Evan replied. "You trying to roll?" Evan asked David.

"Yeah sure, I figured Ryan would pair us up eventually," David replied.

The second round went far better for David than his first round with Ryan. Evan and David had been drilling together a lot lately, and Evan showed him many defensive techniques. Specifically, Evan was showing David how to counter his own attacks because after they would finish sparring, David would ask Evan how to defend certain attacks if Evan submitted or got close to submitting David. Eventually, over time, David got harder and harder to submit for Evan, and this was the first round when David started to feel like he was consistently getting the upper hand on Evan.

David had also taken a few private classes with Terrance and had learned several new techniques that exploited some of Evan's weaknesses. Over time David noticed when he would spar with Evan and establish full mount on Evan, Evan was really good at escaping or getting to half guard. Sometimes

Evan would scramble out from there or fully retain his guard. David would get frustrated because of how good Evan was at escaping full mount, so he started focusing more on attacking from side control.

David had been working with Terrance on attacks from side control or triple attack, and he started developing dangerous arm lock attacks. David started hitting Kimuras and Americana's on many of his training partners, and in this round against Evan, he caught him with each submission twice. After the round was over and David realized he submitted his friend a combined total of about six times, his confidence was through the roof. It was still a bittersweet feeling because Evan had become one of David's best friends, and while David was proud of his own accomplishments, he didn't like having to physically beat his friend. Evan was a really good training partner; David was just a little more physically talented and didn't have to deal with the knee surgery Evan went through after high school. As David sat down to get a drink of water, Evan walked over to him and said, "Damn man, you're really kicking ass. Good shit."

"Thanks man," David replied while breathing heavily.

"That hard work is paying off," Evan continued. David noticed Evan was out of breath as well.

"Yeah, feels good to start going on the attack more instead of just trying to survive all the time," David said.

"Yeah, but you were never really putting yourself in bad positions to get submitted or anything. You have really good grappling instincts; it was just a matter of time before you started learning how to apply different submissions from various positions. Now you're smoking everyone. When you gonna start competing?" Evan asked David.

"Eh I don't know. I kind of want to finish classes before I start competing," David replied.

"That makes sense," Evan said. "Still, with the amount of time you spend in the gym and how you've progressed, I think you can definitely win some medals in grappling tournaments," Evan continued.

"Yeah maybe," David responded before Ryan started pairing people up for another round.

The third round David was paired up with a woman who was a purple belt and competed in grappling tournaments and had an 8-3 MMA record. She had been training longer than him, but he was bigger and much stronger. Trying to be nice, David started on his back and focused on hitting sweeps during most of the round. If he ever got in a clearly dominant position, he would go for a submission. He managed to take her back a few times and applied a basic rear naked choke, careful not to crank on her neck too much. David was glad to have a more technical round where he wasn't forced to use as much explosive energy. It was a good change of pace from feeling like his lungs may explode after each round he had with Evan and Ryan.

David's fourth round of sparring he got paired up with a larger training partner. David recognized him but was hesitant to ask the man's name. David hadn't seen the guy in class for a while, so he couldn't remember his name. David thought it might be Kevin, but he wasn't sure. David had rolled with him before and remembered that Kevin was a pretty good wrestler, but his cardio was horrible, and whenever Kevin managed to get on top of David, he would just kind of lie there instead of trying to pass or apply any legitimate submissions. David understood that it was his responsibility to *not* end up on his back against a much larger opponent, and if that did happen, it was up to him to sweep his opponent or find a way to escape. The first time David rolled with Kevin, he had just started training, so he didn't know as many sweeps or escapes. This round David was determined to not let Kevin establish top position and just lie there. When they first started sparring, David noticed Kevin was already breathing heavily from the previous rounds. David used his speed to his advantage, quickly hitting an arm drag to back take and sinking his hooks in as Kevin rolled over to his side. David trapped Kevin's left arm with his own left leg while maintaining strong back control. While Kevin was trying to get his arm free, David pulled back on Kevin's forehead just enough so he could slide his right arm under Kevin's chin. David decided to grab his own left shoulder with his right hand and start squeezing. *If this doesn't work, then I'll synch up the choke properly,* David thought to himself. It didn't take long for Kevin to tap, however, and then David released the choke and popped back up to start up again. Kevin sat on the mats for a while trying to control his breathing. During the rest of the round, David and Kevin spent the majority of the time on their feet, each man trying to establish a takedown.

Kevin was exhausted and didn't want to end up on his back because he knew how strong David was on top and David didn't want to get taken down because he didn't want Kevin to be able to rest and just lie on him. Eventually David did slip because the mats were slick from sweat, and Kevin pounced on top of him. David immediately retained his guard while Kevin looked over at the clock to see how much time was left. While Kevin was distracted, David tried to set up a triangle choke. Kevin was able to power his way out of it, and just went back to lying on David trying to catch his breath. David started to remember a fight that he had watched when Nick Diaz submitted Takanori Gomi with a rare Gogoplata. David had hit several omaplatas while sparring, but never attempted the Gogoplata. With less than thirty seconds left in the round, David decided to go for it. He pulled Kevin's head down while in guard and pushed Kevin's face to the right while he slid his left leg over Kevin's shoulder. Then David slid his foot and shin through the gap and along Kevin's throat. Once he got his leg through, David pulled down on Kevin's head even harder to squeeze the choke. David felt Kevin try to push his leg away and resist the choke, but eventually Kevin tapped. "Damn man, what the fuck was that?" Kevin asked David.

"Pretty sure it's a Gogoplata," David replied.

"I have no clue how the hell you just did that," Kevin said.

"I don't really know either," said David. "I just watched a fight when Nick Diaz did it and figured I'd try it," David continued.

"Well it worked. That's all that matters," Kevin replied.

"True," David said laughing.

There was only one other person David had not rolled with yet before the final round of sparring, so he assumed that's who Ryan would pair him up with. David had never seen the man before, so he introduced himself before they started rolling. David asked Donnie how long he'd been training because David was curious why he had never seen him before. Donnie explained that this was his first week of MMA training, but he was a black belt in Tae Kwon Do and had been training for six years. Donnie also told David he wrestled a little in high school. Whatever wrestling Donnie learned wasn't very effective because David was able to take him down with ease right from the start of the round. David quickly hit a rear naked choke on Donnie, probably within twenty seconds. David and Donnie were about the same size and age, so David wanted to see how many different submissions he could pull off against a Tae Kwon Do black belt. He wanted to see if Tae Kwon Do had any effectiveness in a grappling situation.

Before he knew it, David had submitted Donnie over twelve times within the five minute round and he began to feel sorry for Donnie. After the round ended, the two shook hands and David walked back to the bench where his bag was and sat down to cool off. Everyone else shook hands or hugged afterward, and David saw Ryan walking toward him.

"Hey man I should have told you, but this was Donnie's first time sparring with us," Ryan explained.

"Yeah, my bad man. I realized pretty quick how inexperienced he was. I just figured if he was a black belt in Tae Kwon Do, he'd be able to handle it," David replied.

"Well, Tae Kwon Do may have its uses when it comes to stand up and striking, but it's essentially useless in grappling situations, and you just fucking mauled that poor guy," Ryan said. David hung his head for a moment before replying, "Shit man. Now I feel bad. Should I apologize to him or something?"

"No you don't need to do that. Maybe just go a little easier on him next time. Just gotta know you're sparring partner's abilities and stuff. If you wreck everyone you roll with, no one is going to want to train with you. Know what I mean?" Ryan said.

"Yeah I got you," David replied. For most of David's life he was somewhat undersized, and because he was smaller than most growing up, he got picked on a lot. David couldn't stand bullying and always considered himself to be the anti-bully. David hated the thought that he was the bully when he was rolling with Donnie. As David sat on the bench, he reflected on his recent sparring session. *It's amazing how different sparring can go with five different opponents,* David thought to himself. Some of the rounds were very competitive and brutal, while others were more technical and experimental. David had moments when he felt confident and like he accomplished something, and then he had other moments where he felt a little bad about submitting his training partners and his friends. David was experiencing the mix of emotions that came with training martial arts. Before he started packing up his gear, Evan came over and asked, "Hey man, what time you wanna head out to hunt tomorrow?"

"Well first of all, where are we going?" David replied.

"My dad's friend from work has over 150 acres we can hunt on, out past 32," Evan said.

"Ok, so that's on the way to your place, right?" David asked.

"From your house, yeah," Evan explained.

"Ok. I can be at your place at seven," David said.

"Holy shit man. We don't need to be up that early to hunt rabbits," Evan laughed.

"What time were you thinking then?" David asked.

"I was thinking more like meet at my place around 8:30 or so. Emma was planning on making a big breakfast anyway; we can grab some food before we head out, so we don't get hungry while we are hunting," Evan explained.

"Hell yeah, that sounds perfect," David replied.

"Alright, I'm gonna head out. I'll see ya tomorrow," Evan said as he held out a fist. David fist bumped his friend and replied, "Sounds good brother; have a good one."

Since David didn't have to wake up as early and worry about making food before he went hunting, he decided to get most of his hunting gear ready after he got home and took a shower. He looked up what the temperature and weather conditions were going to be the next day and laid out the proper camouflage, hunter orange gear, and hunting attire that would be necessary. Then he went to his gun cabinet and got out his Remington 870. Before he put his shotgun in a case, he wanted to make sure he had the right choke for rabbit hunting.

The last time David had used this shotgun was during turkey season, and he was using a full choke. Since he was using a .12 gauge with six shot heavy loads, he decided to use his improved cylinder choke. Even though David was exhausted from sparring earlier that day, when he got home, he was having a hard time falling asleep. For whatever reason, whenever David knew he was going hunting or fishing the next day, he was always so excited he could never fall asleep when he wanted to. It was a similar experience he felt before going into battle in a hostile area, just much more mild.

When David got to Evan's house the next morning, he finally got to meet Evan's fiancé Emma. David pulled into Evan's driveway and over to the side so Evan and Emma could both get their vehicles out of the garage. David noticed the front door was open and when he walked up to their front porch, Emma saw David walking up and hollered, "Hey David, come on in!" David walked through the main hallway to the kitchen where Emma was cooking and setting a table.

"Hi, it's nice to finally meet you," David said as he shook Emma's hand.

"Yeah, likewise. Evan's told me a lot about you," Emma replied.

"Oh shit. I hope nothing bad," David said with a smile.

"Are you kidding me? He thinks the world of you," Emma

said. "He's just finishing up getting ready right now. Gotta get the hounds loaded up in the truck," she continued.

"Does he need help with anything?" David asked.

"I'm not sure. Last I checked he was outside feeding the dogs, so he's probably waiting on them to do their business before he loads them into the truck," Emma told David. "You're more than welcome to go out back and check on him if you want," she continued.

"Alright thanks," David responded. He noticed a sliding door next to the dining room that led to the backyard, so he walked outside and saw Evan standing with one dog on a leash while the other was moving around in the yard.

"Hey! Ain't no rabbits out here," David joked.

"Hey buddy, good morning," Evan replied. "Just waiting on Rocky to take a shit so we can load him up and head out," Evan said when David approached him. David started to laugh.

"So who's this guy," David asked as he knelt to start petting the beagle Evan had on a leash.

"This is Apollo. Rocky's brother," Evan replied.

"You named your dogs Rocky and Apollo? That's fucking awesome," David responded.

"Yeah, I loved the *Rocky* movies when I was younger. Apollo here is the obedient one. Rocky is a shithead. He just does whatever the fuck he wants, but I'll give him credit; he's a workhorse. There is no quit in that damn dog," Evan explained to David. As they were standing there watching Rocky walk around sniffing, David could feel his stomach rumbling.

"Why don't we just go in and eat while we are waiting for Rocky to shit?" David asked.

"Yeah that's fine. I just want to make sure he goes before we leave. Last time I took them hunting, he shit in the crate on the way there and was a fucking mess by the time we started hunting," Evan replied.

"Oh damn; that would be a shitty way to start your hunt," David said.

"Tell me about it," Evan replied as they started walking back toward the house. Evan let Apollo come into the house. Once they sat down and started eating, David asked, "I've heard guys say that letting your beagle inside could ruin their sense of smell; you're not worried about that with Apollo?"

"Eh not really. We let them come inside sometimes. They do spend most of their time outside, and we built the kennel for them, so they have shelter and whatnot, but when it's really cold or really hot, we let them chill with us in the house. Doesn't seem to have messed up their noses," Evan replied.

After they finished eating, Evan went back outside to check on Rocky. David moved his dishes to the sink and started rinsing them off to put them in the dishwasher.

"Oh don't worry about that; you guys gotta get going," Emma told David.

"Please. You cooked this big breakfast for us; the least I can do is clean up after myself. Where I come from the chef doesn't clean up after the meal," David replied.

"Ok, well, I'm fine with you cleaning up your own plate, but you better not touch anything else," Emma said.

"Fair enough," David replied with a smile. Just as he finished cleaning his plate and put the silverware he used in the dishwasher, Evan walked back inside with Rocky.

"You ready to go?" Evan asked.

"Yeah just gotta load up my gear in your truck," David replied.

Once both of them loaded up their shotguns, ammunition

and other hunting gear, they got in the truck and Evan backed out of the driveway. As they began their drive, Evan turned on some country music that played softly in the background while the two started talking. In the beginning of the conversation, Evan asked David how often he had rabbit hunted, and that sparked the conversation about how Evan's father used to breed beagles and train them for rabbit hunting. David learned that Evan's father had injured his shoulder pretty badly through his work as a landscaper and no longer was able to rabbit hunt because he had surgery on his shooting shoulder. The recoil from a shotgun or rifle was too much for his shoulder. Since Evan's father was no longer able to rabbit hunt, he decided to stop breeding and training beagles. Evan explained that Rocky and Apollo were from the last litter of pups Evan's father had his female beagle breed. David was thinking about getting a dog of his own and really wanted to get one that he could take hunting.

"Man it sucks that your dad can't hunt anymore and had to stop breeding beagles," David said as Evan was driving.

"Yeah, I'm just glad I got the picks of the litter from the last one his female had. She was a really good dog too," Evan said. "From the get go, Rocky and Apollo were the two boldest and eager pups from that litter, so I knew they would turn into great hunters," Evan continued.

"Does he know anyone else that still breeds beagles?" David asked.

"Uh, his buddy Jack Stoll might," Evan replied.

"Can you get his number for me?" David asked. "Been thinking about getting a dog or two of my own," he continued.

"Yeah sure. When we get back, just remind me and I'll give my dad a call and get it from him. I haven't seen Jack in a long time, so I'm not even sure if he's still breeding beagles or not. Just be prepared to pay because his dogs ain't cheap," Evan explained.

"I'm not worried about that. Have you ever rabbit hunted at West Spoon?" David asked Evan.

"Hell no. There's too many coyotes and bobcats out there," Evan replied.

"Hmm, sounds like they need to clear out some of those coyotes," David said.

"Yeah, there's just not enough interest in hunting coyotes around there. Even if there was, I'm not a big fan of taking my dogs hunting on public land. Never know who you're going to run into there," Evan explained.

"Got that right," David replied. "Still, we should try it sometime just to see what happens," he continued.

"Wait, you're still trying to figure out what happened to all those people that disappeared, aren't you?" Evan said.

"Hell yeah. Wouldn't you?" David asked.

"Of course I want to know. People go missing all the time though man. There isn't a whole lot we can do about it," Evan said.

"Yeah well, I don't think these disappearances are random. I think they are all connected somehow," David explained.

"What are you talking about? There's no way all those people that went missing knew each other," Evan said.

"No. That's not what I'm saying," David replied.

"What do you mean then?" Evan asked.

"I think there is one person responsible for all the disappearances at West Spoon," David suggested.

"What makes you say that?" Evan asked David who hesitated before responding to Evan because the only person that knew about the stranger that followed David and his brother all those years ago was Michael, someone that David had known since fifth grade. David had only known Evan for about a year and as David got older, he trusted police and law enforcement less and less. Evan certainly didn't give David any reason not to trust him, but that was the problem. David always felt like he had good intuition and was a good judge of character. He was aware that the most untrustworthy individuals were not always obvious at first. "Why do you think there's only one person responsible for all the missing people at West Spoon?" Evan repeated.

"Ok. I only told one other person this, and I want it to stay between us," David started to say. "Back when I was in high school, my brother and I were hunting at West Spoon one day. When it started to get dark, we packed up and headed back toward my truck. While we were walking back on a hiking trail, we noticed a light behind us, and it appeared like someone was following us. When we got closer to my truck, I told my brother to keep going while I hid in the woods in case whoever was following us went after my brother. I was ready to ambush this guy before he got to my brother. Whoever was following us eventually got within like twenty yards or less of me, and he stopped to stare at my brother sitting in my truck. I saw this guy look around scanning the area before I heard him say, "Where the fuck did the other one go?" David explained to Evan who had a shocked look on his face.

"Holy shit! This guy was after you two?" Evan asked.

"It certainly appeared that way," David replied.

"What happened after that?" Evan asked.

"Nothing really. He just kept walking along another part of the trail, and eventually I couldn't see him anymore. I just walked back to my truck quickly and we hauled ass outta there," David said.

"Damn! Sounds like you two got lucky," Evan said.

"I don't consider myself lucky because it sounds like that piece of shit is still out there," David said.

"Yeah, maybe," Evan replied.

"I do feel like I'm getting closer to finding out who it is though," David told Evan.

"What makes you say that?" Evan asked.

"I've talked to a few family members of those who have gone missing," David explained.

"You did what?" Evan was shocked.

"I talked to a couple of the parents of the teenagers that went missing," David said

"Dude, you're not a cop. You can't just go doing that shit," Evan told David.

"Says who?" David replied. "Several of the parents told me the local PD didn't do shit about it, so who's to say I can't do my own investigation?" he continued.

"I don't know man. You gotta be careful with that kind of stuff," Evan said. "I understand you want to find this guy, but I don't want you getting in trouble in the process," Evan continued.

"Don't worry, Mother. I'll be fine," David joked. Just then Evan pulled into a gravel driveway that led up to a large field surrounded by woods in each direction.

"We're here. Let's go bunny blastin'" Evan said.

The two men put on their hunting boots and put on orange vests over their camouflaged coveralls. David also had on an orange beanie, while Evan was wearing an orange field and stream baseball cap. Evan let the dogs out but kept them on their leashes so they wouldn't just run off before they started hunting. David pulled out his shotgun and started loading it.

"Remington 870, hell yeah brother. That's a good shotgun," Evan said.

"Thanks man; it's always worked for me, and I didn't have to spend a whole lot on it either," David replied.

"Yeah, I used to have one too; then I upgraded to an 1187," Evan told David.

"What's the matter? Too lazy to use a pump?" David teased Evan.

"Hey man. I need every advantage I can get. Only downside is sometimes it jams," Evan replied.

As soon as Evan took the dogs off their leashes, they took off toward the woods. There were a few brush piles along the tree line where it looked like some trees had been cut up. The first pile they approached, Evan told David to stand to the left of the pile while he stood to the right between the brush and the woods. The two dogs put their heads down and went to work. David wasn't sure which one it was, but one of the dogs was sniffing around so loud, he sounded like a pig. It didn't take long before both dogs started howling. They picked up a scent.

"Coming your way!" Evan hollered at David who raised his shotgun and saw movement inside the brush pile on the opposite side from where the dogs were zigzagging around. David saw the rabbit take off running out in front of him about twenty five to thirty yards. David put the bead of his shotgun right on the rabbit's nose. David hesitated for a brief moment to make sure the dogs were not right on the rabbit's trail. Once he realized he had a clear shot, David pulled the trigger, *boom!*

"You get him?" David heard Evan call out.

"Yeah," David responded.

"Ok, leave him there and stand by the rabbit, so the dogs can find it," Evan told David. "Go ahead and call to them so they know we got him," he continued.

"*Rocky! Apollo! Here, here, here!*" David called out to the dogs. "*Here, here, here! Rabbit! Rabbit! Rabbit!*" David continued. Almost immediately David saw Apollo come busting out of the brush pile. Apollo had his head up at first and then put his nose back to the ground. David noticed Apollo sniffing as he got closer and closer to him, and eventually Apollo saw the rabbit. When Apollo approached, David raised the rabbit up in the air so the dog could see it without biting into it and tearing up the meat. "Good boy, way to go," David told the dog as he reached down to pet him. Without anyone telling him, Apollo went back to work and busted through into the next brush pile nearby.

Meanwhile Rocky was still sniffing around in the first brush pile, and Evan explained to David that Rocky would need to find the rabbit they just shot; otherwise he would sniff around in the same spot all day. Just to speed things up, David decided to walk over to the brush pile Rocky was still nosing around in and called out to him. Eventually, Rocky did come running out and finally saw the rabbit David had just harvested.

The rest of the day went pretty much the same. Sometimes the rabbit would jump out toward David, and sometimes it would jump out toward Evan. A couple times the rabbit would take off running out in front of them where they didn't have a good shot, so they would just wait and let the dogs run them back, so they could get a better shot. While he was listening to Rocky and Apollo run a rabbit way out in front of them, David thought to himself, *Man, I need to get myself some beagles.* After both men filled their daily bag limit, they walked back to the truck. The dogs were tired, but still acted like they wanted to keep hunting.

"Damn man! You weren't kidding when you said that dog had no quit in him," David told Evan.

"Yeah look at their tails," Evan replied. David looked and noticed the tips of their tails were soaked in blood.

"Damn! Them thorns and thickets cut the hell outta them," David said.

"That's what a good hunting dog should look like. Check their ears. I bet they are all cut up too," Evan told David. Reaching down to pet Rocky and Apollo, David felt their ears and noticed they were both cut up and bloody.

"Both their ears are cut up to hell," David told Evan.

"Yeah, happens every time. I'll clean em up though," Evan said.

"You got yourself some damn good dogs man. I'm definitely going to have to get a beagle or two of my own," David said.

"If you can afford it, I'd get two. That way they will always have a companion and won't get lonely," Evan explained.

"Yeah that makes sense," David replied.

When they got back to Evan's house, Evan told David to just leave the rabbits in his truck and he would clean them.

"Come on man, I'm not going to make you clean all these rabbits by yourself," David said. "I tell you what. Since Emma made us that big breakfast this morning and you took me hunting with you today, let me take the rabbits back to my place and I'll clean them. Then I can have you and Emma over for dinner, and we can eat them. Besides, you're going to have your hands full giving those dogs a bath," David offered.

"Well that sounds good to me, but Emma won't eat rabbit," Evan reminded David.

"Oh shit I forgot. Well let's do this. I'll clean the rabbits and freeze them; then you can come over for the fights next weekend, and we can cook some of the rabbits we got today," David suggested.

"Ok that works for me," Evan replied.

"Alright I'm gonna head out, so I can get to work on these. Please tell Emma thanks again for breakfast," David said as he gave his friend a hug and headed home. When David got back in his truck, he noticed his brother had texted him. Zander was in town for the weekend and wanted to hangout. David texted him and told him to come on over.

While David was on his back deck cleaning and preparing the rabbits, Zander walked out. He brought David a beer and began to help his older brother with the rabbits. With the two of them, things went a lot easier and quicker. David put the rabbit remains in a big garbage bag and explained to Zander that he was going to dump them out in the woods behind his house to see if any coyotes would show up. He planned to pick them off hunting over the bait pile. David soaked the rabbits in a cooler filled with water and sprinkled in some salt to help get the blood out of the meat.

Zander and David chit chatted for a few hours. Zander talked about how classes were going, and David talked more about his martial arts training than anything. Part of David wanted to talk to Zander about the stranger that followed them the last time they were at West Spoon together, but he remembered how rough that was on Zander and considering how good things seemed to be going for Zander at the moment, he didn't want to bring up anything that could possibly ruin his happiness or upset him. David was always very protective of Zander; he wanted the best for his brother. When Zander decided to leave, David said, "You can crash here if you want to man."

"I appreciate it, and normally I would, but Rachel wants to get up kinda early and go shopping tomorrow," Zander replied.

"Really dude, she's already got your balls in a case above the mantel, doesn't she? David teased his brother.

"Nah, I need some new shoes anyway," Zander replied.

"I know. I'm just messing with you bro," David said.

"Yeah I know. Hey, I wanted to thank you for everything you've done for me over the years. You've been more than just a big brother to me, almost like a second father. Especially when Mom and Dad were busy at work and you would cook dinner for us and stuff. You've always looked out for me. I wish there was something I could do to make it up to you," Zander told David.

"You don't owe me anything brother. Just find what makes you happy and be the absolute best person you can be," David replied.

"I will. Love you bro," Zander responded as he leaned in to hug David.

"Love you too man," David replied. As Zander backed out of David's driveway and left, David thought about what Evan had told him earlier that day. *I am lucky that guy didn't go after my brother and I,* David thought to himself.

Chapter 13

After Samuel and Lyndsey got back to Samuel's mobile home, they went into Samuel's bedroom to have sex. As usual, Lyndsey went outside to smoke afterwards. Samuel had given up on getting her to quit smoking; all he asked was that she didn't smoke inside his home. Samuel hated how she always went outside to smoke; he just wanted to hold her and cuddle for a while before falling asleep. Samuel was hoping Lyndsey would return before he fell asleep, but she took her time smoking outside, and before he knew it, Samuel had drifted off to sleep.

Samuel dreamed about the last time he was at The Last Call bar with Lyndsey. They used to go to The Last Call more often, until Samuel got into it with a biker one night. After that Samuel avoided that bar at all costs.

Samuel had met Lyndsey one night after work, and things were going pretty good until Lyndsey went outside to smoke while Samuel finished playing pool. Samuel and Lyndsey were playing against another couple, and they only had one more ball plus the eight ball to win. It was Samuel's turn, and Lyndsey was confident he would finish the game and win, so she decided to go outside for a smoke. At first Samuel didn't notice anything because he was focused on ending the game. After he sunk the eight ball, he went over to shake hands with the couple he just beat; as he was shaking the man's hand, he glanced outside and saw Lyndsey talking with a group of bikers wearing cuts. Since they had just won, they had rights to play on that table again.

Samuel didn't want to lose their spot, but at the same time he didn't like Lyndsey outside flirting with other guys. Samuel decided to go order two more beers at the bar and then head outside to get Lyndsey. As he walked outside Samuel noticed Lyndsey was sitting on a biker's lap. Even though Samuel wanted to sucker punch the guy, he was aware he was outnumbered, and there were at least half a dozen other bikers around them at the time.

"Come on Lyndsey, we're up," Samuel said sternly.

"Oh, ok babe. Hey this is Winston," Lyndsey replied.

"What's up man," Winston nodded toward Samuel who glared back at the man Lyndsey was sitting on and then said, "Come on. Let's go" to Lyndsey.

Lyndsey got up and then said to Winston and the other bikers, "Hey why don't you guys play with us."

"Actually, we are up next on the table right beside you guys," Winston replied. "Maybe after we kick some ass, we can play you two," Winston continued.

"Ok sounds good," Lyndsey replied as she followed Samuel back inside. Samuel really did not want to play against Winston and his friends because he wanted to avoid Lyndsey spending any more time with them. If she was already comfortable enough to sit on Winston's lap after only knowing him for five minutes, who knows what else she would do with him.

Every time Samuel and Lyndsey would finish a game, it seemed like Winston and one of his biker friends would still be in the middle of their game, so instead of waiting for them, Samuel would quickly try to find another opponent and get another game started, so he didn't have to play against them. A couple times Lyndsey would follow Winston outside to smoke when he finished a game, leaving Samuel inside playing pool by himself. Samuel realized they most likely would have lost if Lyndsey stayed inside to play, but at the same time he was more worried about her flirting with Winston than he was worried about winning the pool game.

After a couple of hours had passed, Samuel noticed many of the bikers had left, and eventually they had all left except for Winston who managed to make friends with someone while outside smoking a cigarette. While they played pool, Winston continued to win as well as the night went on. Samuel was hoping Winston would eventually lose and go home, but it seemed like the more he won, the more he wanted to stay and flirt with Lyndsey. It got to the point that while Samuel and Lyndsey were playing pool, Lyndsey was more focused on flirting with Winston than playing pool. Winston seemed fully capable of flirting with Lyndsey and holding a conversation while still winning over and over again.

Samuel was starting to get annoyed and jealous of how easy Winston was winning at pool and flirting with Lyndsey. She was careful not to get too touchy when Samuel was around, but every time they went outside together, Samuel noticed how close they would get. Samuel and Lyndsey were still involved in a game. Winston had just won and asked Lyndsey if she wanted to go outside with him. Lyndsey popped up and quickly followed Winston outside while leaving Samuel behind to finish the game alone. Samuel was furious. He wanted to follow them outside, but he was aware he only needed to hit the eight ball in to win, so he decided to stay and finish the game. After their opponents missed, Samuel sunk the eight ball and stormed outside without shaking hands with the two guys he had just beat.

"We won. Let's go," Samuel told Lyndsey.

"Oh ok, we are going to play Winston and his friend now," Lyndsey replied. *God damnit,* Samuel thought to himself.

Before the game started, Winston went to the bar and ordered a beer for himself and one for Lyndsey. Samuel needed one as well, so after Winston walked back, he went and grabbed one for himself while Lyndsey broke. Lyndsey didn't hit a single ball in the entire game, making Samuel struggle to beat the other two on his own. Winston was very good, and the guy he found to play with was significantly better than a drunken Lyndsey. At this point it was a struggle for her to stand on her own much less play pool. Winston and his teammate won the first game, and Samuel immediately wanted a rematch.

In the rematch Samuel went first instead of Lyndsey, and he managed to knock a few pool balls in to keep things close. Luckily for Samuel, Lyndsey had to use the restroom, and he was able to shoot for her as well which helped Samuel beat Winston and his teammate. After Samuel won the second game, Winston said, "Best two out of three." Samuel broke this time and managed to hit two balls in off the break. Winston and his teammate struggled a little bit more in the third game, but considering Lyndsey was of no help at all, it didn't matter much. The weight of winning rested fully on Samuel's shoulders. After seeing Winston flirt with Lyndsey all night long, Samuel wanted nothing more than to beat this cocky biker and tell him to "fuck off" afterwards.

Unfortunately for Samuel, he failed to knock in the last ball he needed to sink before going after the eight ball. This gave Winston the chance to win the game. The cue ball lined up almost perfectly for Winston, and he only needed to sink the eight ball to win. As he leaned over to take the final shot, he looked at Samuel and said, "After I sink this shot, how 'bout I sink one in your girl later tonight too."

"How about I rip off your head and shit down your throat, motherfucker," Samuel said as he ran up on Winston. The much larger guy Winston was playing pool with was standing between them, and he was able to hold Samuel back.

"Whoa, whoa! Everyone just calm down and relax. Just some friendly trash talk," he told Samuel. Samuel pushed him away and said, "No fuck that he's been flirting with my girl all fucking night. I'm going to end him." By this point a bouncer had walked in to see what was going on, and Samuel noticed most of the bar had cleared out as they were getting ready to close.

"You think you can take me little bitch boy?" Winston sarcastically asked Samuel.

"Guys, guys. Let's not do this here. You'll both get kicked out and arrested," Winston's teammate interrupted. Lyndsey was sitting in a chair watching everything happen with a smirk on her face. She didn't say a word.

"Hey it's closing time. Take that shit somewhere else!" the bouncer yelled at both men.

"You just tell me when and where you fucking pussy,"

Samuel told Winston who smiled right before he sank the eight ball, and then he walked up to Samuel and got right in his face.

"Where you wanna do this, bitch?" Winston asked. Samuel was ready to kill and knew exactly where he wanted to lure this guy in at.

"Vacant parking lot near West Spoon off State Route 56. No weapons. Don't bring any of your butt buddies either," Samuel replied.

"I'll see you soon punk bitch," Winston said right before he chugged his beer and walked back to the bar to close his tab. Samuel had to help Lyndsey walk out so he could close his tab and leave. After they left the bar, Samuel drove Lyndsey home. She fell asleep in the truck on the way back to Samuel's mobile home, and all he could think about was how badly he wanted to beat the shit out of this Winston guy who was hitting on her all night.

After Samuel helped Lyndsey to bed, he went and grabbed his gun from his night stand and put it in his jeans behind his back. Samuel already had a pocket knife on him as well, but he grabbed his larger hunting knife and put it in his spare pocket just in case. The vacant lot Samuel told Winston to meet him at was only about a five-minute drive from his place, and even after all the alcohol he had consumed throughout the night, he managed to get there quicker than normal because he sped out of rage on his way.

When Samuel rolled into the parking lot, he noticed a man sitting up against a motorcycle by himself away from the only lamp post and in the dark. Samuel parked across from the motorcycle, but gave himself enough space to not get ambushed as he opened the door. As Samuel got out of his truck, Winston stood up and walked over to face Samuel. The two were about fifteen feet away from each other. Samuel left his lights on and through what little light was visible, he noticed Winston was holding a large knife in his left hand.

"Thought we agreed no weapons," Samuel said. Winston smirked at Samuel and then replied, "After I shove this knife up your ass and gut you, I'm going to shove my dick up your bitch. Too bad you won't be around to watch."

"Yeah well you know what they say about knives and gun-fights," Samuel responded as he pulled the gun out from behind his back.

"Oh shit!" Winston started to say just before Samuel sent three shots right into Winston's chest. The force and impact from the shots knocked Winston to his knees as he clutched at his chest. While Winston was on all fours, Samuel ran up and kicked Winston in his side as hard as he could. Winston immediately rolled over in pain, gasping for air. Two of the bullets hit Winston's lungs, and they quickly filled with blood, preventing Winston from breathing properly. He was able to inhale slightly, but when he exhaled, a pool of blood shot out from his mouth.

"What, you ain't got shit to say now, do you motherfuck-er?" Samuel taunted Winston as he laid on the ground dying. Samuel walked a full circle around Winston enjoying the pain and agony he saw. Samuel wanted to make Winston suffer and prolong his death, but at the same time he wanted to get out of their quickly, so he could dispose of the body without getting caught. As Samuel was standing over Winston, he looked down at him writhing in pain on the ground and said, "I'll see you in hell you fucking piece of shit" right before he fired one last shot into Winston's head killing him instantly.

Samuel kicked the knife away from Winston's body and leaned over him. Samuel took the cut off of Winston and threw it in the back seat of his truck. As Samuel was standing by his truck, he noticed lights from a car that was driving down the road next to where he pulled into the parking lot. At first Samuel panicked and thought it might have been a cop or someone else who heard the gunshots, but the car kept driving past and didn't slow down at all. Samuel was worried he wouldn't have as much time, so he quickly loaded the body into the back seat of his truck and placed a blanket over the top in case he was pulled over as he was leaving. Samuel was tired and didn't want to hike too far into the woods to dispose of the body. He also didn't want to have to bury or drown the body, so he drove to the northeast corner of the state park; then he dragged Winston's body into a trail that had very thick cover. Samuel knew this would be a difficult spot to dispose of the body but would also be hard to find. Instead of burying the body or burning it, Samuel decided to strip Winston's clothes off of him and leave his body laying naked in the woods.

Before he left, Samuel slit Winston's throat and wrists causing him to bleed out quicker. Samuel hoped that the blood would attract coyotes or some other predators to come and feed on Winston's dead body. On his way back home, Samuel swung by The Last Call and saw the parking lot was empty. It had been at least an hour since close, and Samuel figured the coast was clear. Samuel decided to hang Winston's blood-soaked cut with three bullet holes on a tree behind the bar. Just before he drove off, he looked around to make sure no one saw him or noticed his truck.

Samuel drove home quickly running right through every red light he hit. When he got back to the mobile home, he walked around back to where his fire pit was and loaded it up with a couple of logs and a firestarter log. As the fire started growing, Samuel walked inside to check on Lyndsey. She was still passed out drunk in his bed; she hadn't moved from the position she was laying in before he left. Samuel walked over and kissed her on the forehead before he walked into the kitchen to grab a beer and Lyndsey's pack of cigarettes. Then Samuel walked over to his truck to grab the rest of Winston's clothes. Samuel walked around back to the fire pit, grabbed a chair and sat down.

One by one Samuel threw an article of clothing that belonged to Winston into the fire and watched it burn to ashes as he sat there drinking his beer and enjoying cigarette after cigarette. Once all the clothes were thrown into the fire and burned away, Samuel sat there and finished his beer. By the time he was done, he noticed the sun was starting to come up. *Guess it's time to get some sleep,* Samuel thought to himself as he put out his cigarette and took the last gulp of his beer. Before he got up to go back in however, Lyndsey walked out and said, "Hey baby, where you been?"

"Oh, I just had to take care of some things," Samuel replied.

"Well hell if you're going to sit out here and smoke, I'm going to join you," Lyndsey said as she walked over.

"No you're not. You're going to take your fine ass back inside right now," Samuel replied as he stood up and walked over picking Lyndsey up and carrying her back inside the mobile home as she began to laugh.

Chapter 14

After spending almost every weekend in the woods at West Spoon during the hunting season, David wasn't finding any more clues as to who was responsible for the people who went missing. Often at night he would swing by The Last Call for a beer or two hoping to come across Marcus or another member of the Venomous Riders. David was hoping he could get more information about the guy that Winston Morrow got into it with the night before he went missing.

Sometimes David would go into the room of pool tables just to watch and see if anyone was acting suspicious. He was particularly interested in looking for anyone who smoked Marlboro Reds since that was the cigarette found near the bodies of the father and son who were murdered and then dragged into West Spoon. One night after hunting, David was sitting at the bar when Betty noticed him and walked over to say hello, "Hey sweetie, haven't seen you in a while; how've you been?"

"I've been good. Just busy with work and stuff. How about you?" David replied.

"Well they got me working more during the week because I've been helping my sister with her kids on the weekends. I'm glad you came in tonight and I got to see you," Betty said with a smile as she walked to the end of the bar to help other patrons. David finished his beer and waited for Betty to come back to get him another; he also wanted to ask her a couple questions.

"Hey have you seen any of the bikers from the MC lately?" David asked Betty.

"You talking about the Venomous Riders?" Betty responded.

"Yeah," David said.

"No we don't see them as much during the winter months. Too cold to ride for a lot of them. I know some of them take a trip down south when it gets colder, but we don't see them around here much until it gets warmer," Betty explained. As David sat there thinking about what Betty had just told him, he wondered why the man who got into it with Winston Morrow would avoid the bar when the MC wasn't around. *Does this guy just go looking for trouble?* David thought to himself. David decided to go outside for a little bit while he finished his beer. When he sat down on the patio, he looked around and saw several patrons outside smoking. Without obviously staring at them, David was looking closely at what brand of cigarette each person was smoking. He didn't see anyone smoking Marlboro Reds, and he was beginning to get frustrated. After he finished his beer, he decided to do another walk-through in the pool room. David sat down at a table near the first pool table. After a man and his friend just finished playing, he looked over at David and asked, "You trying to play next?"

"Oh no, I'm just watching," David replied. He scanned the room one more time and tried to listen in on some of the conversations, wondering if he would recognize anyone's voice. Nothing stood out to him, so he decided to close his tab and go home.

The following weekend when David had more free time, he decided to search for the widow of the man who was killed along with his son before their bodies were dragged into West Spoon State Park. David remembered from the article he read online that the two had been hunting on their own property that backed up onto the boundary of the state park. David was very interested in scanning the surrounding area where their bodies were found, but he obviously wanted to talk to the widow first and make sure it was ok. David went back to re-read the article he had found a while back, so he could find the names of the victims. "Thomas and Joey Howe," David said aloud to himself as he wrote the names on a piece of paper. David typed, "Thomas Howe" into the search bar on his Facebook profile, but nothing popped up. David tried "Joey Howe" instead and saw several profiles appear. The profile picture that appeared at the top of the list looked familiar, so David clicked on it. He had found Joey's Facebook profile.

David didn't waste time scrolling through Joey's page; he went directly to his friends' list and typed in "Howe." Three "Howes" appeared in his friend's list. All three of them were women, and David wasn't sure which one might be his mother. One of them looked significantly younger and had to be either his sister or cousin. The other two almost looked like twins. David clicked on the profile that read "Tonya Howe," and immediately he realized he had found the widow. Her profile picture was of herself, but her cover photo was of the entire family. David saw Tonya in a family portrait with her husband, son and daughter in one of the articles he read. After scrolling through Tonya's profile, he discovered that the Howes daughter was named Taylor. David searched for an address for Tonya Howe and quickly found a location that was right next to West Spoon State Park. *This must be it,* David thought to himself.

David drove to the address he found online and as he got closer, he noticed that from the road he was on, a gravel driveway by the mailbox led back into the woods. He looked around before pulling into the gravel driveway, and he didn't see other mailboxes or homes nearby. David noticed the Howe's house was pretty secluded. Once he passed through a row of tall trees, things opened up a little bit, and there was a large yard with a pond in front of the house. As he got closer to the house, the gravel driveway turned into a paved cement driveway with a three car garage and a basketball hoop in the back. Damn, this is a pretty nice setup David thought to himself just before he parked his truck. When he was walking to the front door, he heard barking and could see two dogs eyeing him in the window. David rang the doorbell and Tonya was quickly at the door.

"Taylor get the dogs please," David could hear her say before she opened the front door. "Hello, may I help you?" Tonya asked as she looked up at David.

"Yeah my name is David Celanese, and I'm investigating your husband and son's murders. I was wondering if I could speak with you," David said.

"Oh yeah sure, come on in," Tonya replied. "Don't mind the dogs; they are friendly once they realize you're not a threat," she continued.

"Oh they are fine. I love dogs," David replied. "German Shepherds are great companions," he continued.

"Yeah, we got them a while back and at first I wasn't really thrilled about the idea of getting two dogs, but after what happened to my husband and son, I'm glad we have them now," Tonya said as she sat down at the kitchen table. David sat across from her after Tonya told him to have a seat. "Taylor let them out back please," Tonya told her daughter. After Taylor let the dogs out, she walked back into the kitchen.

"Can I get you anything to drink?" Taylor asked David.

"Yes please. Water is fine," David replied.

"Taylor please pour me a glass of wine. I'm going to need it for this conversation," Tonya said. David wasn't sure if he should laugh or not, so he simply smiled instead.

"How can we help you?" Tonya asked David.

"Well can you start from the top and just tell me everything you remember that happened that day?" David asked.

"We already told the Sheriff everything we know; don't you guys share information and talk to each other?" Tonya asked.

"Yes, I'm just trying to check and make sure everything adds up. Plus sometimes things are accidentally left out right after the initial incident because of the shock and grief. Sometimes important details are remembered later," David said.

"Ok well, Tom and Joey had gone out early in the morning to hunt during the bow season. Usually they get out before the sun comes up, but it had been raining a little bit, and they wanted to wait until the rain stopped before they headed out. We have several stands set up throughout our property, but they decided to hunt out of the two stands all the way to the back that are right up against our property line and the boundary for the state park. Joey had set up some trail cams around that area and kept talking about this monster buck he had caught on the trail cam," Tonya explained.

"Makes sense," David said.

"Yeah, I was cleaning the house, and Taylor was over at a friend's house. No less than about fifteen minutes after they left the house, I heard several gunshots. At first I wasn't concerned because we shoot back here all the time, and I knew they were hunting, but then it hit me, and I remembered that they were bow hunting and didn't even have their rifles or anything with them. The shots came one after the other so quickly as well, so I knew something was wrong," Tonya said.

"Do you remember how many shots you heard?" David asked.

"At the time, no, I didn't remember, but when I found Tom and Joey, I saw four bullet wounds," Tonya replied.

"Oh so you found the bodies first?" David asked.

"Yeah, well the dogs did," Tonya explained.

"Jesus Christ, I'm sorry you had to find them like that," David replied. Tonya hesitated for a moment, took a big sip of her wine and then replied, "Yeah."

"So how exactly did you find them, because they weren't on your property according to the police report?" David asked Tonya.

"I called the cops immediately because I knew something wasn't right, and they told me to sit tight and they would send someone over to check things out. I couldn't just sit there and wait, so I grabbed the AR and went outside with the dogs to find out what happened. We have a fenced in backyard as you can see, so when I let the dogs out, they ran straight to the end of the fence and were barking like crazy. I ran to the gate and opened it, so I could go back to the end of our property where Tom and Joey said they were going to hunt that morning. The dogs beat me to the tree stand obviously, and they started sniffing around immediately. I was calling out for Tom and got no response. That's when I really started to g-g-get worried." Tonya started to get choked up.

"It's ok; take your time," David said as he reached over to put his hand on Tonya's. She took a deep breath. She wiped her eyes and then continued. "I started calling out for Joey as well, but neither of them responded, and the dogs were zigzagging all over the place sniffing. They crossed our property line and went into the park, but I didn't want them going over there without a leash on, so I started calling for them to come back. Obviously they didn't listen to me, so I started to follow them. Before too long I found both dogs standing over my husband and son's bodies," Tonya said. She broke down and put her face in her hands and began sobbing. David hated putting her through this and talking about the death of her husband and son. He gave her a moment and then he stood up and walked over to sit in the chair beside her. As Tonya sat there crying, David reached out and put his hand on her shoulder.

"I'm so sorry," David whispered. He noticed a box of tissues on a nightstand by a couch and walked over so he could hand it to Tonya. When David handed her the box of tissues, she looked up at him and said quietly, "Thank you." Once Tonya had regained her composure, David let her continue.

"I fell to my knees as soon as I recognized them," Tonya said. "I sat there crying hysterically for what felt an eternity. Then the cops showed up, and I could hear them hollering out for me, so I walked back to our fenced in yard to tell them what had happened. They roped off the area pretty quick and brought in a forensics team to look for any clues or DNA I guess," she continued.

"So they are sure the bodies were dragged into West Spoon, correct?" David asked.

"Yeah, the forensics team said it was pretty obvious they were dragged through the woods into West Spoon. They said whoever killed them likely tried to hide the bodies, but when they heard the dogs barking, they just left them and bailed."

"Ok, did the forensics team find anything that might help discover the identity of the killer? Was anything left behind? Did they find any prints or anything?" David asked.

"So they told us that they found tracks along a trail that was near the state park boundary and our property line, but the tracks disappeared because whoever it was ran into the creek and the tracks stopped there," Tonya explained. *This guy knows what he's doing,* David thought to himself.

"Were they boot tracks?" David asked Tonya.

She nodded and said, "Yeah hunting boots."

"Ok, did they find out what size boots?" David asked.

"I'm not sure. Might be in the report," Tonya replied.

"Wait, you said your son had trail cams set up nearby. Did they pick up anything?" David asked.

"Actually, when we went to check them, the SD card was missing. I don't know if Joey was about to replace it or if it was stolen. I have no clue how that guy would have found those trail cams though. Joey was usually pretty good at putting them in tough spots to find," Tonya explained. "He had three total set up around our property; the only one that was near where they were killed didn't have an SD card," she continued.

"What about the other two?" David asked.

"There was a trail cam by the pond. The SD card was full. Then the other one he had set up that was farther away from where they were killed didn't pick anything up, but the SD card was still there and had plenty of space for more photos," Tonya said.

"Damn, kinda sounds like the bastard knew where the trail cam was and removed the SD card," David said.

"Yeah, but if that's the case, he would of had to do that before he killed them. There's no way he would of had time to grab that afterwards with me and the dogs coming," Tonya replied. "I gotta admit, you've been more curious and thoughtful about all this than any of the cops or detectives we initially spoke to," Tonya continued.

"Yeah, the families of those teenagers that went missing told me the same thing," David replied.

"Oh, so you are investigating that as well?" Tonya asked.

"Yeah, I'm kinda on several cases related to West Spoon right now," David said. "The parents of two of the boys that went missing from that group of four believe that their friend Curtis killed the three boys, and then ran away," David said. "But to be honest with you, I'm starting to wonder if there's one individual who is responsible for all these murders and disappearances," he continued.

"Oh my god! Are you serious?" Tonya replied.

"Yeah, it's very weird to me that all of the victims didn't seem to have any connection to each other. Besides your husband and son, the rest have all gone missing," David explained.

"How many have gone missing?" Tonya asked.

"So far there's been eight people who've gone missing and then your husband and son who were found murdered," David replied.

"Holy shit! No wonder why property value around here is plummeting," Tonya said. "I've been trying to sell this house ever since Tom and Joey were murdered, but the value is so low for how much we put into it. I'd be taking a huge loss at this point if we sold and moved," Tonya continued.

"Yeah, it's not good," David said.

"So you don't think one of those boys killed his friends and then ran away? You think the same guy who killed Tom and Joey killed them?" Tonya asked David.

"I do. I have a hard time believing that a sixteen or seventeen-year-old kid can just run away in this day and age. It's not like kids these days know how to hotwire cars and find jobs without being found in the system. His only real chance if he did that would be to go south of the border maybe. I think he would have gotten caught before he could make it there, to be honest. Technology is just too advanced, and eventually he'd be found. He had a pretty long rap sheet too, so we know he's in the system," David explained to Tonya.

"Good lord, I can't wait to sell this place and move the hell away from here," Tonya replied.

"That's understandable. How is your daughter handling all this?" David asked Tonya.

"She won't talk about it. She's terrified that the guy may come back and attack us. She used to be very outgoing and friendly, always spending the night at a friend's house or out doing something. Now she only leaves the house to go to school or if we both leave together. She constantly checks to make sure all the doors and windows are locked. She even sleeps with a loaded shotgun under her bed," Tonya told David.

"Damn. Keeping a loaded gun like that under her bed can be dangerous, but I understand her concern. Do you trust her ability to handle it if need be?" David asked.

"Yeah, we taught both our children how to handle guns and firearms at an early age. She probably would have been out there hunting with them if she wasn't already at a friends house," Tonya explained. "What about the other people that went missing? They didn't find them or find any clues?" Tony asked.

"No, not really. The only other clues that were found were a cell phone from one of the teenage boys that went missing and the motorcycle that belonged to the biker that went missing. There was no DNA or other evidence found on or around those items either," David responded.

"I just can't imagine one person going around killing innocent people in that state park. They didn't even find the bodies. Did they? My god those poor parents," Tonya cried. "They need to find this piece of shit and fucking kill him," she said. David didn't say a word; he simply nodded to agree with her.

As David and Tonya sat at the kitchen table in silence, Taylor walked in quietly and asked, "Hey Mom, what did you want to do for dinner? I'm getting hungry."

"Oh I'm sorry sweetheart. I lost track of time," Tonya replied.

"Yeah I apologize. I'll head out so you two can eat dinner. I appreciate you taking the time to speak with me," David said.

"Oh you don't have to leave. Did you want to stay for dinner?" Tonya asked David.

"Oh no I couldn't do that. I'll make a deal with you though; once I find the one responsible for your husband and son's murders, I'll come over and cook for both of you," David replied.

"Ok, I'm going to hold you to that," Tonya said with a smile as she wiped away tears.

"Alright, have a good evening," David said, and he started to walk down the hallway to let himself out.

"David wait," Tonya said as she followed him to the door. When she got closer, she reached in and gave David a hug. "Good luck finding the fucker; please be careful," Tonya told David.

"I will. If you notice anything, please don't hesitate to let me know," David replied. He gave Tonya a piece of paper with his phone number on it and walked out of the house and headed toward his truck. As he opened the door, he felt a drop of rain hit his arm. He looked up and saw dark clouds hovering above him.

When David got back to his house, he looked at his phone and saw that Michael had texted him several times wanting to meet up for drinks later. David replied and suggested going to The Last Resort. David texted Michael and told him to come on over. Meanwhile David took a shower and changed clothes. Before Michael came over, David started cooking his dinner. He decided to make a little extra in case Michael wanted some. As he was grilling chicken, he heard a knock on the front door. He walked over and saw Michael standing in the doorway, "Come on in," David said.

"Damn dude, you're a hard man to get ahold of," Michael said as he walked in and headed toward the kitchen.

"Ah, I've just been really busy lately," David replied.

"I thought you told me you were done with classes?" Michael asked.

"I am; just been working a lot and going to the gym," David explained.

"So when's your graduation? When do you get your degree?" Michael asked.

"I don't know; I told them to just mail it to me. I have no desire to get all dressed up for that stupid shit," David said. Michael laughed at David's response.

"Why am I not surprised?" Michael said.

"Hey, I got better things to do than waste time sitting for hours," David said. Michael walked over to David's fridge and helped himself to a beer while grabbing one for David as well and handing it to him before he sat back down.

"So where we going tonight?" Michael asked.

"I kinda want to go to The Last Call," David replied.

"Ah come on man. That place is a shithole. Why do you always want to go there?" Michael asked David.

"First of all, it's close. Secondly the drinks are cheaper than most places. Third, it doesn't get as crowded as other bars, and most importantly, the bartender knows me, so she tends to get my drinks quickly," David explained.

"You tapping that?" Michael smirked.

"No, I think she wants to though," David said.

"What makes you say that?" Michael asked.

"Well she gave me her number the first time I went there," David replied.

"Hell, yeah. Why haven't you banged her yet?" Michael asked.

"I don't know; I like a challenge I guess. Kinda felt like she was making it a little easy," David said. He turned around to hand his friend a plate of food.

"Oh damn! This look delicious," Michael said. "I was just planning on grabbing something at the bar. Thanks," he continued.

"No problem man, this is healthier than bar food anyway," David replied.

As they were eating, Michael was texting Avery trying to get her to meet them at The Last Call and bring some of her friends. In particular Michael wanted David to meet Avery's friend Molly. "Dude this chick Molly that Avery works with is a smoke show," Michael told David.

"Well, tell Avery to invite her then," David replied.

"I'm working on it brother. They both gotta close tonight; then maybe they can meet us," Michael said. "You want me to order an Uber?" Michael asked when they finished their meals.

"Nah, I gotta get up early, so I'm only going to have maybe two or three beers tonight. I can drive. If I decide to drink more, we can Uber back and I'll just pick up my truck in the morning," David replied. He wanted to bring his truck in case he came across the man he was looking for. He would need his truck so he could follow him.

David and Michael got to the bar earlier than normal and things were pretty slow. Betty was working behind the bar, so David went over to order a round and introduce Michael to her. After they got their beers, Michael wanted to go outside to smoke before Avery got there. "She wants me to cut back, so I figured I'll smoke a few before she gets here, so it doesn't look as bad," Michael explained.

"I can see why you didn't call her now," Michael said referring to why David didn't call Betty after she gave him her number.

"Yeah, she's really nice. Just not really my type," David said.

"Definitely; she looks like she would be a lot better looking if she didn't drink and smoke as much," Michael responded. "I think you'll be impressed with Molly though," he continued.

While they were waiting for the girls to show up, David and Michael decided to play a few games of Golden Tee. Every time it was Michael's turn, David would look around the bar. He wasn't exactly sure what to look for since he never got a good look at the guy who stalked him years ago, but he had a feeling he could notice specific behaviors that might tip him off. Once the girls showed up, the group of four decided to move to the pool area and play a few games. Michael and Avery played against David and Molly at first, and the matchup was relatively even.

When David first saw Molly, he was impressed; she was very pretty, and throughout the night the two talked often. Molly was very friendly, and David tried to return the favor, but his mind was distracted at times. After covering the typical bases when two people first meet, David was starting to run out of topics to discuss, and Michael began to take over the conversation within the group of four.

"You want another beer?" Michael asked David as he went up to the bar to get the group another round. Michael loved to show off how much money he made whenever he was around friends by continuing to buy round after round. Usually David tried to buy a few rounds to share the responsibility, but since he knew he wasn't going to be drinking much, he let Michael do his thing.

"Nah man I'm good; can you get me a water though?" David replied.

While Michael was up at the bar getting more drinks, the girls went to the restroom, so David decided to rack the pool balls to get ready for the next game. As he sat down to wait for his friends, he noticed an intoxicated woman come into the pool room with a man who seemed quiet and standoffish. The man put a quarter on the table next to the one David and his friends were playing on so they could play the winner at that table. David noticed the woman the man was with was going around hugging random guys and talking to just about everyone she saw.

David looked over at the man she was with. He was sitting in a chair against the wall parallel to David who noticed he was wearing a long-sleeved shirt and dirty jeans that had dirt, grease and oil all over them. David looked at the man's boots and saw how worn and rugged they were. David was used to seeing people wear boots in this bar, but none were quite as beat up as this guy's boots. *Clearly he works somewhere that dealt with vehicles,* David thought. As he was observing the odd man who just walked in, the girl he was with came over to David and asked, "Hey are you waiting for an opponent?" startling David slightly.

"Yeah, my friends are in the restroom right now."

"Ah gotcha, what's your name baby," the woman asked with a smile.

"David," he replied with his hand extended.

As the woman shook his hand, she said, "Nice to meet you cutie. I'm Lyndsey."

"Nice to meet you Lyndsey," David said.

"Do you come here often?" Lyndsey asked.

"Nah, not really," David replied. He glanced over at the man Lyndsey came in with, and he was giving David a dirty look. David was trying to be polite, while not engaging with Lyndsey too much and potentially causing a problem.

"I don't think I've ever seen you here before. Where you from?" Lyndsey asked David.

"Newtown," David replied as Michael walked back in the room. "Lyndsey, this is my friend Michael," David continued as Michael walked over to them. After he sat the beers down on a table nearby and handed David his ice water, Michael introduced himself to Lyndsey. While Michael and Lyndsey were talking, David looked over at the man she came with. At this point he stood and was staring directly at them. *This dude looks fucking pissed,* David thought to himself. Just as the man started walking toward them, Avery and Molly walked into the room right in front of him and cut him off. David immediately started talking to Molly hoping to calm the guy down. Michael introduced Avery and Molly to Lyndsey, and the girls immediately started chatting. Once the women were talking, the man sat back down, but he kept his eyes glued on Lyndsey.

Since Michael and Avery had just won the last game, and Avery was talking to the other two women, Michael broke to start the next game. David started off really well and managed to sink a couple shots while the women were busy chatting away. Once it was Avery's turn, David noticed Lyndsey walk outside, and the man she was with followed her. *This guy was watching Lyndsey like a hawk,* David thought. The game lasted longer than expected because the women kept talking between turns. While David was waiting for his turn, he would often glance outside to see what Lyndsey and the guy were doing. David noticed the man sat down at a table by himself while Lyndsey went around talking to other people.

Sometimes she would walk over and sit in his lap and they would talk; then she would see someone she knew and run over to greet them. While Lyndsey was talking to a group of women, the man walked back inside and headed over to the pool table where he placed a quarter earlier. David looked over at the men currently using the table and realized the game was almost over.

The man Lyndsey was with quickly turned around and walked outside to get her. Lyndsey was busy talking, so he grabbed her by the arm and started to lead her back inside. Lyndsey didn't resist; instead she moved her hand down to hold his and they walked back into the pool room together. "Alright Sammy, looks like we're up!" Lyndsey said aloud.

"Ok, we are going to switch up teams," Michael told David after they had just finished their last game.

"What? Why?" David replied.

"Because Avery and I are kicking your ass," Michael joked.

"It's not a big deal man; I'm just here to have fun," David replied.

"Oh I know, you and I are pretty even, but Avery is a lot better than Molly," Michael explained. "Besides, I figured I could talk you up a little bit while Molly's my teammate," Michael continued.

"Ah you don't have to do that man. I can talk to her myself," David said.

"You sure about that?" Michael asked. "Because you keep looking at that Lyndsey chick and the guy she's with. You've barely even talked to Molly," Michael continued.

"My bad. They just looked familiar, and I was trying to figure out where I might know them from," David explained. Deep down, David knew there was something off with the guy Lyndsey was with and he was very suspicious of him.

From that point on David remained focused on playing pool and the conversation with Michael, Molly and Avery. Throughout the night a couple of songs came on that Avery and Molly would dance to, and David liked that Molly had good taste in music that was similar to his. David and Avery did manage to win the next two games, so Avery suggested they change teams once more. This time she suggested the girls play the guys. Earlier in the night that matchup wouldn't have seemed fair considering David and Michael were clearly the two best at pool within the group of four, but after Michael started slamming beer after beer, he started to struggle.

It became clear that David was the most consistent and

would most likely end up carrying Michael when they became teammates. Molly started to get the hang of it and was improving significantly the more they played pool. Once the next game started, David noticed Lyndsey and the guy she was with had won several games in a row because they were still on the same table. Lyndsey wasn't always in the room while they were playing, so David assumed the guy she was with was doing most of the work.

After David and Michael won the first game between the girls vs the guys, Avery and Molly went to grab a round of beers and use the restroom again. Michael decided to use that time to go outside for a smoke.

"Hey man, I'm going to try to go outside and smoke before the girls get back," Michael told David.

"Alright," David replied as he was re-racking for the next game. David sat back down and started to watch the man Lyndsey was with. David quickly realized he was extremely good at pool. The guy rarely missed, and even if he did, Lyndsey was usually busy talking to other patrons at the bar, so he would shoot for her and ended up sinking the ball he was going for anyway. As David was watching the guy play pool, Avery and Molly walked back in.

"Where did Michael go?" Avery asked David. David didn't want to lie, but he didn't want to out his friend for smoking either.

"I think he went outside," David replied. "I'll go ahead and break, so we can start though." He continued hoping it would change the subject. *Avery probably knows what Michael is doing out there anyway*, David thought to himself. On the break David managed to knock in the three ball.

"Looks like we are solids," he told Avery and Molly. David

missed his next shot, and it was the girls' turn. Avery let Molly go first while she went outside to find Michael. Molly made her first shot, but missed her second. The timing worked out perfectly though because right after she missed, Michael and Avery walked back in.

"You're up," David told Michael. As Michael began to line up his shot, David heard a pool ball bounce off the table next to them and he saw the cue ball roll under his feet. David reached down to pick up the cue ball. When he turned around, the man Lyndsey was with was standing over him.

"Oh here you go," David said.

"Thanks," the man replied. "You see the other one roll over here too?" he asked.

"No I didn't know there was another one that rolled over here. I only saw the cue ball," David replied. "I'll help you look for it though," David continued. He started looking underneath the table and then moved closer to the corner of the room to search for the ball. As David was looking under the table in the corner, the other man started looking underneath the pool table David and his friends were using. The two men were not far from each other.

David had his back turned to the guy when David heard him say, "Where the fuck did the other one go?" Immediately David felt a chill go up his spine, and he had goosebumps. David recognized the man's voice. David jumped to his feet and turned around wide eyed and in shock. After all this time searching for the man who had stalked him and his brother the day they went hunting years ago, he had finally found the stalker. David was certain this was him. He was also convinced at this point there was only one person responsible for all the people that went missing at West Spoon. As the man was looking around underneath the pool table, David stood over him and looked down at the back of the man's head. David thought about how easy it would be to attack him from this position. *I could drop an elbow on the back of his head and knock him unconscious instantly, or I could jump on his back and choke him out,* David thought to himself.

"Ah here it is," the man said as he stood up. When he turned around, David was staring at him. David didn't make a move toward the man, but his hands were shaking. The man froze for a split second because of the intense look David was giving him. "Thanks for your help," the man said before he walked back to the pool table to finish his game. David tried not to be too obvious about it, but at this point he was more focused on the guy Lyndsey came with than playing pool or speaking to his friends.

The stalker finished his game quickly and walked over to whisper something to Lyndsey. David could tell the guy was trying to leave. Lyndsey was very drunk so she didn't object, but the guy she was with did have to her walk outside into the parking lot. David decided to go to the bar to see where they parked and what the guy was driving. As he ordered a water from Betty, David saw Lyndsey and the man she was with get into an old gray Ford Ranger pickup truck. Before Betty could even bring David the water he ordered, David decided to go out to his truck. While he was in his truck, he decided to text Michael real quick, so he didn't worry or think David had ditched him and the girls. "Hey man I'll be right back. I had to take care of something real quick."

David saw the direction the stalker drove toward and slowly started to follow him after sending the text to Michael. Since it was late at night and there were few vehicles on the road, it was easy for David to find the stalker's truck. David was also aware that it would be easier for the stalker to notice he was being followed, so David tried to keep as much distance as possible. The only time the vehicles got close was when they came to a red light, and David was right behind the truck the stalker was driving. When the light turned green, the stalker sped off quickly, and David took his time catching up so he could see where they were going.

Before long David saw the stalker turn left and head into a trailer park. The area was dark, and there were few street lights nearby, so David was hesitant to follow because he knew his headlights would give him away. David remembered seeing a gas station on the road before they pulled into the trailer park. Instead of pulling in there, he waited a few minutes to see if the stalker was going to stay in the trailer park. David decided to go back and park his truck at the gas station, so he could head into the trailer park on foot. David grabbed his pistol and headed toward the trailer park.

He searched for the gray Ford Ranger as he walked through the trailer park. Most of the lights inside the mobile homes were turned off, but a few were still on. David figured it would be pretty obvious which trailer the stalker went to because none of the mobile homes had much of a driveway. The trailer park wasn't very big, but David still did not see the truck he was looking for. The main road of the trailer park was "T" shaped, so after David walked down the main stretch, he headed back to search the other section for the stalker's truck. David was walking down the road and didn't see what he was looking for. Once he got to the very end of the road, he noticed a small, short driveway that went off the main road into the far back corner of the trailer park.

There it was; David found the truck he was looking for. There was a big tree in front of the yard by the mobile home, so David decided to go hide behind it and wait. He wanted to make sure the stalker lived here before leaving. David noticed the lights inside were on as he was waiting, and he heard loud music coming from the mobile home the gray truck was parked by. As he was hiding behind the tree waiting, Michael started calling David's phone. David quickly hung up so the phone wouldn't make too much noise. Before Michael could call back, David turned his phone on silent so no one could hear it.

David looked up from his phone after he turned it off and saw Lyndsey walk outside to smoke on the front porch. *This has to be it,* David thought to himself. Just then the stalker opened the front door and asked Lyndsey, "You want me to get a fire started?"

"Yeah sure," David heard Lyndsey reply. *Bingo,* David thought to himself. *Oh I got you now motherfucker,* he whispered to himself. David waited for Lyndsey and the guy she was with to walk around to the back of the mobile home before he headed back to his truck.

Once he got out of the trailer park, he checked his phone and noticed Michael had now texted and called him about half a dozen times, "Dude! Where the fuck did you go?" Michael had texted David.

"I'm on my way back. I'll explain when I get there," David replied. When David got back to his truck, he wanted to call Evan and let him know what he had just discovered. As the phone rang, David realized how late it was and assumed Evan was already asleep. "Damnit," David muttered. He was so eager to go after this guy.

When David got back to The Last Call, Michael was pissed. "Bro you can't just up and leave us all like that! Where the fuck did you go?" Michael asked David.

"Sorry. I had to find something," David replied.

"What the hell are you looking for?" Michael asked.

"Remember that guy I told you about that was following Zander and me all those years ago at West Spoon?" David asked Michael.

"Yeah, so what?" Michael said.

"Well I think that guy playing pool next to us earlier was him. Actually I know it was," David explained.

"The guy that left with Lyndsey? How the hell could you know that?" Michael asked.

David nodded and then said, "I heard him say something, and I immediately recognized his voice."

"So what? You just ditched us to go follow him?" Michael asked.

"Yeah, I wanted to see where he lived so I can help the authorities find him," David explained.

"Dude, what if he saw you following him. He could have killed you too," Michael told David.

"He could try," David replied.

"What's going on? Is everything alright?" Avery interrupted.

"Yeah, we're good," David said. "Ready to play another game?" he asked.

"Yeah, but this is probably going to be my last game. I'm getting kinda tired," Molly said.

"We can head back to my place now if you'd rather do that," David offered to the group.

"Yeah let's get out of here. I just need to close my tab first," Michael replied. Avery followed Michael to the bar. While David and Molly were sitting there waiting, she approached him and put her arms around his shoulders.

Molly gave David a look as she stared into his eyes and then asked, "So where did you go?"

"Ah, it's a long story," David replied.

"Gotcha, can you tell me when we get back to your place?" Molly asked.

"That depends; how long you staying?" David replied with a smile. Before she responded Molly leaned over and started kissing David. He responded and pulled her body in closer to his.

She pulled back slightly and replied, "Well I was planning on making you breakfast in the morning."

"Sounds like a plan to me," David said as he gave her a wink and smiled.

"Alright, let's get you two a room," Michael said as he and Avery walked back in the room.

The four of them got into David's truck and headed back to his house. Michael and the girls were talking about sitting outside, so David started a fire when they got back. Instead of sitting in her own chair, Molly decided to sit in David's lap while they were outside talking. David told Michael and Avery they were more than welcome to spend the night, and Michael was the first one to pass out after David helped him to the guest room. Once Michael went to bed, things started to die down a little bit, and Avery followed Michael to bed shortly after.

Once David and Molly were outside and alone, she asked him about why he left the bar earlier. He was hesitant to tell her what happened because he had just met her and didn't want too many people finding out about him searching for the one responsible for all the missing people at West Spoon. Still,

David was starting to pick up on the fact that Molly was attracted to him, and they were about to hook up. David wasn't sure where things were going from there, but if there was any potential that the two of them were going to start dating, David didn't want to lie to her at the start of their relationship.

David decided to tell Molly about the time he went hunting with his brother at West Spoon and the stalker followed them. He explained to her what he heard the man say and how he heard the stalker repeat the same thing at the bar while they were playing pool. David admitted he found where the man lived, but he didn't go into detail about what he planned to do next.

"So are you going to report that guy or anything?" Molly asked David.

"Yeah probably; not really sure how I want to handle this," David replied. "Let's go to bed though. I'm tired," David said as he picked Molly up and carried her inside to his room. Molly kissed him as he carried her upstairs and when they got to his room Molly started pulling his shirt off. They both undressed quickly before they started having sex. Since it had been a while for David, he was able to go several times before they decided to go to bed. David lay on the bed and Molly laid her head on his chest. While they lay there together, David turned *Scrubs* on Netflix so they could watch something as they fell asleep.

"Do you usually sleep with the TV on or off?" David asked.

"I usually turn the TV off, but I love *Scrubs,* so its fine," Molly replied. David chuckled and then replied, "Yeah me too."

"I had a lot of fun tonight," Molly told David.

"Me too. I'm glad I finally got to meet you. Michael and Avery had told me a lot about you before tonight," David replied.

"Well I was a little worried when you left. I thought you didn't like me. You have no idea how happy I was when you came back," Molly explained.

"Oh yeah. Me leaving had nothing to do with you. If I hadn't found the man who stalked my brother and I, there was no way I was leaving," David replied.

"I understand," Molly said. Then she got up and sat on top of David and continued, "I don't mind if you leave, as long as you promise to always come back." David sat up and put his hands around the back of Molly's head, so he could pull her in and kiss her. When he finished kissing her, David said, "I think I can do that."

Chapter 15

The next morning Samuel woke up earlier than normal after the dream he had reminding him of the time he killed a biker from The Last Call. Samuel rolled over and saw Lyndsey was asleep, so he tried to go back to bed. After about fifteen minutes, he decided to get up and go make coffee and watch TV out in his living room area. Samuel was watching *Law and Order SVU* and thought about how sloppy some of the perpetrators were in the show and how easily they got caught. *If they had half the intelligence and ability to cover up their crimes as I did, they would never get caught,* Samuel thought to himself. Samuel was very secretive about the people he murdered; not even Lyndsey knew about what he did. Samuel had told Lyndsey about how Stephen was raping his little sister, but he never told her that he killed Stephen in retaliation. Samuel was crazy about Lyndsey and wanted to spend the rest of his life with her, but he didn't fully trust her, and he knew if he told her the truth about all the people he murdered, she could use it against him.

After watching a few episodes of *Law and Order SVU,* Samuel fell asleep on his couch. Since Samuel had been thinking about all the people he murdered recently, he dreamed about his most recent murder spree while he was taking a nap. Samuel had overheard several people talk about how the hunting north of the lake was better than trying to hunt south of the lake. Typically, Samuel had hunted more in the south part of the park because it was closer to his home, and he knew if he harvested a deer, he wouldn't have to drag it as far. Samuel had poached many deer in the southern part of the park, and he was starting to have a hard time finding anything.

After a lousy start to squirrel season, Samuel decided to try his luck in the northern part of the state park. Before bow season opened up, he went out and started to scout the area where he planned to hunt. Even though bow season hadn't opened up, Samuel brought his rifle with him anyway while he scouted and planned to shoot a deer regardless. Samuel would have brought his crossbow, but he had to get it re-strung. While he was scouting the northern section of the state park, which was actually the largest section that allowed hunting, he noticed several tree stands along the park boundary line on private land. Several larger trees on the private land had "Private Property, No Trespassing" signs on them. "Man, these stands are in perfect spots," Samuel whispered to himself while he was in the woods scouting. He had seen many large rubs and scrapes around the area and knew there was at least one large buck, possibly several roaming the area.

Samuel started to walk to the stand to inspect it, but as he was walking onto the property, he noticed a trail cam pointed out in front of the ladder by the stand. Samuel walked behind the tree where the trail cam was set up on and slowly reached around the tree to pop it open and remove the SD card that was inside. Samuel also removed the batteries before walking over to check out the stand. As it started to get dark, Samuel headed back to his truck and decided the opening day of bow season he would hunt out of one of the stands he found near the state park boundary even though he was fully aware he would be trespassing.

Samuel got up earlier than normal to make sure he could get to the stand under the cover of darkness and hopefully be unnoticed. He got to the stand about an hour before sunrise. As the sun was coming up, Samuel started to take notice of his surroundings. The stand he was in was along the tree line that separated the state park from the private property. Out directly in front of him, Samuel could see a large open field that eventually led to a fenced in yard and a large house nestled between heavily wooded areas. Just as Samuel was settled in and ready to hunt, he noticed someone dressed in camouflage from head to toe walking across the field and toward the stand. Just about the time the hunter got within firing range for Samuel, the man looked right up at Samuel and stopped dead in his tracks. Instead of advancing, the man who was alone turned around and started walking back toward the house. There was a large pine tree out in the middle of the field by itself, and the man walked behind the tree where Samuel could no longer see him.

Unknown to Samuel, the hunter was texting his father asking him if he had decided to hunt out of the stand he was heading toward. When his father replied, "No," the hunter decided to walk into the heavily wooded area and walk around his tree stand to sneak up on Samuel. Samuel thought about getting out of the stand to avoid getting caught trespassing, but decided to stay and hunt anyway because he didn't know where the guy went.

Just as Samuel decided to stay in the stand and continue hunting, he saw the man in camouflage walk to his right into a thicker part of the woods and disappear once again. Samuel spent half the time looking around for deer and the other half looking for the hunter he saw walking in the field. Samuel assumed whoever it was probably lived in the house and owned the land he was trespassing on. Samuel kept looking in the direction the man walked, but couldn't see anything. Every now and then, Samuel could hear a twig snap or leaves rustle in the woods behind him and would turn around in the stand to see what it was. One time he saw a squirrel bouncing around making a bunch of noise, so from then on he just assumed anything he heard behind him was probably the squirrel looking for an acorn or hickory nut. As Samuel was staring out in the field in front of him, he heard a voice from behind him to his left, "Hey you're in my stand." Samuel looked down and noticed there was a young man probably in his late teens or early twenties looking up at him in full camouflage and carrying a compound bow.

How the hell did he sneak up behind me? Samuel thought to himself. "Oh my bad man, I thought this was still public land," Samuel replied.

"No this is my parents' land; there's no trespassing signs all over the place. I don't know how you missed them," the young man said.

"Well when I got up here, it was pretty dark. Couldn't really see anything," Samuel said. "Since I'm already up here, is it cool if I just hunt the rest of the morning?" Samuel asked. The young man sighed and hung his head.

"You know what? Good luck hunting now, jackass," the young man said as he placed his bow on the ground and walked over to the tree the stand was attached to. As he stood directly below Samuel, the young man unzipped his pants and started to urinate directly on the tree. Samuel looked down and noticed he was waving his body back and forth trying to cover as much area as possible with urine. *Well there goes my morning hunt,* Samuel thought to himself. He thought about shooting the guy right in the head with his shotgun as he looked down and watched him pee, but as the young man was peeing, another man on a dark green ATV pulled up.

"Is this the tree rat?" the older man asked the younger man who just peed on the tree.

"Yeah. He's trying to hunt out of my stand, Dad," the younger man replied.

"The fuck he is," the father replied. As the father got closer, he drew his bow and aimed directly at Samuel.

"What the fuck are you doing on my property, and what the hell are you doing with a shotgun during bow season?" the father angrily asked Samuel.

"Look man I didn't know this was your land or your tree stand. If it's going to be a problem, I'll leave," Samuel replied.

"Oh no, you're not going anywhere just yet. You're going to throw down your hunter license to my son and then stay right where you are while I call the game warden," the father told Samuel.

"Ok, can't we just be civil about this. No need to get the game warden involved," Samuel started to say.

"*License now!*" the father yelled at Samuel.

"Ok, ok," Samuel replied. He moved slowly while he thought about what to do next. Instead of tossing his hunting license down to the son like the father had asked, Samuel went to open his wallet and then threw it directly at the father's face distracting him. Samuel immediately reached for his shotgun while the father dodged the wallet. This gave Samuel enough time to get his shot off first. Samuel aimed his shotgun directly at the father and shot him once in the chest knocking him to the ground immediately. Since the son's bow was still on the ground, and he was shocked at what had just happened, he panicked.

"*Dad nooo!*" the son cried out as he ran over to his father. Samuel was using his pump action shotgun, so he chambered another round quickly as the son ran to his father. While the son was knelt down over his father with his back to Samuel, Samuel shot again. The second shot hit the man's son in the upper part of his back severing his spine, leaving him paralyzed and unable to escape. Samuel got out of the tree stand and grabbed the shotgun shells from the two slug rounds he just shot before he walked over to the two men he mortally wounded. Instead of using his shotgun, Samuel placed it up against the tree stand and drew his pistol. As he got closer to the two men, the father was facing him and the son was lying face down desperately trying to crawl away.

"Please, let my son go," the father pleaded as blood began to fill his mouth.

"Should have just let me hunt," Samuel replied as he shot the man's son in the back of the head killing him instantly.

"*Noooooo! Fuck you!*" the man screamed as loud as he could just before Samuel shot him in the head killing him as well.

Samuel was sure all this noise attracted someone's attention, so he quickly picked up the shell casings from his final two shots and stuffed them in his pockets. Since he was already wearing gloves, he quickly started dragging the father, who was larger, into the woods out of plain sight. After he drug the father's body onto the trail he had followed to get to the tree stand, he headed back onto the private property and started to drag the son's body into the state park as well. Samuel could hear a woman yell from the house, and he immediately panicked. After all the murders he got away with, Samuel was worried this would be the one that got him caught.

He could hear dogs barking, and he knew he wouldn't have enough time to get both bodies away from the murder scene and dispose of them without getting caught. "Son of a bitch. Fucking damnit," Samuel said out loud to himself. He was kicking himself for getting greedy and trying to hunt on private land. Once he got the son's body into the woods and onto the hiking trail, he peeked through the trees and could see two large German Shepherds sprinting toward him. *Oh fuck! I gotta get out of here,* Samuel thought to himself as he grabbed his shotgun and took off running through the woods, heading back to his truck. Without realizing it, Samuel's pack of cigarettes had opened while he was carrying the bodies and a cigarette fell between the bodies.

Samuel managed to get back to his truck without getting caught, and he was pleased when he returned to the parking lot where he left his truck and realized he was the only one there. Samuel backed out and drove away, trying to drive the speed limit to not attract attention to himself. When he got back to his mobile home, he checked himself and noticed he still had a little blood on him from the two men he just killed. As much as he hated to get rid of his camouflaged hunting clothes, he knew he had to dispose of them so he wouldn't get caught. Samuel quickly burned them in his fire pit behind his mobile home and then went inside his trailer to watch TV.

After he was done disposing of the clothes he was wearing, Lyndsey texted him and asked if she could come over. Samuel hadn't seen her much lately, but apparently she got into a fight with her mom and was looking for somewhere to stay. Later that night while he was watching the news to see what the weather was going to be like the next day, the news ran a story about the two men he had just killed. Lyndsey sat in bed next to him while the news anchor explained that a father and son had been killed on their property while hunting, and they had not found the suspect.

"Oh my god," Lyndsey said. "Sammy I don't like you hunting at West Spoon. There's too many people that have been killed or gone missing around there," she continued.

"Don't worry about it. I can take care of myself," Samuel replied.

"I'm serious babe. That place is fucking dangerous. I don't like you going there alone," Lyndsey said.

"Then why don't you come hunt with me. Keep me safe," Samuel sarcastically replied.

"Come on, you know I could never kill an animal," Lyndsey told him.

"What about a human?" Samuel asked.

"If I had to, yeah sure," Lyndsey quickly replied.

"What do you mean if you had to?" Samuel asked.

"Well, like if someone was trying to kill me or rape me. Then yeah, I wouldn't have a problem killing them in self-defense," Lyndsey explained.

"Do you know how to shoot a gun?" Samuel asked Lyndsey.

"No, not really," Lyndsey said.

"Maybe I can show you sometime," Samuel replied as he smiled.

"Oh yeah that'd be fun. You should take me on a date to the gun range," Lyndsey told Samuel.

"We don't need to waste money at a range; we can just go out back into the woods and practice shooting," Samuel explained.

"Is that legal?" Lyndsey replied.

"Yeah it's a state park; it's public land. Besides if anyone hears gunshots around this area, there's no way they are going to fuck with us," Samuel told Lyndsey.

"That's true," Lyndsey said as she leaned over to kiss Samuel goodnight.

Chapter 16

The next morning when David woke up after Molly spent the night, he rolled over and checked his phone. He noticed he overslept and he also got a text back from Evan after trying to call him the night before, "Hey man. Sorry I missed your call. What's up?" David didn't want to call Evan back while Molly was still there, so he got out of bed and walked downstairs to his kitchen to start making breakfast. Considering David had three guests over, he made a large pot of coffee and started scrambling some eggs. He laid out some bacon to cook next and started making toast for everyone. He had finished cooking the eggs, but the smell of the bacon must have woke up the rest of them because once he started cooking the bacon, Michael and Avery walked out of his guest room.

"Damn that smells good," Michael said.

"Hell yeah brother. Can't have a proper breakfast without some bacon," David replied.

"Especially when you're hungover. Holy shit. I can't believe I didn't puke last night," Michael said. David and Avery started laughing. "I'm serious. It hurt just opening my aching, fucking eyes this morning," he continued.

"You came pretty close babe," Avery said. "Don't you remember jumping up out of bed and heading to the bathroom?" Avery asked Michael.

"Yeah kinda," Michael replied. He held his head up with his hands while sitting at the kitchen table.

"Hey man, you puke in my guest bed, you're getting choked," David joked.

"Trust me bro. I know better," Michael replied. Molly walked downstairs and saw that everyone else was already up, and David was cooking breakfast. She walked up to David and put her arms around him hugging him while he was cooking.

"I thought we agreed I was going to make you breakfast," Molly said.

"I was just helping you get a head start," David replied. "Besides I wasn't sure what everyone would want. I got some fruit in the fridge if anyone wants that to go along with what I've already made," he continued.

"Here, let me take over. You go sit and enjoy your coffee," Molly told David. When he turned around, she gave him a long kiss, and then he grabbed his coffee and sat down next to Michael at the kitchen table. Michael turned his head toward David and gave him a look.

"Well looks like you two are getting along pretty well," Michael said while smiling at David. "Hope you two had fun last night," he continued.

"Thanks captain obvious," David joked.

"So am I going to be an uncle?" Michael replied.

"Michael leave them alone," Avery said while shaking her head.

"Oh come on, I'm just kidding," Michael said. "Besides I know David better than that, I'm sure he wore protection," Michael continued.

"Condoms? What are those?" David sarcastically replied. Michael and Molly laughed although Avery did not seem amused.

"You hit her with the old pull and pray didn't you? No wait, I know you better than that. Your couch pulls out but you don't," Michael joked.

"Jesus Christ," Avery said as she put her hand to her forehead. David was laughing so hard he was almost crying.

"Alright, I don't think that's appropriate table talk," Molly said right before she turned around and handed everyone plates.

"Here let me help," David said. He stood up to help Molly carry the rest of the food to the kitchen table. The four of them started eating and David was quickly scarfing down his food.

"Damn man, you hungry?" Michael asked David.

"Mmmm," David replied trying not to talk with his mouth full of food. The girls started talking while David and Michael listened. David ate so fast that his stomach was full before he knew it.

"Did they teach you culinary arts while you were in the Army?" Avery asked David.

"No, why?" David responded.

"Because this is really good," Avery told him.

"Yeah this is amazing," Molly agreed.

"I'm telling ya, David knows how to cook. Just wait until you try something he kills and grills," Michael interrupted. David couldn't help but smile.

"I just really like breakfast food, so I got used to cooking it often," David said.

"Well as good as this is, I'm afraid to take another bite. I still feel like I'm going to puke," Michael said.

"Yeah well that's what happens when you buy round after round and slam shots in between beers, man. You don't have to fly today, do you?" David asked Michael.

"Nah, that's why I drank so much last night. It was my first full day off in weeks," Michael replied.

"Will you be good to drive, or do you want me to?" Avery asked Michael.

"Nah, I'll be alright," Michael replied.

"Ok, well can we head out soon? I have a lot of errands to run today," Avery said.

"Yeah let me grab my wallet and keys," Michael said as he walked back into the guest room. While he was grabbing his stuff, Avery used the restroom, and David went to sit on the couch. He turned on the TV and Molly sat next to him, cuddling up against him. David put his arm around her and kissed her on the forehead.

"Alright man, we are going to head out. Thanks for letting us crash here," Michael said to David who stood up and gave his friend a hug.

"No problem man. You know you two are welcome any time. Glad we could all go out last night. I had fun," David replied.

"Damn right you did," Michael joked. David then went over to give Avery a hug while Michael hugged Molly. The girls said their goodbyes right before Michael and Avery left. Once David and Molly had the house to themselves, they talked a little bit more and got to know each other better. They talked about their likes and dislikes and what hobbies and activities they enjoyed. David discovered that Molly was a cheerleader when she was in high school and loved to watch football and basketball. She was a fan of basically anything to do with Ohio sports and especially rooted for Cincinnati teams. David was a little bummed to find out how much Molly loved baseball because while he respected the sport, he always thought the pace was a little too slow. He talked to Molly about martial arts and she was intrigued. She asked him if they could watch a movie about martial arts.

"If you want to see the greatest martial arts film of all time, you need to watch *Enter the Dragon*," David told Molly.

"*Enter the Dragon?*" Molly asked.

"You've never heard of *Enter the Dragon*? How about Bruce Lee?" David asked Molly.

"Oh yeah, who hasn't heard of him?" Molly replied.

"Ok, well that's a start," David laughed. "Bruce made four films while he was alive, and in my opinion each film just got better and better. The dialogue in the films wasn't the best, but people weren't watching Bruce Lee films for the dialogue," David explained.

"Ok, do you have *Enter the Dragon?*" Molly asked.

"Shit, do I have *Enter the Dragon*. Who do you think you're talking to?" David joked. He went upstairs into his room to find the movie, and then the two of them spent the next few hours watching the film and talking about martial arts. David got completely distracted at first and forgot to call Evan back. Toward the end of the movie, he remembered and was trying to think of a nice way to ask Molly to leave so he could call Evan. After the movie was over David asked her, "You got anything else going on today?"

"Eh, not really. Why are you trying to get rid of me already?" Molly joked.

"No, absolutely not. I was just hoping to go to the gym later, and after watching Bruce Lee kick ass, I really want to train now," David replied.

"Ok, that's cool. I probably should get home and clean up a bit anyway. Are you doing anything tonight after you go to the gym?" Molly asked David.

"No, probably just come back here and chill," David replied.

"How about I come over after you're done training, and I can finally cook for you," Molly offered. "Or if you want, you can come over to my place, and we can have dinner there," Molly suggested.

"Yeah that sounds good; you want me to just text you when I get back from the gym? I can shower, change and then head over," David said.

"Yeah that'll work. I can start cooking while you're getting ready," Molly said.

"Sounds good," David replied right before Molly leaned over to kiss him.

"Alright, do you mind giving me a ride home before you go to the gym, so I don't have to Uber?" Molly asked.

"Yeah, sure," David replied. He forgot that Molly Ubered to the bar with Avery before coming home with him after they left the bar. As David was packing up his gym bag and getting ready to go to the gym, he texted Evan to see if he could meet him at the gym to train for a little bit. David wanted to talk to Evan, but he didn't want Molly around when he did. David packed his bag for the gym and then gave Molly a ride back to her place.

Molly actually lived pretty close to his parents, so David was familiar with the area. David and Evan got to the gym about an hour before classes started, so they decided to drill some techniques on their own before they sparred a few rounds. After they finished sparring, they stuck around for one of Greg's Muay Thai classes which lasted a little over an hour. When the class ended, David walked over to Evan and asked, "Hey man can we go outside to talk real quick?"

"Sure man, everything alright?" Evan asked David. He sensed something was off.

"Yeah," David replied. He packed up his gear, but took his time as he was hoping the parking lot would clear out so they could talk in private. David was sitting on the back of his truck when Evan walked out.

"So what's on your mind? You called me at a weird hour last night," Evan laughed.

"I think I found the person responsible for all the missing people and murders at West Spoon," David said confidently.

"Are you serious? What makes you say that?" Evan asked.

"Last night I was at The Last Call with some friends," David started to explain.

"Wait that's the bar where they last saw that biker that went missing isn't it?" Evan interrupted.

"Yes. So I was at the bar playing pool with some friends, and this creepy guy comes in with his intoxicated, flirty girl-friend. I mean she was a complete shitshow man. Just going around talking to everyone, flirting with every guy at the bar right in front of him. He looked like he was ready to fight right then and there. He had a look in his eye like he was ready to kill. Anyway while I'm outside with my friend Michael, I no-ticed he was smoking Marlboro Reds," David told Evan.

"No fucking way," Evan said, remembering that was the brand of cigarette found near the bodies of the father and son who were murdered.

"Then when we went back inside, he was playing pool right

next to us. He knocked a ball over by our table, and while he reached down to look for it, I heard him speak. I swear to god his voice sounded exactly like the guy I heard the night when my brother and I were being followed at West Spoon. I know it's him," David said.

"Jesus Christ man. What happened after that?" Evan asked.

"I waited for him to leave the bar, and then I followed him," David replied.

"You followed him? Where to?" Evan asked David.

"I followed him to his home. He lives in the back of the trailer park south of West Spoon. His backyard is basically right up against the boundary of the state park. I wrote down his address," David explained as he handed Evan a piece of paper with an address on it.

"He didn't see you following him, did he?" Evan asked.

"No, I was very cautious. You think you can look up who lives there and find out his name?" David asked. Evan was looking at his feet puzzled by what he had just heard.

"You can go after him, right?" David asked.

"I can find out who he is, but I don't think we have enough probable cause to do anything man," Evan replied.

"Oh come on. At least bring him in for questioning or something," David said.

"It doesn't work like that. There's no proof he was at the scene of any of these crimes, and the only thing we can prove right now is he smokes the same cigarette that we found at one of the murder scenes, which I'm sure thousands of other people smoke. Then you're claiming his voice sounds identical to the voice of the guy who stalked you and your brother. Neither of you reported that you were being followed, so there's nothing we can do about it now. We are going to need more evidence if this is in fact the guy we are looking for," Evan explained. David wasn't happy about Evan's response, but he knew he was right. They didn't have enough probable cause or evidence to issue a warrant or bring him in for questioning. David knew he would have to keep an eye on this guy and do his own reconnaissance to prove he was the one responsible for all the disappearances at West Spoon.

"Alright man, I gotta go. I got a hot date in about an hour," David told Evan.

"Ah, atta boy. Who's the lucky lady?" Evan asked.

"Her name's Molly. I just met her," David replied.

"Good for you. Looking forward to meeting her soon," Evan said.

"For sure man; maybe we can go on a double date or something," David suggested.

"Yeah. I'll talk to the wife and let you know," Evan replied.

"Alright, take it easy brother," David said as he reached over to hug his friend.

"You too man," Evan said before walking to his truck. David started his truck and noticed the time. *Shit! I need to get moving,* he thought as he raced home so he could shower and change before heading to Molly's.

While David was over at Molly's, they talked about their upbringing. David let her do most of the talking even though every now and then she would ask him questions that forced him to talk more. David learned that Molly's family was from Chicago and that she came to Cincinnati to study medicine at UC. Molly wanted to become an orthopedic surgeon, and she still had about two more years of school left. David explained that he had just finished up his online classes and got his degree in Criminal Justice.

"So are you going to be a cop and work with your friend Evan?" Molly asked.

"No, I think I'm going to look more into becoming a conservation officer or something along those lines. I don't really have any interest in being a cop like Evan. Too much bullshit to deal with," David explained.

"Yeah I don't think I could be a cop either. Although compared to what you had to go through in the military, being a cop would probably be pretty easy, wouldn't it?" Molly asked.

"Eh, I don't know to be honest. As far as training goes, it would probably be a lot easier. In the military it was usually pretty easy to be aware of where the danger was; over here it's not always obvious who is a threat and who isn't. I feel like when guys let their guard down is when shit happens," David explained.

"Yeah that makes sense. Why did you decide to leave the Army?" Molly asked David.

"That's a long story," David replied.

"That's ok; we got time," Molly pressed.

"Yeah, I guess I just don't really want to talk about it right now," David said. Molly could sense it was a sensitive subject, so she moved closer to David and put her arms around him.

"It's ok; you can tell me when you're ready," Molly told David as she leaned in to kiss him. David kissed her back, and then Molly stood up and held her hand out for David to follow her. She led him to the couch where they began to kiss and undress each other.

"Wait, is your roommate home?" David asked Molly causing her to laugh.

"No, she's out of town," Molly said. After they had sex on the couch, they decided to go upstairs and watch Netflix in bed. They decided to watch *Wedding Crashers,* and then they both got ready for bed.

"Hey, I'm going to set my alarm for 7 a.m. I have to get up early for class tomorrow," Molly told David as he was brushing his teeth. "You can sleep in if you want. I don't know what your plans are for tomorrow," she continued.

"No that's fine; I'm used to being up early," David told her.

The next morning after he left Molly's, David decided to do some scouting around West Spoon. First, he wanted to explore the trail that he and his brother used the night they were followed. The trail led through several different creeks that fed into the lake, but David had never gone past the third creek because according to the trail map it led to a non-hunting zone and was along the boundary of the park. David didn't want to shoot a deer and then have it run into someone's backyard or a neighborhood, so he avoided going beyond that location, but he was curious where it led to, so he decided to check it out. After he got past the creek, the trail got smaller and smaller to the point where there really wasn't a trail left.

There was a small trail that wasn't very wide and led through thick foliage, and then things opened up into an area that was surrounded by many very tall oak, maple and hickory trees. David could see some light shining through the trees to the south and decided to head in that direction. After zigzagging through the trees, trying to avoid spider webs and thickets, David eventually realized where he was. He reached the boundary of the park and was looking at the trailer park. He continued to walk along the edge of the woods to see if he could find the home of the man he believed was the killer. He could see through the tall trees and thick cover, and before too long, he noticed the gray Ford Ranger he had followed two nights ago. David took out his phone and decided to ping the location. He looked around the woods to try and locate some landmarks that would help him navigate through the area later, if necessary. As he was scanning the forest, he heard the screen door on the back of the trailer swing open, and Lyndsey sat down in a chair next to an old fire pit to smoke. Without making too much noise or drawing attention to himself, David decided to head back and look for clues along the way.

On his way back, David thought about riding his motorcycle and heading over to the trailer park to see if he could find out where the man went during the day. David was curious about what he did for a living and thought finding out might help prove his suspicion about him being the killer. David decided to jog back to his truck instead of thoroughly searching that area of the park for evidence. *I can always search more later,* David thought to himself as he was running up a hill and then back down toward a ravine.

When he got home, he realized this was the first time he rode his motorcycle since the riding season ended, and it got too cold to ride. *I hope this damn thing starts,* David thought. Luckily the engine fired up right away, and he drove off toward the trailer park. Not wanting to be too obvious, David decided to park at the gas station on the corner of the street that led into the trailer park where the man lived. David wasn't sure, but he was assuming the man had to head that way to get back on the main road to go to work. While he was waiting David decided to go inside and grab a coffee. Every time a vehicle drove past, he was looking outside to make sure he didn't miss the gray Ford Ranger. David walked outside and found a bench to sit on near his bike. The bench faced the main road, so he could clearly see who was coming and going. When he was about halfway finished with his coffee, David saw the stalker. The man had pulled up to the red light by the gas station in his truck, so without being too obvious, David threw his coffee away and got back on his motorcycle. The light was long, and it gave plenty of time for David to get back on the road. As he pulled out of the gas station parking lot, he saw the man in the gray truck turn left, so he followed him keeping at least two cars between them at all times.

After following him for about fifteen minutes, David saw the gray truck turn into an empty parking lot with a small building in the middle. As he drove by, he saw that the sign out front read, "Ron's Auto Body." There was a Waffle House across the street, and David turned around and headed there so he could grab some food and watch to make sure he had found where the man worked. When David finished his breakfast, the gray truck was still over in the parking lot of the auto body shop, so he felt confident the man worked there and was not just getting work done on his truck. When David got back to his truck, he noticed he got a text from Evan asking if he wanted to go turkey hunting over the weekend when the season opened. David really wanted to spend more time looking for clues and evidence at West Spoon, so he replied, "At West Spoon?"

"Hell no, my buddy Val has over two hundred acres we can hunt on, and he said he's been seeing some massive Toms out at his place," Evan replied. David was slightly disappointed Evan didn't want to join him in looking for more evidence at West Spoon, but still wanted to turkey hunt with Evan considering how much success and how much fun they had rabbit hunting together. The rest of the week went by pretty fast for David because he was starting to really enjoy spending time with Molly. They took turns spending the night at each other's place, and she stayed the night with him before he got up Saturday morning to go hunt with Evan. David woke up long before she did, and after he had everything packed up and loaded into his truck, he walked upstairs to his bedroom to give Molly a kiss before he left. He was very quiet and cautious so he would not wake her up. He got to Evan's house long before the sun came up and noticed Evan was already in his truck waiting for him.

"Morning buddy," Evan said as David opened the passenger door to get in Evan's truck.

"Still feels like night," David replied.

"Yeah? Your girl must be keeping you up too late," Evan joked.

"Nah, we were both pretty tired from a long week. We didn't stay up too late. I just have a hard time falling asleep the night before I go hunting. I'm always too excited," David explained as Evan laughed.

"That just means you're doing it right. If you're not excited to hunt, then you got no business hunting," Evan said.

"True. Hey, I'm pretty sure I found out where that guy works," David told Evan.

"The guy who followed you and your brother at West Spoon?" Evan asked.

"Yeah. Did you find out what his name is?" David asked.

"Yeah his name is Samuel Ryan. He has a pretty clean rap sheet, but that dude's been through a lot," Evan said.

"What do you mean," David asked.

"When I looked into his files, the report I found noted that his mother was arrested for possession with intent to sell, and then she overdosed after she got out of prison. The guy she was dating was murdered in his mobile home after Samuel's mother died, and shortly after his stepdad was murdered, his sister committed suicide. His dad wasn't in the picture; I'm not sure what happened to him," Evan told David.

"Good lord. Do you think he could have killed his stepdad, then his sister to keep her from exposing what he did?" David asked Evan.

"No, the report on his stepfather's murder stated his stepfather owed rival drug dealers a massive debt, and they had been gunning for him for a while. I don't even think he was home when his stepfather was murdered according to the report because Samuel was the one that called it in. There's no way he killed his sister either; he found her hanging from a swing set at a nearby park, and EMS had to pry him away from her because he was hysterical when he found her," Evan explained.

"Damn, that's brutal. Wonder what happened to his father?" David said.

"Yeah, how the hell did you find out where he works?" Evan asked.

"I followed him to Ron's Auto Body shop on 125. I ate breakfast across the street, and when I was finished, his truck was still over there. There's no way he just dropped it off or anything. I think he's a mechanic. When I saw him at The Last Call, he had engine grease and oil all over his pants," David explained.

"Hmm, that makes sense. I can probably look into that. Shit man, you should join the FBI as a detective or something," Evan told David.

"Fuck that," David replied as Evan started laughing again. Evan turned onto a long, gravel road that led to a house on top of a hill overlooking several large fields and rolling pastures. As

Evan drove toward the house, David looked around and saw cows and other livestock on the property. Several fields had large ponds in them as well.

"Man this place is beautiful," David said.

"Yeah, Val has a nice set up," Evan replied.

"How do you know this guy?" David asked.

"He's friends with my dad. Dude is an avid turkey hunter. He even makes his own calls as a hobby," Evan said.

"Oh wow! That's cool. Is he hunting with us?" David asked.

"He will probably go out on his own," Evan explained.

Evan introduced David and Val, and then the three walked out beyond the pasture that was closest to the house. Val was explaining that he tried to keep his cattle near the house during turkey season, so the turkeys would have more room to roam away from the house. Val would move his cattle from the fields further away and tried to time it so that there would be plenty of cow pies out in the fields that the turkeys would be tempted to flip over and pick at. David had heard turkeys did this, but never witnessed it himself. David had only been turkey hunting a few times and only harvested one bird before coming out to hunt with Val and Evan. Just walking from the house to the fields where they would be hunting, David could tell Val was an expert when it came to turkey hunting as he listened to Val talk.

"Alright, when we get to the gate up here, I'm going to let out a shock call and see if we can't locate some birds," Val explained. Val grabbed a crow call out of his hunting pack and let out a couple loud yells. The three men heard several gobbles from out in the distance; David was surprised to hear that many responses.

"Oh yeah it's gonna be a good day boys. Evan, you and

David head out to the right. Walk along that tree line, and there's a holler at the top of that field. If I were you, I'd set up a couple hens and maybe a Jake decoy to draw a big ol' Tom out to fight that sum bitch. I'm going to head to our left; there's a creek down through the woods over here where I've been seeing a monster Tom," Val told them.

"Could you tell where all those gobbles were coming from?" David asked Val.

"Yeah, I heard at least three over in the direction you and Evan are going. I think I heard one, maybe two over here by the creek where I'm heading. Gotta get moving though; they are about to head down from the roost. Get your decoys set up before they see you moving around," Val said.

"Ok, good luck man," Evan said as he patted Val on the back and then started walking along the tree line like Val suggested. David grabbed the bag full of decoys and followed Evan. Evan and David walked quickly to get to the location where Val suggested they set up for their hunt. Evan started setting up the two man pop up blind while David walked twenty yards out in front of the blind to set up the decoys. David wasn't sure how far away Evan was willing to shoot, but he had practiced shooting with the new shotgun shells he decided to try out because he liked the tight pattern it left at about forty yards. David harvested his first turkey at about that distance and felt comfortable he could do it again if he got the opportunity.

"You want to do the calling first, or do you want me to?" Evan asked as they sat inside the blind.

"You invited me. I feel like I should let you shoot first," David offered.

"Ah I don't mind calling, I've harvested plenty of turkeys over the years, man," Evan replied.

"Alright, that's up to you. I'll admit I'm not the best at calling anyway, so maybe I can learn some pointers from you this morning," David said.

"Ok, I got you," Evan replied.

"Actually, I'm going to go sit by that bush over there sticking out into the field," David said as he stood up and unzipped the blind.

"You sure? You're going to be covered with ticks if you sit on the ground in that thick shit," Evan told David.

"I'll be alright. I lathered up with some bug spray before we left," David replied.

"Oh so that's what that smell is. Better hurry up," Evan told him. David quickly gathered his gear and moved to his new location. When David was sitting in the blind, he didn't feel comfortable with the angle he had to shoot from the blind in regard to how he set up the decoys. David was confident there were turkeys roosting up in the trees directly behind them, and he was hoping a Tom would fly down into the middle of the field out in front of the decoys. If the Tom was interested and if Evan did a good job calling to bring him in, David would have a very easy shot hiding behind the honeysuckles. When David got closer to the bush that would provide cover, he noticed a downed log and decided it would be a perfect place to sit up against. David sat with his back up against the log and leaned slightly to his right placing his right leg against the ground and he propped his left leg up, bent at the knee so that he could use his knee as a stand for his shotgun. David had a mouth call with him, so he could keep his hands free, but he was counting on letting Evan do most of the calling. David sat waiting, looking around while wondering exactly which direction a turkey could fly from.

As David and Evan were sitting and waiting, David could hear a turkey gobbling far away and wondered if Evan could hear it as well. Just as David was hoping Evan might let out a couple calls to get that turkey's attention; he could hear Evan start using his box call which was louder and carried further than his push call and slate call. When Evan stopped, the Tom responded immediately with an even louder gobble. *Oh shit this guy's fired up*, David thought to himself. He looked over to the blind Evan was sitting in and could see Evan looking over his shoulder trying to locate where the gobble was coming from. David looked to his right, up into the trees and was trying to spot the turkey as well, but the sunlight wasn't shining through the trees enough to see anything yet.

David looked out to his left into the large field and noticed some sunlight was coming from over the tree tops and lighting up the field, so it was more visible. There was a little bit of fog out toward the creek that Val was hunting near, but closer to the decoys it was starting to become very clear. After waiting a few more minutes, David heard movement coming from the trees, and it sounded like a giant bird was flapping its wings. David saw the bird's shadow just before he saw the large body of the turkey swoop down and land about one hundred yards out in front of the decoys. "Holy shit!" David whispered under his breath. He had never seen a turkey come down from the roost, and watching this magnificent bird fly down from the trees reminded him of watching a plane land on an airstrip.

David regretted not bringing a video camera to film what he just saw. Evan noticed the turkey land out in front of him as well and let out some quiet purrs on his slate call hoping it would get the Tom's attention and bring him closer. For the first fifteen minutes or so, the bird just zigzagged around at about eighty yards, and David could see him pecking around trying to find food on the ground. Evan knew the Tom wasn't interested at the moment, so he hesitated to call again in case it might spook the bird and drive him away. Just as David was starting to lose hope, the Tom started walking back toward the holler and was facing Evan in the blind almost head on. David could see the Tom strutting with his feathers fanned out, but the grass was tall, and the turkey was walking in a diagonal direction taking himself further away from David and closer to Evan.

David could see a deer trail about thirty yards to the right of the blind Evan was in and started to wonder if the Tom would head back into the woods avoiding them entirely. David worried that the Tom was no longer interested in Evan's calls, so he decided to try using his mouth call and let out a couple loud yelps. Immediately, the Tom poked his head up, and David saw the long, white head looking around in his direction. The decoys were still ten to fifteen feet away from David, so he felt confident that if the Tom continued heading in his direction and got closer to the decoys, he could take a shot. There was a slight breeze, and every now and then it seemed like the Tom's head would disappear over the tall grass and then pop back up again in a slightly different location. *Come on you bastard,* David thought to himself. With his tail feathers fanned out, the Tom was turning back and forth just before he stepped forward a couple more steps and into David's firing range. *Boom!*

David saw the bird drop and start flopping around on the ground. Evan came busting out of the blind without his shotgun and ran across the field. David stood up and walked over quickly reaching the downed bird shortly after Evan did. Evan had his right knee down on the body of the turkey and his left over its neck. David stood over Evan while the bird kicked around a little bit before it died.

"Not worried about getting hit by one of its spurs?" David asked Evan.

"Nah, just trying to speed things up a bit, so it doesn't suffer. I've seen them run off after being shot and then die long after," Evan said.

"Yeah, I gotcha. I don't want any animal to suffer," David replied. Evan stood up and let out a deep breath to relax.

"Hell yeah man, that was a great shot!" Evan said as he high fived David.

"Thanks, how far do you think it was?" David asked.

"Well let's find out," Evan replied. He started walking over to the bush that David was sitting behind. Evan could see the imprint in the grass from where David was sitting, so he stood there with both feet and then started walking back to where the bird was lying on the ground. Counting in his head and whispering to himself, Evan reached David and said, "About fifty-five yards."

"Oh shit, that's further than I thought," David replied.

"Oh yeah? Doesn't matter. Only thing that matters is you filled your tag brother," Evan said.

"Damn straight. Now let's go get you one," David said.

Evan decided to leave the blind where it was but brought one hen and the Jake decoy with them as they looked around for another location to hunt. David brought some rope, so he hung his turkey up in a tree high enough off the ground so that nothing could get to it, and then they followed the tree line along the field before finding another holler to hunt. Evan wanted to go into the woods a little bit because there was a slight incline, and it helped set up a good vantage spot to take a shot.

"I'm going to stay here, but go up the hillside about ten yards, so you can call behind me and bring them in," Evan told David. David had his own slate call, but Evan let him borrow his box call and push call as well to mix things up. David was starting to get better at using the slate call, but didn't feel as confident with the box call as he did the push call. The push call Evan had was probably the easiest call to use for any hunter no matter how much experience they had. David was also using his Vortex binoculars, so he could see much farther out into the fields. The two men waited there for about an hour while they heard faint gobbles far in the distance every twenty or thirty minutes. Because David wasn't great at calling yet, he remembered some advice he got from other hunters in the past; *Sometimes less is more*, he thought to himself.

Eventually, anticipation got the best of David, and he started to think, *Evan did a great job calling and helping me bring that bird in. I need to return the favor.* David decided to start letting out some yelps with the slate call every fifteen minutes. After a half hour of light calling, David noticed two dark spots out in the field. He raised his binoculars and saw two turkeys walking across the field heading toward the woods. As he was glassing the field, Evan asked, "Those turkeys out there in the field?"

"Yeah," David replied trying to be quiet.

"Toms or hens?" Evan asked.

"I'm not sure. Neither one of them are fanned out, but one is definitely larger than the other. Almost looks like the bigger one is following the smaller one," David described to Evan.

"Could be a Tom that just mated with a hen, or maybe he's trying to mate," Evan whispered.

"Yeah," David replied. As he was trying to follow the two

turkeys way out in front of them, he was startled when he heard an extremely loud gobble behind him. *Holy shit that was loud,* David thought as he slowly looked over his shoulder. He was trying to locate the bird without making too much noise or movement.

He looked down toward Evan and noticed Evan didn't move an inch. David wasn't sure if he should try calling again or wait to see if the Tom gobbled again and got closer. Knowing the gobble came from behind him to his left, David slowly shifted, so he could see up the hillside. As he was slowly turning, he noticed Evan was doing the same.

Before he could get turned all the way around, David could hear Evan very quietly whisper, "Wait." David decided to stay still, not moving at all and reluctant to call at this point. Looking up the hillside out of his peripherals and then back down toward Evan, David saw Evan slowly raise his shotgun and point it up the hill to David's left. Just as David was wondering if Evan could see anything, Evan pulled the trigger, *Boom!* The sound from the shotgun was very loud, but David didn't flinch. He was used to the sound of gunshots regardless of whether he was being shot at or simply around others while they were shooting.

"My bad, man," Evan said when he stood and started walking up the hill to get his turkey.

"No worries. I'm used to it," David replied.

"Can't believe that fucker snuck up on us," Evan said before chuckling.

"Yeah, I didn't hear any gobbling all day from behind us; that surprised the hell out of me," David said.

"Stupid bird. Fuck around and get busted right in the mouth," Evan joked as David started to laugh.

"Yep they can be pretty dumb sometimes, but other days they outsmart even the most experienced hunters," David said.

"True. Most animals are creatures of habit. You never know what the fuck turkeys are going to do though," Evan replied.

"For sure man. Ready to head back and see how Val did?" David asked.

"Yeah, can you carry the decoys?" Evan asked David, "I'll grab the blind on the way back while you're getting your bird down from the tree," he continued.

"Yeah, man that works," David replied.

David and Evan got back to the truck before Val finished hunting, so once they had filled out their transportation tags, they loaded their gear and put their turkeys in the back of Evan's truck. They waited for about another hour before Val showed up carrying a turkey over his shoulder.

"How'd you boys do?" they heard Val yell as he got closer.

"Look in the back of the truck," Evan replied. When Val got to the back of Evan's truck, he placed his turkey on the ground and peeked over the side of the truck.

"Oh damn! Got some big fuckin' birds this morning," Val said while Evan and David walked over.

"Yeah David got his first probably within the first hour after sunrise, and then I got mine a little while after when we moved to a different spot," Evan told Val.

"Where did you get yours?" Val asked Evan.

"Back along the next holler over from the one you told us to go to this morning. There is a steep hill through the trees where we set up, but the damn thing snuck up behind us. We were expecting them to come across the field," Evan explained. Val started to laugh and then said, "Yeah these birds are fun to hunt, but damn; they can be frustrating sometimes. You just never know what the hell they are going to do. You need some recipes?" Val asked David.

"I usually just smoke them, but if you got some recommendations, I'm willing to try something new," David replied.

"I got a couple recipes. Have Evan send me your number, and I'll text it to you," Val replied.

"Ok, thanks. I appreciate it," David said.

"Did you grab your empty shells?" Val asked them.

"Oh, shit. I forgot," Evan said.

"No you didn't. I grabbed both of them," David said as he pulled two empty .12 gauge shells from his pocket.

"Atta boy. Come inside; we gotta do a shot to celebrate," Val told David and Evan.

"What?" Evan replied.

"Yeah after you kill a bird, you gotta take a shot out of the shell you used to harvest it," Val explained. Val led them into the kitchen and washed the empty shotgun shells in the kitchen sink. After he was done drying them off, he went over to his liquor cabinet and asked them, "Alright what will it be? I got rum, bourbon, vodka, scotch. What sounds good to you?"

David and Evan looked through the collection before Evan blurted out, "Oh we gotta take a shot of Wild Turkey."

"Yeah that seems very fitting," David agreed.

"Good answer young man," Val said as he filled up the shotgun shells with bourbon whiskey. Val handed David and Evan their shot and said, "Cheers boys! Congrats on a successful hunt."

"To pussy and gunpowder. Born by the first, killed by the second, and we love the smell of them both," David added. Val and Evan started laughing before all three men downed their shot.

"Damn, man. That was pretty good; where did you come up with that?" Evan asked.

"It's classified," David replied with a grin.

Chapter 17

During the week following David and Samuel's encounter at The Last Call, Samuel felt somewhat suspicious that he was being followed. He was also starting to feel the pressure of possibly getting caught for all the murders at West Spoon after he was unable to dispose of the bodies of the father and son he killed. With everyone else he murdered, Samuel was successful in disposing of the bodies and hiding the evidence.

While he was sitting in his mobile home watching TV with Lyndsey, he started to wonder if he was still wearing his gloves when he dragged the bodies off their property and into the state park. If Samuel wasn't wearing gloves, there was a chance his fingerprints or DNA would be on the bodies, and authorities could identify him as the killer. *No I'm sure I was wearing my camouflaged gloves,* Samuel thought.

When the sun came up, Samuel decided it was time to teach Lyndsey how to shoot in case anyone ever came after him or if she was being attacked. Samuel didn't have his CCW, but he still kept a handgun on him or in his truck at all times. Samuel was glad Ohio was an open carry state. As he was packing up his handguns and rifles, he handed Lyndsey his Glock 19 since he had a holster for it.

"Here, put this on your hip," Samuel said.

"Ok, but I don't have my concealed carry permit," Lyndsey replied.

"You don't need one; open carry is legal in Ohio," Samuel explained.

The two walked about a half mile into the woods, and Samuel set up four targets against a pile of logs so there was a backstop. Samuel showed her how to shoot the handguns first, mixing in shooting several different calibers and letting her feel the difference between a standard semiautomatic pistol and a revolver. After Samuel felt comfortable in her ability to shoot handguns, he taught her how to load and shoot his shotguns and rifles. Samuel had her start at close range, and as she started to get more consistent hitting center mass, he would back her up more and more so she developed greater marksmanship at longer distances.

"I think the squirrel slayer is my favorite," Lyndsey said referring to Samuel's Remington .22 long rifle.

"Oh yeah? Why's that?" Samuel asked.

"Because it's not very loud, and it doesn't kick," Lyndsey replied.

Samuel laughed, "Yeah, a .22 doesn't have much recoil, does it?"

"No, not at all," Lyndsey said.

Meanwhile David started exploring West Spoon more often trying to find evidence or anything that might help him prove who the killer was. David would spend time with Molly in the evenings after training. Then in the mornings after she left for class, David would hike along the trails at West Spoon and survey the surrounding area on days when he wasn't scheduled to work. At first he spent more time surveying the area closer to the trailer park hoping there might be clues closer to where Samuel lived.

David found several old campfire locations that were littered with garbage and other trash that people had left behind, but nothing led him to believe the killer was frequently using those locations. *This guy is too smart to leave stuff behind,* David thought. Around one of the hiking trails that was in an illegal hunting zone, David noticed a few makeshift blinds that were far off the trail and harder to spot. When he approached the makeshift blind, he could tell someone had been using it because there was an old, beat up chair still in the middle. David thought about taking the chair and turning it in to authorities so they could maybe get prints off it, but he decided not to because if the killer noticed the chair missing, David was concerned the killer would think someone was on to him.

After scanning the majority of the southern portion of the state park, David decided to survey the area near where Winston Morrow was killed and his motorcycle was left in the parking lot. David suspected that the killer could have possibly tried to dispose of the body near the parking lot somewhere deep in the woods. He walked around looking for clues, and after spending several hours each morning three days in a row, he found nothing. The woods closer to that parking lot were extremely thick, and David suspected it would be difficult for anyone to be able to drag a body through that area. As David walked back to his truck, he was wondering if the killer could have moved the body somewhere else that would be easier to dispose it.

Since David had already tagged one bird, and he was allowed to harvest one more turkey in the spring, he decided to hunt the northeast corner of the state park where he hadn't searched for clues yet on his day off. While He was out searching for clues and evidence, he didn't notice many signs of turkeys south of the lake, so he was hoping he would have more luck finding them to the north. The evening before David headed out to hunt, Molly spent the night. Even after David tried to be as quiet as possible so he wouldn't wake Molly as he was leaving, she still woke up.

"Be careful out there," Molly told David when he was packing up to leave in the morning.

"Don't worry. This is what I'm best at," David replied as he leaned over to kiss Molly on the forehead.

"No, what you did last night is what your best at," Molly smiled at David before rolling over to go back to sleep.

David arrived at the state park a little later than he wanted to, but he still could hear some gobbling as he was walking into the woods, so he felt confident the Toms hadn't come down from the roost yet. David brought a Jake and a hen decoy with him, and he got them set up quickly so he could get into position. After the first two hours of not seeing anything and hearing gobbling far off the distance, David decided to pack up and walk a little farther into the woods hoping he could bring a Tom in.

As David was following a hiking trail, he looked to his right and saw the sun shining through the trees up alongside a hill. Curious to see what the landscape looked like at the top of that hill, David decided to hike up and see if there were signs of turkeys moving in that area. When he got to the top of the hill and it leveled out, he noticed things opened up quite a bit. He looked straight ahead and could see a large fenced in field with cows roaming around across from the edge of the nearby tree line. *This seems like a good spot for turkeys to roost,* David thought. As he was walking around looking for a spot to set up his decoys and start calling, he started to see turkey scat and areas where they were scratching. David was in the middle of an area with many tall oaks, maple, and hickory trees. It looked like there might be several deer trails that turkeys could travel as well, and there was some thick cover to his right, so David decided to set his pop up blind against the bushes and other thick cover. Then he put his decoys out toward the middle where he had several open shooting lanes and could see if anything was approaching.

David decided to set up his decoys first and then started walking over toward the bushes and thickets so he could set up his blind. There wasn't a great spot to set up his blind, so he started walking into the thick cover looking for a spot where he could possibly set up his chair and use the natural vegetation as cover. As he got to a spot that was a little more open, he saw bones scattered on the ground.

At first David wondered what animal the bones used to belong to, but as he got closer, he noticed these did not belong to an animal. These were human remains. *"Holy shit!"* David whispered to himself. He immediately put his shotgun and backpack down, so he could get the plastic bag he brought with him in case he harvested a turkey. Some of the bones looked like they had been chewed on and were pretty damaged. David was careful not to move too much around, and he put as many bones as he could into his bag. He wanted to save the skull for last because when he found it, he noticed it had a bullet hole. In order to help find the location later, David grabbed two large sticks and made an X with them nearby and left his orange hat up in a tree branch, so he could see it from a distance. He also decided to leave his decoys where they were, so he could carry the bag of bones back and get the decoys later. When he got back to his truck, David immediately called Evan.

"Hey man you're not going to fucking believe this," David said over the phone.

"Why, what happened?" Evan asked David.

"I just found some bones from a dead body at West Spoon," David said.

"No fucking way! Where?" Evan asked.

"Up near Sugarmill Road. I went up that way to hunt the northeast area of the park and found the bones when I was trying to find a spot to sit and call," David explained.

"Ok, don't touch them. I'll meet you, and you can show me where you found them," Evan said.

"I already bagged some of them," David replied.

"No! Dude you can't do that. That's tampering with evidence," Evan told David.

"Don't worry; my fingerprints aren't on them. I was wearing gloves. I didn't get all the remains; there are still some," David told Evan.

"Damnit man, you still should have left them there for our forensics team to check it out," Evan said.

"Don't worry. I took pictures. I just want to get them to a lab as quick as possible. You on duty right now?" David asked.

"Yeah, I can meet you at the station. Drop off what you got and then go show me where the rest of the remains are," Evan replied.

"Ok. See you in about twenty minutes," David said.

David met Evan in the parking lot at the police station, and the two walked inside so Evan could drop off the bag of remains that David had found. Then David got into Evan's police car and they sped off to collect the rest of the remains. David led Evan through the hiking trail he had followed and then up the hillside toward where he left his decoys and orange hunting hat.

"Damn man, why'd you walk this far?" Evan asked as they were walking up the hill.

"Hell, this isn't even that bad," David replied.

"We almost there?" Evan asked.

"Yeah, you need to work on your cardio bro," David said.

"It's not that; my damn knee is acting up again," Evan explained.

"Oh shit, my bad. I forgot," David replied.

"No worries." Evan grunted as he struggled to keep up with David.

"Here we are; the rest of the bones are right over there," David said as he pointed to the "X" he made with sticks and his orange hat hanging on a tree branch. Evan followed David as they walked up on the remains.

"Damn man! I can't fucking believe you found this," Evan said.

"Tell me about it. I've been scanning this park all fucking week trying to find something and, go figure when I actually come out here to hunt, I finally find the evidence I've been constantly looking for," David replied.

"Yeah, but who the hell could this be?" Evan asked.

"I'm not sure. Based off the reports and articles I read, there weren't any missing people reported in this area of the park," David said.

"Yeah, all of the abandoned vehicles were found elsewhere," Evan replied.

"Maybe the killer moved the body to throw off the authorities," David suggested.

"Could have, but there were still several pretty extensive searches throughout the park. Especially after the park ranger went missing," Evan explained.

"Well hopefully we will find out after the remains are sent to the lab," David said as the two began to collect the rest of the bones and put them in evidence bags. They got into Evan's squad car and headed back to the station.

"I got some good news brother," Evan told David.

"Oh yeah, what's that?" David asked.

"Emma is pregnant," Evan said.

"Oh congratulations man. You finally figured out where to put it," David replied.

"Yeah all those charts and videos Emma showed me finally paid off," Evan joked as David laughed.

"Seriously though, I'm happy for both of you. Know if it's going to be a boy or girl yet?" David asked.

"No, we both want to be surprised," Evan replied.

"Gotcha. What time does your shift end? We gotta go celebrate," David said.

"Four, but I wanted to go train later this evening, so maybe we can grab a beer or two after class," Evan suggested.

"Yeah man. That should work. You mind if Molly comes? I'm sure she will want to see me tonight. I don't want to blow her off," David said.

"No that's cool. I'll tell Emma where we are going, so they can finally meet," Evan replied.

"Ok, sounds good," David said.

"So when are you two going to start making little minions of your own?" Evan asked David.

"Hey man, don't put that evil on me yet. I just met the girl. She will probably get sick of me in a couple months anyway," David laughed.

When David got back to his house, he texted Molly and explained to her that he wanted to go out with Evan and Emma after Jiu Jitsu class, so they could celebrate the pregnancy. As David waited for Molly to reply, he checked his phone to see what the weather would be like the next day, and since it looked like it was going to rain throughout the day, he figured it would be easier to spend the night at Molly's house after they went out. He decided to pack a change of clothes for after class. Eventually Molly replied, "That's great! I can't wait to meet them."

David texted back, "Is it cool if I shower at your place after class? I can just leave my stuff there so we can stay the night at your place after we go out with Evan and Emma." David was running late for class, so he packed his stuff before her response anyway and headed to the gym.

Right when he rolled into the parking lot, Emma texted him back, "Yeah that works."

David and Evan partnered up for drills during Gi Jiu Jitsu class, and David noticed Evan was moving slower than normal. David didn't want to embarrass him, so he decided to move a little slower when they were doing hip to hip drill. He didn't want to make Evan look bad. Terrance had the class do a drill where the person on their back practiced transitioning from armbar to triangle choke, then to omaplata from full guard. David went first to let Evan rest a little bit and then when Terrance had them switch, Evan started moving a little faster. When Terrance told the class to start doing knee on belly switches, Evan muttered under his breath, "Fuck. Son of a bitch."

"Don't worry man. I'm not that fat," David joked.

"I know. My knee is still fucking killing me though," Evan explained.

"Oh from hiking through the woods earlier today?" David asked.

"That and just life in general I guess," Evan said.

"Well just take it easy if you need to then," David suggested.

During the knee on belly drill, David could tell Evan was in significant pain when he had to put any pressure or weight on his right knee. Evan eventually walked off the mats and sat down to give his knee a rest. David started to walk over until he saw Terrance going to check on Evan. David couldn't hear every word that was said, but he did manage to over-hear Terrance tell Evan to take it easy and participate when he could. Terrance also suggested that Evan sit out when they started rolling. Evan nodded reluctantly. David could tell not being able to spar later was bothering Evan. After Terrance showed a few sweeps from various positions, he had the class grab drinks and use the restroom if needed before they got ready to spar. When David walked over to grab a drink, he noticed Evan had started packing up his gear and looked like he was ready to leave.

"You heading out?" David asked.

"Yeah. I don't mind watching you guys drill because I can at least visually learn the technique and stuff, but if I stick around, I know I'm going to want to get back on the mats and roll, and I probably shouldn't right now," Evan explained.

"I understand man. We still meeting up for dinner and drinks later?" David asked.

"Yeah. I'll shower and change and then text you when we are heading out," Evan replied.

"Sounds good brother," David said as he gave Evan a fist bump.

After David finished sparring, he drove over to Molly's house. The front door was open, so David could see through the screen door. When he looked inside, he didn't see Molly, so he knocked before opening the door and walking in.

"Hello?" David called out.

"In here," Molly responded from her bedroom. David walked down the hallway and saw Molly sitting in a chair putting on her makeup in the corner of the bedroom.

"Damn. I was hoping you'd join me in the shower," David joked.

"Aw I'm sorry. I just knew it would take me longer than you to get ready, so I figured I'd shower and get dressed before you got here. I'll make it up to you later tonight," Molly said as she smiled at David.

"Sounds great," David said right before he walked to where she was sitting and kissed her on top of her head.

"How was class?" Molly asked.

"Pretty good. I'm a little worried about Evan though," David replied.

"Why? What happened?" Molly asked.

"His knee is bothering him, so he sat out for most of the class and headed home early," David explained.

"Oh that sucks. What happened to his knee?" Molly asked as David stepped into the shower.

"He had knee surgery after he injured his knee playing football. I guess it acts up every now and then," David said. He quickly showered and changed into his clothes while Molly was still getting ready. He combed his hair, splashed on some cologne and threw on a hat. David walked over toward Molly and sat at the foot of the bed near her vanity.

"How do you get ready so fast?" Molly asked.

"Because I don't give a shit what I look like," David replied. Molly turned around, stood up to walk over to David.

"Well I think you look damn good," Molly told him.

"Why thank you. You know you don't need all that stuff," David said as he pointed to the makeup Molly had spread out on her vanity.

"You're sweet," Molly said as she placed her hands on David's face and leaned over to kiss him. David moved his index finger up to his mouth and said, "Shh, don't tell anyone. You ready to go?"

"Yeah, let me grab my purse real quick," Molly replied as David walked out the door and headed to his truck. He opened the passenger side door and waited for her to lock her front door and walk down the steps toward her driveway.

When David and Molly got to the restaurant, Evan and Emma were already there and had gotten a table while they waited for their friends. David expected to find Evan toward the back of the restaurant as he walked in, and sure enough it didn't take him long to find his friend. David and Molly approached their table while Evan and Emma stood up to greet them. David jokingly walked right by Evan pretending to ignore him and went over to give Emma a hug.

"Congratulations, Momma!" David said to Emma.

"Oh hey, Evan. Didn't see you there," David joked.

"Yeah, long time no see, jackass," Evan smiled.

"Evan. Emma. This is Molly. Molly this is Evan and Emma," David said introducing Molly to his friends.

"Nice to meet you," Emma said as she shook Molly's hand. Evan followed Emma's lead before the group of four sat down at the table. The ladies sat inside the booth by the windows while David and Evan sat at the end of the table across from each other. Before the group ordered their food, they exchanged pleasantries and Evan and Emma took turns asking Molly questions so they could get to know her a little more. While they were waiting for their food, the conversation shifted, and the women spent most of the time talking about Emma's pregnancy while David and Evan talked about jiu jitsu and hunting. David wanted to talk to Evan more about what they had discovered at West Spoon earlier in the day, but he was hesitant to bring it up when Emma and Molly were around.

David waited until they both went to the restroom and then he asked Evan, "So how long do you think it will take before they run the DNA test and find out whose remains we found today?"

"I have no idea man. I'm not sure how long it takes the coroner or whoever to determine that kind of stuff. I would imagine if the person has a record and if they are in the system, then it will be easier to find," Evan explained.

"Yeah, well, I hope they figure it out soon. Whoever it is, their family deserves to know the truth. I'm sure finding out will suck, but at least they might have some closure," David said.

"Yeah," Evan agreed as the girls returned, prompting David to change the subject once again. After dinner the four walked out of the restaurant together. David and Molly followed Evan and Emma to Evan's truck since they had parked closer.

"Thanks again for dinner," Evan told David.

"No problem man. I'm just happy for both of you," David replied.

"It was nice finally meeting you," Molly told Emma.

"Yeah for sure; we will have to do this more often," Emma replied.

David gave Emma and Evan a hug and while the girls were saying their goodbyes, he asked Evan, "Can you let me know who it is when they run the DNA?"

"Yeah, sure," Evan replied.

Overhearing part of the conversation, Molly asked, "What are you talking about?"

"I'll explain on the way home. It's a long story," David replied. He and Molly walked back to his truck holding hands and David noticed Molly was squeezing his hand a little harder than normal. David looked over at her, and she looked back at him with a concerned look on her face. He opened the door for her and then walked around his truck to get in on the driver's side. Once he sat down and started his truck, he began explaining, "Ok, so I found the remains of a body today while I was hunting at West Spoon."

Molly was shocked, "Oh my god, are you serious?"

"Yeah, I contacted Evan, and we brought the bones and remains back to the lab, so they could run the DNA test and hopefully identify the body," David replied.

"Who do you think it is?" Molly asked.

"I'm not sure. Considering we scanned the surrounding area and didn't find anything else, I'm going to assume it is either the park ranger or Winston Morrow, the guy from the motorcycle club that went missing after his motorcycle was found in a parking lot near the park," David said.

"Jesus Christ, I can't believe you found a human body," Molly said.

"I know. There's probably more out there too," David replied.

"Do you want me to help you look for them?" Molly asked.

"Oh no, I don't want you out there," David said.

"Why not?" Molly asked.

"It isn't safe," David said quietly.

"If it isn't safe, then why are you going there?" Molly asked.

"Because I need to find the killer. I need to find the truth."

"David, please be careful," Molly said softly. He looked over at her and could see her starting to tear up. He pulled over to the side of the road.

"Hey, I'll be fine. I know what I'm doing," David said as he leaned over the center console and put his arm around Molly.

"I know you do. I'm just scared. I'm worried about something happening to you," Molly said.

"I understand. If there is someone out there killing people and I could possibly stop them, I couldn't live with myself if I did nothing," David explained.

"Why can't the cops just arrest that guy you think is the killer?" Molly asked.

"Evan doesn't think we have enough proof or probable cause to go after him," David explained. He pulled back onto the main road, and the two continued their conversation all the way back to Molly's house.

"Can't you at least bring someone with you when you hunt there? What about Michael or Evan?" Molly asked.

"Michael doesn't hunt and Evan refuses to hunt on public land. He has enough connections and access to private land; he doesn't need to bother hunting at West Spoon," David replied.

"Ok. What about your dad or your brother?" Molly asked.

"My dad works too much; he can't get away long enough to go hunting, and my brother refuses to go to West Spoon after what happened when we were younger," David explained.

"He must be the smart one," Molly said.

"What? Are you saying that I'm dumb?" David laughed.

"Little bit, yeah," Molly joked.

When David and Molly got back to her house, they went to her bedroom where they both undressed and got ready for bed. After brushing their teeth they started to kiss; then David laid her down on the bed. He started to kiss her neck and began moving his way down toward her chest when she stopped him. "Can you just hold me for a while. I'm not really in the mood right now," Molly said.

"Yeah sure, you alright?," David replied.

"Yeah, I'll be fine. So what's your plan?" Molly asked him as she laid her head on his chest.

"What do you mean?" David replied.

"How do you plan to get this guy?" Molly asked.

"Just going to keep looking around West Spoon, see if I can find any clues while I'm hunting. There's two more weeks of spring turkey season, and I got one tag left. If the killer is who I think he is, he may be out there during the turkey season as well. One thing I've noticed is most of the people went missing during hunting season," David explained.

"Well, I hope you get him before he gets you," Molly said quietly.

"Don't worry. He ain't going to bag me," David replied.

Chapter 18

Samuel had been busy at work for most of the spring Turkey season and was unable to get out to West Spoon to go hunting. As the season was coming to an end, he was getting impatient and decided to take some time off work once the weather cleared up, and he had a good day to hunt later that week. He woke up about forty-five minutes before sunrise, so he had plenty of time to hike the trail toward the area he planned on hunting that morning. Samuel remembered he left a chair in one of his makeshift blinds, and he had seen several turkeys moving around in that area last fall during deer season. Samuel didn't have a turkey tag on him at the time, but he still considered shooting one of the hens that he thought might come his way; however none of the turkeys he saw got close enough for a shot with his crossbow.

Samuel saw more turkeys moving around in that area in the evening during the fall season, so he figured there might be some up there roosting, and maybe he would be able to call one in that morning. By the time he reached his makeshift blind, Samuel realized he still had about thirty minutes before sunrise. He walked out about twenty yards in front of his blind so he could set up his decoys. He was using two hen decoys. At this point in the season, he didn't care if he harvested a Tom or Jake; he just wanted to shoot something. When he got back to his makeshift blind, Samuel sat down and waited. He was exhausted from lack of sleep and was having a hard time keeping his eyes open even as the sun was rising. Samuel had grabbed a bag of cocaine that Lyndsey bought from one of her coworkers before he left his mobile home that morning. Desperate to stay awake once the sun was up, Samuel decided to snort a line off his hand between his thumb and pointer finger.

Meanwhile David was preparing to turkey hunt at West Spoon that morning as well. Molly had spent the night, so she was still in bed when David woke up and started getting dressed to go hunting. For whatever reason, David had a weird feeling that he should wear his armor plated vest under his camouflage. Since he already had his hunting clothes laid out, he had to go to his closet and find his armor plated vest. He quickly turned the light on so he could find his vest, and it woke Molly. She rolled over and asked, "What's that?"

"Armor plates," David replied.

"Do you always wear that when you go hunting," Molly asked.

"Depends on what I'm hunting," David replied with a smirk.

David could tell Molly was confused about what he meant and was struggling to understand because she was still half asleep. Before David headed downstairs to grab the rest of his gear and head out, he sat down on the bed next to where Molly was lying. He put his hand on her forehead before he brushed her hair back and leaned over to give her a kiss.

"You think he might be out there today?" Molly asked.

"I don't know. Just feels like I'm getting closer to proving this guy is the killer. I'm going to try to hunt closer to where he lives, and if we cross paths, I don't see him being too welcoming," David explained. Molly sat up and placed both her hands on David's face. He still had a beard although it wasn't as thick as he usually let it get during the winter. Molly's hands on his cheeks sent a tingling feeling through his face.

"Please be careful," Molly told him.

"I will," David said right before he leaned in to kiss her again. He held her tight as they embraced. When they both pulled back slightly, she looked at him and said, "I love you"

David had never heard that from a woman before, so he hesitated at first. After all the time they spent together, David realized how strong his feelings for her were, and he felt like she really meant it. "I love you too," he replied softly. Before he loaded up his truck with his hunting gear, David also grabbed his gun case with his Daniel Defense DDM4 and a couple of magazines just in case he might need it later, then he backed out of his driveway.

David decided to park in the same lot where he parked years ago when he was deer hunting with his brother. Since it was still dark, he wore a head lamp while he was walking along the trail into the legal hunting zone. He brought his Jake and hen decoys with him, but opted not to bring his pop up blind. He set up at a location near a creek, downhill from many tall trees hoping that a Tom may fly down near him from the roost. About fifteen minutes before sunrise, David could hear gobbling in the distance, but couldn't exactly tell where it was coming from. He let out some calls, but after the sun came up, the gobbling stopped. He didn't want to be too eager about calling, so he waited an hour and decided to relocate because he could hear more gobbling in the distance farther to the southeast.

The cocaine Samuel snorted was effective, and he began to feel very alert to his surroundings. As he was sitting in his makeshift blind, Samuel noticed his hands were shaking a bit as the high began, and he hoped it would wear off eventually. The last thing he wanted if he saw a bird was for the bead at the end of his barrel to be bouncing around. Before the sun came up, the woods were very quiet, but within the first hour, Samuel started to hear gobbling. At first he heard gobbling coming from his right to the east which sounded closer, and then he started hearing some gobbling to the south, and occasionally he could hear a faint gobble from the west. Samuel wanted to focus on the gobbling he heard to the east, so he got out his slate call and started responding with some soft yelps hoping it would still carry through the woods and bring in a Tom or Jake. With his shotgun across his lap, his slate call in his left hand, and the striker in his right, Samuel started to hear something moving toward him from downhill from the north.

At first Samuel thought it might be a squirrel or deer because whatever it was didn't seem to care about moving quietly. *There is no way this is a turkey; turkeys aren't this damn loud* Samuel thought. Still, whatever was approaching Samuel made him anxious, so he moved his slate and striker out of the way and raised his shotgun over a branch in front of him to stabilize the barrel of his shotgun. Whatever was coming uphill was getting louder and Samuel started hearing voices.

"I heard them over here Dad," a young boy's voice echoed through the woods.

"Hang on Benny" an older man's voice replied.

"Come on. There's a gobbler over here. I heard him," the boy said.

"We still need to find a spot to set up; otherwise, he's going to see us coming, and we are going to spook him," the father explained.

Samuel first saw the boy's head. Then his upper body. Followed by his short legs. He was covered in camouflage except for the orange vest he wore over his camouflaged hoody, and he carried a small shotgun that Samuel assumed was a .20 gauge. Samuel was waiting to see where the father was, but before he found the father, the boy called out to his dad.

"Hey Dad, I think there's some decoys over here," the young boy said. He turned to look downhill at his father who was following him up the hill.

"What? Are you sure?" the father replied.

"Yeah. Look! They are right over there," the boy replied as he pointed toward the decoys Samuel was using.

Samuel was pissed. He kept the bead of his shotgun on the center mass of the young boy walking up the hill, and once the boy shifted his weight to face the decoys out in front of him, Samuel realized the boy was within range. Without hesitation, Samuel exhaled and pulled the trigger. *Boom!*

The loud blast woke up the woods, and when Samuel stood up, he looked over the decoys where he could see the young boy's body fall backward. Then he could hear the body rolling down the hill.

"*Noooo!* Oh my God, Benny! No, no, no, no, no," the father screamed as he ran up the hill to his son. When the father approached his son, his son was lying face down so he rolled his son over and he could see the boy had been shot.

David heard all the commotion as he was relocating to a

new spot to hunt, and he took off running toward where the dad's screams were coming from. The gunshot didn't sound too far off, but David knew moving uphill would present a challenge. He crossed the creek and started running up the hill as fast as he could. He was moving at an angle because the hill was very steep, and he knew if he tried to run straight up the hill, he might slip, and it would be harder for him to return fire if necessary. Once David could see the father kneeling over his son, he started running even faster.

Samuel walked toward the edge of the hill where he last saw the boy before he shot him. Samuel passed his decoys and raised his shotgun as he scanned the area for the boy's father. At first, Samuel didn't see either of them because the father grabbed his son and moved him behind a large tree for cover. The young boy was struggling to breathe, and his father was panicking. All the noise and commotion got Samuel's attention, and he quickly found them, but where he was standing, he had no shot. Samuel started to walk to his left to sneak around a thicket, and when he got through the foliage, he raised his shotgun and pointed it at the father. David saw what was happening as he got closer and now the father was aware Samuel was walking down the hill toward him.

"*Stay down!*" David hollered to the father. David shot at Samuel knowing full well that Samuel was out of range for his shotgun to be effective, but David wanted to deter Samuel from shooting the boy's father. The plan worked. As soon as David shot, Samuel turned and started to run back uphill toward a large tree for cover. David continued running up the hill and passed the wounded boy and his father, so he could continue pursuing Samuel. When Samuel ran behind the tree and out of David's sight, he wasn't sure if Samuel had kept running away or if he was getting ready to return fire, so David started to slow his pace and walk up the hillside with caution.

David zigzagged up the hill trying to use trees and bushes for cover. He stopped when he reached a spot where the next tree or cover was too far away. David moved to the right of the tree he was behind and pointed his shotgun directly toward the tree he last saw Samuel hide behind. David noticed Samuel shot pool right handed, so he expected him to do the same with a rifle or shotgun. As David was staring at the right side of the tree he expected Samuel to be hiding behind, he saw Samuel spin out to the left side of the tree and start to raise his shotgun to his shoulder. David was quicker, but Samuel slipped as he turned, and the majority of David's buckshot went right over Samuel or hit the tree he was hiding behind. David chambered another shell, and Samuel scrambled to hide behind the tree again.

Samuel stuck his shotgun out to the other side of the tree and shot at David without even looking. David took a knee as Samuel's shot was too high and to his left. Samuel stood to the right of the tree and shot three more times quickly, forcing David to take cover behind a tree. When Samuel realized he needed to reload, he took off running up the hill. Before David could get another shot at Samuel, he ran out of sight, and David started to sprint up the hill hoping to catch him.

David got to the top of the hill and noticed the makeshift blind he saw earlier in the season and realized where he was. He also saw two decoys out in front of the blind that Samuel had left behind as he retreated to his mobile home. David slowly approached the blind expecting Samuel to pop out again. When David reached the makeshift blind, he recognized the chair Samuel was using and something under the chair caught his eye. David knelt down quickly and saw a baggie containing cocaine. David pulled out his phone and took a picture of the bag before picking it up and putting it in his back pocket. Realizing that Samuel had gotten away, David headed back down the hill to help the young boy and his father.

"Oh my God, my boy," the father kept crying out as David approached them. David looked down at the poor boy and could see blood dripping down the side of his lips, and he struggled to breathe.

"Grab my shotgun. Let's go," David told the father.

"Wait. Should we move him?" the father asked.

"Paramedics won't be able to find us here. We gotta get him to the nearest road. Follow me," David replied as he picked up the young boy and started quickly moving up the hill toward the hiking trail so he could follow it to the road.

David was running as fast as he could while carrying the wounded boy, and he could hear the father sobbing behind him as he struggled to keep up. David was breathing heavily from carrying all the extra weight, but the adrenaline pushed him to keep moving quickly. David could see a car drive by through the trees and he knew they were close. He pushed through low hanging branches and thorn bushes to reach the edge of the road that led to the parking lot where his truck was. David placed the boy on the ground and lifted his hoody. His chest was covered in small bullet wounds from all the buckshot that hit him, and the blood had now soaked through his clothes. The father pushed through the woods and immediately fell to his knees seeing how severe his son's condition was.

"Oh my god. Please help him. Please do something," the father pleaded.

"I'm not a medic. We need to try to stop the bleeding,"

David replied as he called 9-1-1. The boy's father wept and David realized the boy wasn't going to make it when he started coughing up blood. As the phone was ringing, David asked the father how old his son was.

"I got an eight-year-old gunshot wound victim at West Spoon State Park. We are on the side of Slate road. He's been shot by a hunter likely using a .12 gauge shotgun within twenty-five yards, and there's buckshot all over his upper torso. Send EMS immediately," David told dispatch.

David knelt next to the wounded boy and his father. David took off his camouflage pullover and started to wipe the blood away from the boy's mouth. David could see the fear in the young boy's eyes and noticed he was crying and struggling to breathe. The boy's father was hysterical and not helping much at all. David wanted to remain positive, but he was aware of the reality that was about to happen. David also wanted to go after Samuel, but he didn't want to abandon the boy and his father before EMS arrived. The boy started shaking and coughed up more blood.

"Hang on buddy," David told the boy as he lifted his head off the ground. More blood came pouring down his chin as David lifted his head up. The boy's father was still kneeling beside him.

"Come here; hold his head up," David told the boy's father. The father sat with his legs crossed and held his son's head in his lap. David could now hear the sirens of the paramedics approaching and decided to call Evan who answered immediately.

"Yo, are you at West Spoon right now?" Evan asked David.

"Yeah. I'm with the boy and his father," David replied.

"Holy shit! You were there when it happened?" Evan asked.

"Yes, get your ass over here. We are going after this guy right now," David said.

"Just hang on man. I'm almost there," Evan replied just before David hung up the phone. The paramedics parked on the side of the road as they approached, and a few EMS came out running toward the father and his wounded son. Before they could do anything, the boy stopped breathing, and his head fell back into his father's lap as his neck went limp. The boy's father immediately began weeping, and David yelled out in anger, "*Ahhh fucking damnit!*" David's outburst scared the paramedics that arrived on scene, and they all looked at him before he took off running toward his truck. He left his shotgun behind, so he could run faster.

"Where are you going?" one of the paramedics yelled out as David sprinted away from the scene.

"To find the bastard that killed that kid!" David hollered back.

"So he wasn't the shooter?" the confused paramedic asked the boy's father.

"No, he tried to save my son," the boy's father cried.

David quickly got to his truck and loaded up his rifle as he peeled out of the parking lot. He had to pass the ambulance where the paramedics parked, and one of them tried to wave him down to stop him. Before David could reach the park exit, Evan pulled in and saw David speeding down the road toward him. Evan turned his car sideways to block the road, and David slammed on the brakes.

"Dude, you need to calm down!" Evan said as he got out of his squad car.

"No. We need to get this guy right now! Not tomorrow, not next week. Right fucking now!" David sternly replied.

"Did you see his face?" Evan asked.

"No, he had a mask covering it, but I know it's him," David said.

"I can't just go and arrest someone without legitimately identifying them. You just admitted you couldn't see his face," Evan explained.

"What about this?" David asked as he pulled the bag of cocaine from his back pocket.

"Where the hell did you find that?" Evan asked.

"The stupid fucker had it on him while he was hunting. I found it right next to the chair he was sitting in," David replied.

"Ok, let's go to his home, and I'll see if he will come in for questioning. If he refuses, I'll have to get a warrant," Evan said.

"He's not going down without a fight." David warned Evan before he got back in his truck and waited for Evan to lead the way.

Evan stopped his car just before turning left to head toward Samuel's home. David sat in his truck as Evan stepped out and started walking toward him. As Evan was approaching, David rolled his window down.

"Park your truck back here, so he doesn't see you. His truck is still in the driveway. I am going to park behind it so he doesn't try to drive away. Since you don't have a badge, don't approach the house with me. Sit back a bit and wait. If he's hostile, back me up," Evan explained.

"This isn't going to work. I'm telling you he's going to come out shooting as soon as he sees you or any cop for that matter," David said.

"I gotta do this by the book," Evan replied. David wasn't happy.

"Alright, just be cautious. Check your corners and peek the

windows before approaching the front door," David said.

"Yes sir, I got it," Evan replied. David turned his truck off as Evan parked behind Samuel's truck in his driveway. David grabbed his rifle out of the back seat of his truck, stuffed a couple extra magazines in his pockets and jogged over to a tree in front of Samuel's yard, so he could provide cover for Evan if necessary.

Samuel had ran back to his home as quickly as possible and woke Lyndsey as he came busting through the front door. "Oh my god, you scared the shit out of me," Lyndsey said. Samuel tossed his shotgun on the bed next to Lyndsey.

"Quick, load up my shotgun," Samuel said as he looked through his closet for a handgun and his Smith and Wesson M&P 15.

"What? Why?" Lyndsey asked.

"Just do it!" Samuel yelled at her.

"Samuel what the hell is going on?" Lyndsey replied.

"There might be someone coming for me, and we need to be prepared," Samuel explained.

"Who is coming for you?" Lyndsey asked.

"I don't know who he is. Just load that damn thing and help me," Samuel said.

After Samuel threw a box of shotgun shells on the bed, Lyndsey started to load up the shotgun. "Sammy, I'm scared. What the hell is going on?" Lyndsey asked.

"I'll explain later. We just gotta grab some stuff and get out of here. Grab your bag and some clothes. I'll pack food. We may need to leave town for a while," Samuel told Lyndsey.

"And go where?" Lyndsey asked.

"I don't know, just away from here," Samuel said.

Samuel grabbed a suitcase and started throwing clothes

into it. After he loaded up his suitcase, Samuel put the suitcase in his truck and walked back inside to help Lyndsey finish packing. Samuel grabbed a grocery bag from the kitchen and started filling it with chips and other snacks he could bring with him on a road trip. He walked back into the bedroom where Lyndsey had just finished packing her own suitcase, and he grabbed his pistol from the nightstand to put in the back of his pants. Just then Samuel and Lyndsey heard a knock on the front door.

"Oh shit," Samuel whispered as he put his index finger up to his mouth and motioned for Lyndsey to be quiet. She froze, so Samuel walked over to her.

"Take the shotgun and follow me. I want you to stay low and hide behind the couch when I answer the door. If anyone comes through, blast them. If I give you the signal, shoot at anyone you see," Samuel explained. Lyndsey was afraid, so she nodded instead of replying. Samuel slowly walked down the hallway and looked through the window to see who was at his front door.

On his porch Samuel could see a cop who at first was peeking through the window, but then began to stare at the front door. There was a smaller window to the left of the door, so Evan shifted his weight and peeked into that window instead. With his back turned to them, Samuel realized this was the perfect opportunity to move. He quickly walked across the living room and was now hiding behind the kitchen cabinet across from the front door while Lyndsey crawled toward the couch by the window. Samuel slowly rose up to point the barrel of the shotgun at the cop standing on the front porch.

David saw movement through the window to Evan's right, but he didn't want to yell to Evan and blow his cover. It was dark inside the trailer, and David couldn't tell if he had just seen one or two bodies move across the room. As David had his eyes fixated on Evan at the front porch, he was also scanning the surrounding area, almost expecting to see the killer sneak around the mobile home and try to ambush Evan. David looked back at Evan and saw him standing sideways on the front porch instead of facing the door. David knew Evan was wearing body armor, but it was essentially useless if he was shot from his side. As David was watching his friend knock on the front door for the occupant to come out, he desperately wanted to tell Evan to face the door instead of standing sideways. David suddenly saw more movement in the window to Evan's right.

"Evan get down!" David tried to warn him just as he heard a loud gunshot come from the mobile home. Evan immediately fell to the ground and rolled off the porch. David returned fire in the direction of the muzzle blast and laid down a barrage of gunfire into the larger window to the right of the front door. David could see Evan trying to crawl away and take cover behind another tree in the front yard.

David stopped firing for a moment right before more gunshots came from the mobile home. It appeared as if gunfire was coming from both windows out front of the mobile home, so David focused on returning fire toward the right window as he moved closer to help Evan. Evan was sitting up against the tree next to Samuel's truck when David reached him, and as David knelt beside Evan, the gunfire stopped.

"Ah fuck, what are you doing? Don't worry about me. Go get that fucker," Evan told David.

"You sure? You ok?" David replied looking down at Evan.

"Yeah man I'll be good," Evan replied. Suddenly more

gunfire started coming from the mobile home. David ducked and moved behind the truck to use it for cover as he started to move toward the mobile home. David decided to sneak around back and pretend he was trying to get through the back door. Realizing it was probably locked, he decided to shoot a few rounds at the lock and handle of the back door. *I wish I had a damn flashbang to throw in there*, David thought to himself as he circled around the mobile home. He wanted to throw Samuel off and make him think he was trying to get in through the back of the mobile home. Samuel immediately unloaded the rest of his magazine through the back door trying to shoot David. David quietly approached the front door of the trailer that had been shot up from the initial gunfire after Evan was shot.

David kicked the front door to bust it open and he could see directly into the mobile home. He shifted his weight to check the corner to his left and saw nothing. When he moved over to check the corner to his right, he could see a woman's dead body lying on the floor with a gunshot wound to the head and several to the chest.

David recognized Lyndsey's face from when he met her at The Last Call the same night he realized Samuel was the killer. David took a few steps into the mobile home and looked around for Samuel. As David walked toward the kitchen, Samuel jumped out at him and attacked. Samuel grabbed the barrel of David's rifle and pushed it away, throwing an over-hand right and punching David in the face and knocking him to the ground.

The force of Samuel's punch also forced David to drop his rifle, so he could brace himself as he fell to the floor. Samuel was in a fit of rage after witnessing Lyndsey die, and he pounced on David as soon as he hit the floor. While Samuel was on top of David, he started punching him as hard and fast as he could. When David went to cover up, Samuel started dropping elbows instead hoping they would get through David's defense and bust up his face. David's head was up against the couch, and he had nowhere to go as he tried to escape from Samuel. David managed to trap Samuel's right arm just after he created a little space away from the couch. David had his left foot over Samuel's right leg trapping it as well.

Once David had Samuel's right arm locked up, he turned over his left shoulder and bridged off his head rolling Samuel over. David ended up inside Samuel's guard and started dropping elbows on Samuel in retaliation.

"*Where did you hide the bodies?*" David yelled at Samuel between strikes while he was inside Samuel's guard.

"Fuck you! You'll never find them," Samuel grunted as he tried to cover up.

"Tell me now or I'll cave your fucking skull in!" David yelled at him. David was stronger and starting to get the upper hand on Samuel when Samuel pulled out a pocket knife and stabbed David in his left leg.

"*Ahhhhh!*" David yelled out loud in severe pain. Distracted by the knife, Samuel was able to place both feet inside David's hips and kicked him away as hard as possible forcing David to fall backwards. David wanted to pry the knife out of his leg, but Samuel was back on top of him before he knew it. David focused on pushing Samuel's right knee away so he could get back to half guard. While Samuel was focused on punching David, it allowed David to hand fight a little bit so he could adjust and get his full guard back.

Samuel was starting to get winded, and now that David

had his guard back, he went to work. David isolated Samuel's right arm and pulled it across his chest as he hip escaped trapping it between their torsos. David then reached around Samuel's back with his left arm and grabbed whatever cloth he could find behind Samuel's left armpit. Now that David had Samuel's right arm trapped, he reached underneath Samuel's left knee with his right hand. David made a quick circular motion with his left leg as he started to open up his guard; then he completed a perfect pendulum sweep ending up on top of an exhausted Samuel.

Realizing that Samuel would never confess to the murders nor where he hid the bodies, David knew what he had to do. He had full mount on Samuel and dropped a few elbows causing Samuel to cover up. With Samuel's forearms up covering his face, David decided to reach around the back of Samuel's neck with his left arm. David leaned forward as he grapevined Samuel's legs so Samuel couldn't bridge and sweep him. David then reached into the sleeve of the shirt he was wearing on his right arm with four fingers on his left hand. Samuel relaxed for a moment to take a deep breath as he got a break from David's onslaught.

David then curled the back of his right hand around, driving the edge of his hand into Samuel's throat like the blade of a knife. With a very tight grip on the sleeve of his shirt and the back of his hand pressing into Samuel's neck, David straightened his arms creating a tight Ezekiel choke on Samuel. Samuel started kicking, desperately trying to escape. Blood was dripping down David's face from the cuts he sustained when Samuel was punching and elbowing him. David could feel the blood dripping down by his mouth while he was choking Samuel.

"Ahhhh! Die you fucking bastard!" David yelled spitting blood all over Samuel's face.

Samuel looked up at David in shock and desperately trying to breathe. Both of their faces were covered in blood, and David was trying to ignore the sharp pain and burning sensation in his leg from where Samuel stabbed him. David had his hand placed in a position on Samuel's neck where he was cutting off both the blood and air supply to Samuel's brain. While David was on top of Samuel, his arms were shaking as he was finishing the choke; Samuel kicked and tried desperately to escape before his body went limp. David knew it was over. He rolled off of Samuel and sat between Lyndsey and Samuel's dead bodies on the floor inside of the mobile home. David wiped the blood off his face and took a deep breath trying to calm down and process what just happened. He looked over at Lyndsey and saw that she was wielding the shotgun that he saw her use to shoot Evan.

David initially thought Samuel was the one that shot his friend; he couldn't believe Lyndsey would do such a thing. David was sore and beat up from his fight with Samuel, but he remembered Evan was wounded, so he stood up to exit the mobile home and go help his friend. As David walked down the porch, he looked over and saw Evan slumped to his left against the tree.

"Oh no, no, no. Come on man get up," David said as he ran to his friend. Evan was barely breathing at this point.

"I don't think I'm going to make it brother," Evan struggled to tell David who was checking Evan's side trying to inspect the wound. As David ran his hand down Evan's side, he realized Evan wasn't hit with buckshot; Lyndsey had loaded a slug into the shotgun first. Realizing that Evan was just hit with a slug at close range, David hung his head. David was trying to keep his composure and not expose his emotions, but grief was starting to overcome him, and he could feel tears welling up in his eyes. Evan coughed and spit up more blood. David reached for the radio on Evan's shoulder, but Evan stopped him and grabbed David's hand instead.

"Please don't. I don't want those fucking sirens to be the last thing I hear. I can't stand that sound," Evan said. David didn't know what to say. He wiped his eyes with his right hand and then put both his hands on his head as he looked down at the ground hoping this was all a bad dream that would end soon. David looked back at Evan and struggled to muster enough strength to speak.

"I'm sorry man," David struggled to say.

"Don't be. You got him, right?" Evan replied. David couldn't speak, so he nodded in response.

"Good. West Spoon is safe then. You just did the community a huge service," Evan told David.

"Please, please tell Emma I love her," Evan struggled to tell David just before he took his last breath.

"Come on man, you gotta tell her yourself. Evan. Evan?" David replied. David hung his head and he started crying softly. Unable to contain his emotions, he began to cry harder as he held Evan's body and sat against the nearest tree. While David closed his eyes, he thought about his friend Danny who died in Afghanistan. David felt like the two people he had met throughout his life that he had most in common with were now taken from him. David's grief was uncontrollable after two of his best friends were killed in action. The anger and grief David felt after losing Danny changed his life forever and pushed him toward an earlier than expected exit from the Army. Now that he lost his friend Evan, he wasn't sure what was going to happen next. David held his friend in his arms as he could hear sirens finally approaching in the distance.

Chapter 19

David woke up in a hospital bed and looked around the room to find his father was asleep in a small recliner next to his bed. David felt groggy and his left arm was in a sling. His left shoulder felt stiff, and when he reached underneath his gown to feel his shoulder, he noticed it was bandaged. He could tell it was raining outside when he looked out the window, and he started to wonder how long he had been in the hospital.

"Dad. Hey, *Dad!*" David said.

"Oh hey, yeah. What's up kid," his father replied as he suddenly woke up from his nap.

"How long have I been here?" David asked.

"They took you here right after they found you and Evan. You had to get a couple stitches on your forehead, and they cleaned out the stab wound on your leg. You also got shot in your left shoulder, but the docs said it didn't hit bone or anything. You got pretty lucky; they said it will just be sore for a while. You lost a lot of blood and passed out in the ambulance on the way to the hospital; luckily you're O positive, and they could give you a blood transfusion pretty quickly," his father explained.

"I don't even remember getting shot in the shoulder."

"Damn! Must have been the adrenaline kicking in," his father suggested.

"Where's Mom?" David asked his father.

"She's out in the waiting room with everyone else talking to doctors and nurses," his father explained.

"Who all's here?" David asked.

"Michael and Avery, your brother and his girlfriend and then the girl you've been seeing that you didn't tell us about," David's father replied.

"Ah shit, I didn't know how serious it was or where it was going, so I didn't want to say anything," David explained.

"Hey, I get it. Your mom is the one that interrogated her when she found out about you two dating," his father said.

"Jesus Christ," David replied forcing his dad to laugh.

"I'm just glad you're ok. I love you son," David's father said as he leaned over to give him a hug. David could only move his right arm as he embraced his father.

"Love you too Dad."

"I'll go grab your mom and let them know you're awake," his father continued.

When his family came in the room, one by one they gave David a hug while he sat up in his hospital bed. David's mom was crying as soon as she stepped in the room and saw her son. David hated seeing her upset. Michael, Avery and Molly stepped up to hug David next.

"Glad you're ok buddy. I told you to stay the hell away from that place," Michael said shaking his head.

"I know. I may have to take you up on your offer next time you ask me to golf with you. Seems a little safer," David joked.

"Yeah, maybe you should stay off public land," David's father suggested.

David turned his head toward his father as his eyes looked at the ground; he thought for a moment before replying, "Yeah, maybe."

Avery hugged David next and said, "I'm glad you're ok." When Molly came over to give David a hug, she had tears in her eyes and instead of leaning over to give him a hug, she sat beside him, grabbed his face with both hands and kissed him. David moved his right arm around her waist and held her.

"I'm sorry about Evan," Molly told David.

"Thanks babe," David replied softly.

"Are you ok?" Molly asked.

David was holding back tears trying not to cry in front of his family and friends. He nodded before replying, "I will be." Zander's girlfriend Rachel came over to give David a hug next, and then Zander approached his older brother. After the two hugged, Zander stepped back and leaned against the wall.

"Was it him?" Zander asked David.

"Yeah," David replied.

"What are you talking about?" David's mother asked. David and Zander looked at each other for a moment and neither of them spoke. David realized Michael and Molly knew about the guy David was searching for at West Spoon, but David never spoke about it with his parents. David remembered how scared his brother was and didn't want to bring it up and make him relive that moment. Now that the threat was gone, David figured it was time to let his parents know what happened.

"A while back when Zander and I were younger, some guy

was following us one night when we were walking back to my truck after hunting at West Spoon," David started to explain.

"Oh my god are you serious?" his mother interrupted.

"Yeah, I never spoke about it because I didn't see who it was, and I knew Zander was pretty shaken up about it. When I moved home for good and found out that a bunch of people went missing at West Spoon, I started to look into it on my own. I suspected there was only one person responsible, and I had a feeling the same guy who was following us that night was the one out there killing all those people," David explained.

"What made you think that?" his father asked.

"Not sure. Just a gut feeling I guess. The guy had to know the area, and he knew how to hide evidence. If there were just a bunch of random murders, I don't think the authorities would have struggled to find the perpetrator as much as they did with this guy," David replied.

"Tell them about the night when we were playing pool," Michael said.

"Oh yeah. One night when the four of us were at The Last Call playing pool, I noticed this creepy guy come in with his girlfriend, and while we were playing pool, he knocked the cue ball over by me, so I reached down to pick it up and hand it to him. After I heard him speak, I recognized his voice and knew it was him. I followed him to find out where he lived and worked, but Evan said I still didn't have enough evidence to prove anything. I definitely kept my eye on him and was constantly searching around West Spoon for clues. By the time I found anything, it was too late," David said with a somber tone in his voice.

"I can't believe he shot a little boy," David's mother said.

"Yeah, dude sounds like he was a fucking psychopath,"

Michael said. "He clearly had some issues and apparently he had a rough past; still doesn't excuse what he did," David stated.

"I'm just glad you found him before he killed even more people," his mother said.

"He probably would have gotten caught eventually. I just didn't want any more innocent people to suffer, and I had to know the truth. My only regret is not being able to find all those he killed," David said.

Later that night after everyone except Molly and his parents left, Emma showed up. David was eating when she walked in the room, and he immediately moved his food to the side and started to get out of bed. David's parents tried to stop him and tell him to stay in the hospital bed, but David wanted to show his respect to Emma. When David reached over to give Emma a hug, she immediately started weeping, and David helped her to sit on the bed beside him. He put his arm around her and let her collect herself.

"Thank you for being there with him," Emma told David.

"No, it shouldn't have happened. I'm sorry," David tried to explain while holding back tears.

"He was just doing his job, and you were there helping him. David please understand, I don't hold you responsible for what happened to Evan. He chose this line of work, and he embraced the risk every day. You were like a brother to him, and I'm so glad you two met," Emma said with tears in her eyes.

"If you ever need anything, please don't hesitate to reach out," David replied.

"Thank you. I know it isn't what Evan wanted, but I asked my doctor what the sex of the baby is," Emma said.

"Oh yeah, boy or girl?" David asked. Emma smiled before

replying, "Boy. I'm going to name him after his father." David's eyes began to tear up and his lip quivered a bit as he smiled; then he reached over to give Emma another hug.

After David was released from the hospital and went home, Molly started staying with him to help him out as he recovered from his injuries. After dinner one night at David's home while Molly was putting the dishes in the dishwasher, David asked her, "When is your lease up at your place?"

"End of next month, why?" Molly replied.

"Why don't you just move in with me?" David suggested. Molly turned around and appeared shocked.

"Are you sure?" Molly asked.

"Hell yeah; I wouldn't bring it up if I wasn't sure." David replied. Molly walked over and sat on his lap; then she gave him a kiss. Holding her with one arm, David looked at her as she replied, "I'd love to move in with you."

The next couple of weeks, David tried to take it easy as he let his wounds heal. Once he could take the sling off, he started doing more yard work and helped Molly move her stuff in so she could live with him. David had the house furnished for the most part, but he didn't have many pictures or decorations, so he was glad Molly moved in and had some stuff she could put up on the walls so they weren't empty.

Eventually, the parents of the teenage victims Samuel murdered at West Spoon came to David's house to visit and thank him. Logan Miles and Mark Blaser's parents were the first to visit him once word got out that authorities believed they had found the culprit responsible for the murders at West Spoon.

When the parents of the victims came to visit David, they would ask why he didn't come to them and tell them what happened. He explained that he felt bad that he was not able to find the bodies. As much as he wanted the parents to know he got the killer, he felt like he failed to accomplish what he set out to do. Despite David's frustration with how things ended, the parents of the victims were very grateful for his efforts, and they felt they finally got some justice. Even Damien Young's father, who slammed the door in David's face, came to thank him for finding the killer. David also kept his promise to Tonya Howe. David and Molly visited her and Taylor at their home and made them dinner.

David was thrilled Molly moved in with him, and he started spending more time at home instead of searching around West Spoon and constantly going to the range to improve his marksmanship. David took time off from sparring and training at the gym and managed to spend more time with his family and friends who he started to invite over to his home more often. David continued to work at the gun and ammo store, but he was still unsure if he wanted to apply for the academy so he could become a conservation officer. It was something that interested him at first when he came home from the Army, but after losing another friend in the line of duty, David was searching for something else.

One summer day, David and Molly had Michael and Avery over and while David was out back cooking on the grill, Molly heard someone knock on the front door, so she went out to let David know. "Hey babe, someone is at the front door asking for you," Molly said.

"Who is it?" David replied half expecting it to be another parent or relative of one of the victims.

"I'm not sure; he just asked if he could speak with you," Molly replied.

"Alright I'm coming. Mike keep an eye on the steaks, would

you?" David said as he walked back inside and headed down the hallway. When David got to the front door, he saw a man in a suit standing on his front porch. A black sedan was parked in his driveway behind Michael's navy blue Jeep Cherokee.

"Can I help you?" David asked as he opened the door.

"Yes sir. My name is Peter Hoover. I'm an agent with the FBI. We looked into your files after we heard what happened at West Spoon State Park, and I would like to extend an invite to you to enroll at the FBI Academy in Quantico, Virginia," the man in the suit told David who hesitated for a moment before replying.

"Fuck off Fed boy" David told him before slamming the door in the man's face so he could go join Molly and enjoy the company of his friends.

Made in the USA
Columbia, SC
25 April 2023

15771810R00167